refugees

refugees

Catherine Stine

Delacorte Press

Published by
Delacorte Press
an imprint of Random House Children's Books
a division of Random House, Inc.
New York

Visit us on the Web! www.randomhouse.com/teens
Educators and librarians, for a variety of teaching tools, visit us at
www.randomhouse.com/teachers

Library of Congress Cataloging-in-Publication Data
Stine, Catherine.
Refugees / Catherine Stine.
p. cm.
Summary: Following the September 11, 2001, terrorist attacks, Dawn,
a sixteen-year-old runaway from San Francisco, connects by phone and email
with Johar, a gentle, fifteen-year-old Afghani who assists Dawn's foster mother,
a doctor, at a Red Cross refugee camp in Peshawar.
ISBN 0-385-73179-5 (trade) – ISBN 0-385-90216-6 (lib. bdg.)
[1. Refugees–Fiction. 2. Runaways–Fiction. 3. New York (N.Y.)–Fiction.
4. Afghanistan–Fiction. 5. Musicians–Fiction. 6. September 11
Terrorist Attacks, 2001–Fiction.] I. Title.
PZ7.S86017Re 2005
[Fic]–dc22
2004010128

The text of this book is set in 11.5-point Baskerville BE.

Book design by Angela Carlino

Printed in the United States of America

February 2005

10 9 8 7 6 5 4 3 2 1

BVG

For my mother, who understands endurance,
and my father, who taught me the
nonviolent Quaker path

Special thanks to Sulaiman Zai, Abdul Raheem Yaseer, Shaista Wahab, Farzana Sayed, Michelle, Joe, Andrea, Stephanie, Norris, Jack, Nate, Ellen, my New School MFA classmates, Barbara's group, and Ziad from way, way back

NOTE

While the characters in *Refugees* are totally fictitious, I was careful to rely on my direct experiences of that difficult September day, and of the days following. I felt that it was the only way to avoid the temptation to sensationalize or distort the events.

It was on the corner of Fifth Avenue and Thirteenth Street that I witnessed the towers' demise. I waited in the lines snaking down the block for the dwindling supplies in the East Village bodegas and heard the drone of military jets overhead as I wandered through smoke-filled streets. I visited the Union Square memorial nightly.

And it was on the insurance company stairs, on a park bench on Greenwich Street, and in the greenish light of St. Peter's that I wrote the first paragraphs of this novel.

prologue
Dawn and Johar
2005

Subj: A Surprise!
Date: May 7, 2005
From: dawnmusic@usa.com
To: johar.maryamsch@afg.net

Johar! Are you sitting down? If not, brace
yourself. I just bought my ticket to
Afghanistan! I'm returning in June! Can you use
a pathetically overeager music teacher at
Maryam School? I have often thought of our time
in Baghlan—the way the sun beat down, how we
filled burlap with rubble to make way for your
new school. I remember how we came and went
with a hundred loads, how every day was a
revelation of new emotion for you, for my
mother, for the chance at a new life.

Do you still think as much of me? I am
scared, Johar; I never want to be as lonely as
I was. Your letters have warmed me the way the
sunrise warmed the Afghan sky those years ago.
Can't wait to see you!
Dawn

Subj: Happy Day!
Date: May 8, 2005
From: johar.maryamsch@afg.net
To: dawnmusic@usa.com

Dear Dawn—
Khub ast! Can it be true? Four years have flown
and our days in Baghlan so vivid as if they
happened yesterday. I waited for this moment!
You will not be alone. We have much to talk of
and do together.

Finally, you will hear my students' happy
laughter, when they find at last that perfect
word to complete their poem, or play the rubab
with sweet sound they so struggled for. And
such a talented music teacher they will gain.

In your e-mail before, your final project in
musical composition sounded most inspiring. And
I am glad you had much fun to organize the Red
Cross fund-raiser with your mother. How did the
audience respond to your new orchestral piece?
How my cousin Bija has grown! She too will be
thrilled to see you.
Fondly, Johar

dawn

San Francisco,
September 4, 2001

The marina-style house up ahead, with its crud-brown roof tiles and tiny concrete yard painted green to simulate grass, never failed to fill Dawn with dread. She'd forgotten an umbrella, so she gripped her jacket over her sandy hair as she broke into a weary jog. Rain pummeled against the jacket's nylon fabric. She swung the rusty gate closed, went inside the house, and kicked her dripping shoes onto the rubber floor mat. Victor's pipe tobacco smelled of overripe fruit. No doubt he was puttering around, but she couldn't bring herself to say hello. Victor had been ignoring her ever since he returned from his state research job. It was Dr. Louise who was always trying to *connect*.

Dawn trooped upstairs to her room, slammed the door, and locked it. Picking up her flute, she ran through some scales, then cracked opened the Vivaldi. Too mechanical, she thought, and put a book of Russian folk tunes on the stand instead. She gave herself to the song's mournful B-minor as the rain softened to a patter on the window and broke into rivulets, winding its way down the glass. Music was everything life was not—it loved her, and if she played to its moods, it would leap to her anytime she needed it. In a catharsis of sound, she could whisper a pianissimo and sob an adagio. Playing flute and being with her friend Jude were all Dawn cared about.

The muffled din of angry voices filtered into her room. She inched open the door. Her foster parents, Victor and Louise, were at it again. Lately they were always arguing. Dawn glanced at the wall clock. Why had Louise come back so early? It was only four. Dawn crept into the hall near their bedroom and listened.

"This couldn't be a worse time for you to go," Victor was saying. "I turn in my statistical research in October. Dawn's shenanigans will be a major distraction."

"What shenanigans?"

"Her nasty attitude, her cold stares. Having to drag her back from that faggy boy Jude's day after day."

"OK, OK, you've made your point. But it's never a good time, is it, Victor?" Louise shot back. "Look, I postponed my trip to the Afghani camps when Dawn arrived. Meanwhile, you ran off to the CDC in Atlanta for some conference completely unrelated to your research."

"Well, you managed to slip out to Texas the second I got back."

Louise gave a wry laugh. "Yes, for that very unnecessary tornado rescue!"

It was always like this: a debate over whose job was

more important, who would get to travel, and who would have to stay with Dawn. Louise went on. "Look, it's not like this is something new. We've always traveled for our jobs."

"We used to have time for each other," murmured Victor. "We used to go to lectures."

"And museums," added Louise.

Victor's voice resumed its edge. "Now it's always Dawn this, Dawn that."

"It's not really about the trip, is it, Victor?" Dawn pictured Louise's owl eyes staring down his nearsighted ones.

"No. It's about Dawn," he admitted. "I said I'd do this foster thing to make you happy, but we both know it's been a disaster. I told you it would never work. Foster kids Dawn's age are set in their patterns. And you let her get away with murder."

"Well, I don't see you making any attempt."

"I'm not good at this. Take her with you," Victor said. "You said you'd consider that at some point."

There was a long pause. Dawn feared her ragged breaths were as loud as sandpaper on wood. Travel with Louise? Getting to see new countries would be cool, but if they were stuck in a plane together, they might just bring it down.

"Victor, she's got school, she's got flute practice, she's–"

"Louise, admit it," Victor cut in. "You can't stand to be around the girl for more than a few minutes."

"That's not it," Louise shouted. "It's my *duty* to see that she goes to school–"

"Your duty?"

"What's wrong with duty?"

"It's fine until it involves real human beings," Victor snapped. "I've washed my hands of it. The girl is a hazard.

One minute she's all bottled up and the next minute she seems ready to explode. Send her back to Epiphany, where she belongs, before your sense of duty ruins us."

Dawn inhaled sharply and stumbled into the side table as she sneaked back to her room. Their fights had been awful, but she'd never heard it get this ugly.

Their door opened abruptly and thwacked against the wall. "Dawn, is that you?" Louise's strained voice called.

Dawn picked up her flute. Her fingers trembled as she tried to slip back into the ambiance of the Russian folk song. Her face felt flushed. She wouldn't let this get to her, but sometimes there were hot parts she couldn't freeze. Tears were for suckers. She hadn't cried for years and had probably forgotten how. "I'll never go back to that hellhole," she whispered. She didn't often allow herself to think about Epiphany House. When she did it was so hard. She remembered the excited and nervous departures, the defeated returns. It wrecked her and her friends, in stages. Dawn had paced back and forth in Little Mo's room just before Mo left. Dawn's heart just about broke with that last hug before her friend sped away in her new foster family's car. But it was worse when Mo returned, after not even lasting a month with her new family. Dawn tried her best to convince her that she'd find another family, but Mo's canceled-out eyes stared right through Dawn. Watching her friend slide her suitcase back under the threadbare mattress hurt so badly.

"Dawn?" Louise called from downstairs. Then, louder, "Dawn?"

Dawn unlocked the door and opened it a crack. "Yes?" she called.

"Hi, dear. How was school?"

Dawn slipped to the head of the stairs. "It was fine, Louise." There was no way she'd ever call this woman mother. She *had* a mother—blood relations—somewhere.

"Can you come down for a minute? I need to talk to you about something."

"Can it wait? I'm practicing." When she'd come here a year ago and realized that Victor wasn't one bit interested and Louise's interest seemed phony, she decided to hide herself like a bear in winter. Hibernate until she turned eighteen.

When Dawn was seven and in second grade, her first foster mother had slammed her against a hot oven and into a window that cracked with the impact. Dawn recalled the shame of walking into a strange new classroom with bruises. Even so, when the family had returned her to Epiphany she'd felt like a failure. It took ages to get another foster family after that, but finally the DiGiornos had taken her when she was twelve. They hadn't hit her, and Dawn had settled in—slowly.

"That girl will never trust anyone," she had heard Mr. DiGiorno say once when they thought she was asleep. "Permanently withdrawn," Mrs. DiGiorno agreed. Dawn couldn't help it if she had nightmares and couldn't bring herself to hug them right off. They had announced she wasn't working out and returned her to the group home, the way someone would return damaged goods to the store. She wouldn't settle in so easily next time.

Still, she'd held secret hopes that first month with Louise and Victor—of a family huddling close, needing each other. But in the morning Louise would just pore over her case notes, and after dinner she would hurry to her study. The only time Louise's voice hummed was when she spoke to her co-workers behind that closed door. And Victor? Well, he never even attempted a conversation. Day after day Dawn struggled over homework in the living room, tapping her foot to the lonesome beats of the clock. She wondered how long it would take before they pulled the same dirty trick the DiGiornos had.

"It will just take a few minutes," Louise called up.

"Coming, Louise." Dawn hadn't realized how cold the rain had been. Her socks and hair were still damp. She pulled on a sweatshirt and hurried downstairs to the kitchen. Dawn studied Louise from across the checkered tablecloth. Louise wasn't an ugly woman, just plain, with graying hair in a blunt cut and Ben Franklin spectacles. She was square-bodied and wore prudish ironed blouses under cable-knit cardigans.

Louise offered tomato juice. Dawn must've told her ten times that it made her gag.

"Thanks." Dawn took it without sipping. "What's up?"

"How was school?"

"Fine."

"Do you like your new math teacher?"

"He's not so bad." *So, I'm your duty,* Dawn repeated to herself. "Is there anything else?"

"There is." Louise pushed her glasses up the bridge of her nose. "I have to go on a trip with the Red Cross for five weeks or so."

"Oh!" Dawn tried to sound disinterested, but her throat tightened. "To where?"

"To Pakistan, near the Afghan border." Louise stirred lemon into her tea.

"That's on the other side of the world!" The DiGiornos had scheduled a trip before hauling Dawn back to the group home. Mrs. DiGiorno had claimed she needed space, but all that distance probably made it easier for her to dump Dawn. Well, if Louise wanted distance that badly too . . . "How long have you known about this?"

"I just found out."

"Like the time you found out a week before your trip to Kansas and didn't let me know until the *day* before?" Dawn's face grew hot.

"No, not like that." Louise hesitated. "I realize it's far from San Francisco."

"What's in Pakistan, anyway?" Dawn felt herself flip off like a switch.

Louise adjusted her glasses. "The situation in the refugee camps has been deteriorating." She leaned forward. "Afghans have been fleeing from civil war for years, and the border camps are stretched to bursting. Drought has worsened, and food will run out by winter if the International Committee of the Red Cross doesn't intervene. Malaria and pneumonia are rampant." Her owlish gray eyes fixed on Dawn. "How do you feel about me going?"

Dawn said, "They need doctors."

"But does it matter to you?" Louise asked.

Dawn's muscles clenched. "Do whatever you want. You'll do that anyway."

"Well, if you *hate* the idea . . ." Louise wouldn't stop staring at Dawn with a pity that made Dawn's skin crawl.

"It's your duty, right?" Dawn replied. "And the refugees need help."

The ticking clock punctuated their silence.

"I can *see* you're upset."

This routine was beyond exhausting. But Louise had

never traveled so far. Usually it was a weekend of Louisiana flood relief or tornado relief in Kansas. And being alone with Victor for all that time would be awful.

"Who said I was upset? You're the one who's losing it," Dawn snapped.

"Listen, Miss Rude, I've had enough of you!" Louise shouted. She breathed in deeply, exhaled, then spoke in a gentler tone. "I'll cancel my flight, Dawn."

"Absolutely not." Dawn was surprised by her own fierceness.

Louise seemed relieved and gave a tense smile. "Well, dear, as I said, it will only be for five weeks, just until food and medicine are distributed—you'll hardly know I'm gone. Victor can take you to some restaurants. You can bring along your friend Jude—"

"Please leave Jude out of this." Dawn checked the clock. "Are we done?"

"Almost." Louise held up a stack of papers etched in neat script. "Here's all my contact information—my numbers, the address for the ICRC's Suryast camp in Peshawar, my e-mail address. They say the Internet goes in and out, but a letter may get intercepted. E-mail and phone are the best," she explained. "I'll show you how to use the sat phone in my office. Oh, I almost forgot." She pulled out something from her cardigan pocket and handed it to Dawn. "A SIM card in case you need to call while you're away from the house."

Victor shuffled in, puffing on his pipe. "Hello," he said, taking a seat.

"How soon are you leaving?" Dawn asked, pocketing the card.

Victor started to cough, then glared at Louise.

"Tomorrow night." Louise tapped the papers on the table to straighten them, then fastened them neatly with a paper clip. "You know I'll miss you, Dawn."

Sure, just like the DiGiornos had said. "You won't miss me and I won't miss you," Dawn blurted. "Go. Do your Mother Teresa thing."

Victor stood up. "That's enough! What's wrong with you?"

"Let her be." Louise's look pinned Victor back to his seat. "There's a lot she needs to absorb."

"I've absorbed." Dawn raced upstairs, anger and fear blurring her vision. Falling onto the bed, she curled into the fetal position. She hadn't meant to be so mean, but at times she just snapped. The argument between Victor and Louise and this sudden news only added two more off-key octaves to the discordant symphony of the day.

Earlier the math teacher had handed back Dawn's pop quiz with a C-minus. Urban had decent classes, but algebra, no matter how it was candy-coated with games and gimmicky charts, was hell. Then in orchestra Dawn found out that she had only placed as third flutist. *Third flutist!* Just because the other two kids' parents were PTA clones who spent their lives repping their doubtful prodigies didn't mean their brats could waltz right in and grab her rightful chair. It was guilt that had clouded the music teacher's eyes as he mumbled, "You know I think the world of your talent, but these two flutists have been at Urban since way back in the first grade."

But the worst was what had happened after last period. Dawn had turned down the hall, slipped past some giggling classmates, and hurried toward her friend Jude. He was bending over his locker, stuffing books in his bag.

Back when Dawn was new at Urban, Jude had rescued her from the sorry quagmire of freaks and geeks. They had formed a misfit musician-and-actor duo. The previous spring they had hung out at his house in the Haight, where every day Dawn swore she could feel the vibes of old hippie musicians like Hendrix, the Airplane, and the Grateful Dead–ghost trails of brilliant lyrical maniacs. They would sit on Jude's shag rug and plot their fantasy escape to New York, where they would take the plunge into professional music and theater. With each plotting, it grew more elaborate–her in a famous band, him a stage diva. This summer she had worked the counter at Melody's Music Store and Jude skipped off to acting camp. The summer hung on like a crusty scab, and Jude wrote only one half-baked letter. She wasn't quite sure where she stood with him now, but then she was never quite sure of things like that.

"Jude," she called when she was almost to his locker.

He swung around. His hair was stylishly windblown, and he had on one of his trademark silk shirts. "Girlfriend, am I glad to see you!" Jude's chiseled features relaxed into a broad smile. "It's *so* depressing to be back among the heathens. I'm ready to blow this town for New York. Broadway needs the soon-to-be-infamous me, Jude Hahn." He leaned in, his bony hands moving expressively as he spoke. "Pax would let us crash with him in New York. And you're so hot on flute that as soon as he heard you play, he'd get on his knees and beg you to join his band."

"Every time you talk about crashing with your brother in Manhattan I get so charged," Dawn admitted. "I mean, can you imagine? Me in a real band, you a real stage actor."

"Let's do it," said Jude. "No more hokey drama class, no more piddly high school band. You and I, we're destined for greatness." He twirled and dipped in a spacey jig.

When he danced, his androgynous body held a sinewy charisma.

Dawn laughed. If only Jude meant what he said about leaving, she'd be on that next train or bus. But she doubted he was capable of following through; he was such a serious mama's boy. "What would your parents think? Your mom would just die."

"Don't remind me," he sighed operatically. "Dame Edith would have a cow." Jude threw more books in his bag and shut his locker. "Even though she did the same thing when *she* was seventeen."

"She actually ran away to New York?"

"Yup. Hard to believe, huh?"

"Hmm," Dawn replied, then decided to change the subject. "Let's go to the Haight for some cappuccino, then go to your place and play." At Jude's, Dawn could belt out salsa on her flute while he danced like a stripper, flinging Edith's fake furs around his giraffe-like neck. Or Dawn could switch to a flute concerto in between Jude's recitations from *Amadeus*.

"No can do. Dame Edith scheduled a dental appointment for me without asking."

"Can't you call to cancel?" Dawn didn't want to seem clingy, but she dragged with heaviness at the thought of spending the afternoon without him. And this was their first day back together.

"Believe me, I tried. I whined, I threatened." Jude's face became animated in true drama-major vamp style. "Mom wouldn't budge, and to top it off she accused me of cheap melodramatics." He flipped his long hair. "She said I was carrying on like *her* at sixteen. I'm sick of being treated like a baby. I'm ready to go, I really am."

"I'm with you on that," said Dawn. "But don't knock

your mom. She's an awesome painter." And Edith wore flamboyant clothes—so different from Louise and Victor, thought Dawn. She felt her face go slack. "Hey, it's no biggie if you have to go."

"Ah, I envy you." Jude gazed fondly at Dawn. "Nothing fazes you. Maybe it's lucky that you're adopted. You'll never cringe when you hear yourself repeating your mother's most irritating phrases. You'll never have to deal with seeing the worst of yourself in your parents."

"You mean foster, not adopted."

"Oh, right. Sorry. Sometimes I talk without thinking." He paused. "You OK?"

"Sure." Dawn's hands clenched. He was trying to make her feel better, but sometimes Jude was clueless. It wasn't totally his fault; she'd never gone into details about her former life—the foster homes, the never knowing when she'd be out in the cold. If Dawn found her real mother, things would change. "Got to practice for my lesson," she said crisply.

"Adios," said Jude. "Same time, same locker, tomorrow."

Dawn watched him stride down the hall, taut body swishing under his shirt, bookbag bouncing against his narrow hips. Then she bolted the school in a daze.

Now, as she curled into a tighter ball on her bed, the memories of earlier that afternoon merged with her present resolve. There was nothing for Dawn here unless she counted dread. She turned over on her bed and listened for sounds outside the bedroom door. Victor and Louise must still be downstairs, she thought. Dawn picked up the phone and dialed.

Jude's machine clicked on: "If I don't pick up, it's because I'm rehearsing *Hamlet,* or *Death of a Salesman,* or whatever, but leave a shout-out at the tone."

"Jude," Dawn whispered, her voice cracking. "I'm leaving San Francisco, and if you're serious about it, come with me."

johar

Baghlan, Afganistan,
early September 2001

Johar's clan had once spiraled out from the village of
Baghlan like vines from a Zanzibar pea. Most of his tribe
had withered; only a handful survived. He'd not forgotten
the dead—his mother stirring pilau over the cooking fire, his
father telling stories as they leaned on the mattresses bordering the den in their mud-brick hut.

Johar, now fifteen, and his older brother, Daq, lived in
the hills with their sheep. The world was colder with so few
of his tribe to warm him. Johar's mind would have frozen
like the caps of the Hindu Kush if he'd not persisted in his
passions: his knitting and his poetic rambles.

*Women's work. Language of unbelievers. A shepherd's mind
stuffed with trifling patter.* That's what the boys in Johar's village whispered. They called him rose and flower, brainboy
and Inglestani. They claimed he put on scholarly airs.

He couldn't help it if Aunt Maryam had been a brilliant teacher. She had taught Johar and Daq when they came in from the fields at night, no matter how tired she was from a full day of teaching her regular girls. She and her young daughter, Bija, still lived down the road toward the village. Johar's aunt had always been a well in a desert of sand. She had taught him to weave, to knit, to read, and to speak languages—Pashto and English as well as Dari, which was their native tongue. Her most inspired gifts to Johar were the books of poetry by Rabi'a, Rumi, Farrukhi, Khushal, and Durrani. And of course the English textbooks. It was a miracle that her brother, Tilo, had been able to bring in such textbooks from England. No one else had so much as a notebook. Maybe that's why the other boys resented Johar. Words and languages were more essential than food or friends. But try explaining that to most village boys, who waited excitedly for their first guns at five. Johar could tolerate the name-calling, but at fifteen, with Johar now a man, these things he so loved—poetry, language—were becoming embarrassments.

The hills above Baghlan were pocked, and when Johar herded the sheep he had to tread carefully, inching around land mines and old battle trenches. This soil had witnessed many years of battering, army against army, faction against faction. But Johar could forget his troubles here, even these days when a group of humorless clerics called the Taliban were raiding towns and taking young men at gunpoint to train for the new jihad. Keen to install their punishing brand of sharia in the land, they decreed no laughter, no music, and no vices. *No vices? Pah,* thought Johar. Vices were reserved strictly for the Taliban. They had seized many villages and the hubs of power—Kandahar, Kabul, advancing on even the northernmost towns—and now they wanted unwilling boys to help them gain even more. Johar's heart hammered fitfully when he thought about it. The greedy goats would not be satisfied until they had taken the whole of Afghanistan and the shreds of his family in the bargain.

Johar was called a coward by the villagers because he shied from guns, because he was afraid to join the Alliance to fight these Taliban, because he preferred to spend his time with children rather than soldiers. *Call me coward, then,* Johar thought, *for that is what I am.*

• • •

"Will they come to our house?" Johar asked his brother on one of summer's last sunny days. He pictured their black-lined eyes and cane sticks rapping sharply at their door. So far the Taliban kept to Baghlan, but Johar and Daq lived just an hour from town on their family's farm. Johar took shallow breaths as they climbed further up the ochre rock passes to find more sparse clumps of grass for the herd of sheep they were leading.

"So what if they come?" Daq prodded the sheep back as they wandered from the path. "I am not afraid. Besides, they've kept order in Baghlan. Who knows, maybe I will even go fight for them." Johar did not know what to make of this new side of his brother. Daq had always been moody, but after their father's death he had grown distant and willful. And since Daq had run into his old friend Naji at the chaikhana, he had become even worse. Now he flew into anger over nothing. His behavior frightened Johar.

"Well, I hate their ways," Johar replied, spitting on the dust. "They beat Aunt Maryam at the fountain for laughing." Johar worried constantly about Maryam and Bija's welfare, especially now that Maryam's home school, where she continued to teach a dozen girls, was illegal under Taliban rule. The brothers visited their aunt and cousin at week's end to help with chores, but it wasn't enough. She needed more help with Bija, and they all needed more time to rest. Johar marveled at Aunt Maryam's perseverance with Bija. She was three and as hard to contain as a shooting star.

Johar went on, "If they come, I'll tell them how people ridicule them. Clerics, nonsense! Most learned nothing at madrasah but Quran. Not even how to spell. Talibs are illiterate as toads. I would tell them they would do well to learn how to read and to study the basics of human decency."

"You? Face up to them?" Daq burst out laughing. "You're as flimsy as unspun wool. I would have to shield you from a beating with their canes."

Johar couldn't believe his brother was seriously thinking about signing on with the army. Maybe it was just talk. "What about your radio?" he asked. "Do you like them enough to hand it over?"

"No, my radio stays with me," Daq said firmly. The streets of Baghlan were silent after the Taliban had shut the music stalls and smashed all the popular records and tapes. As they seized the villages, they took over the radio stations and played only their insufferable sermons. Strange, Johar thought, that the Taliban forbid one to own a radio, yet they still preached their propaganda over the airwaves. Thankfully there were still free stations in the north. And Daq still played his radio every night, so softly that only the two brothers could hear, long after the night sky was strewn with stars.

"I made a better hiding place." Daq grinned.

"Where?" asked Johar.

"Shh! Later." Daq peered through the passes to make sure no one stood near. Johar nodded and stroked Marqa, the old ewe with the crooked jaw, as she passed. He would never forget Marqa's first day of life, years ago—the way her pink nose had quivered and her limbs had swayed as she nursed. That first day of Marqa's life in their sunny courtyard, with Aunt Maryam and his mother, had been his mother's last.

Johar recalled everything about that afternoon—how he had drunk the warm sheep's milk his mother saved for him. How he had danced around the new lamb and buried his face in her curls as the distant sound of gunfire shattered the clouds, how his aunt and mother laughed by the back door. He had watched his mother sew an ankle-length coat, called a chupa, and his aunt knit socks, thick and warm to wear under yak boots in winter. After an hour or so, everyone had been thirsty and hungry.

"I will prepare chai and gabli pilau," Johar's mother announced.

She returned with chai but no food. "I have lamb and rice for the pilau, but the oil has run out. I'll go collect more."

"Let me come with you," Johar offered.

"Not this time, son. Stay and keep your aunt company." His mother closed the gate behind her, singing with a voice as high and pure as a wooden flute. They waited for her until the sun slipped behind the stone wall, then his aunt said, "Stay here, child. Wait for Daq and your father to come with the sheep. I must go and fetch your mother. Which direction is her neighbor?"

Johar explained the way, then asked, "Has something happened?"

"No, Johar, she must have stayed to talk. Try not to worry." Then Aunt Maryam hurried out of the gate. The last thing Johar could bear to recall was a vision of himself, crouched by the old pistachio tree, trembling. It had been simple and cruel. On her way to the neighbor's to borrow oil, Johar's mother had stepped on a buried land mine.

"Bless Mother and her music," he murmured now as he walked with his brother.

Up, up, and up he and Daq climbed. Here Johar liked to imagine he could touch the roof of the world. The valley below was dotted with sheep and the few mud-brick houses of the neighbors. The blinding dust of the plain was replaced by rose-colored cliffs. There were no streams here, and it wasn't the Matari Pass, yet this place made him think of the poet Khushal every time:

O! Of Lundi's streams the water and of Bari,
Is sweeter to my mouth than any sherbet.
The peaks of the Matari Pass rise straight up to the heavens,
In climbing, climbing upward, one's body is all melted.

Johar sat and took frugal sips from his water jug. Daq joined him as the sheep grazed on the dry grasses. Soon there would not be enough grass and water. Autumn was coming on, and the drought was worsening. Still, when the winds blew the clouds in a lazy eastward dance, Johar imagined he could hear his father's laughter and see his proud face looking down. His mother gazed down on them too but did not speak. Her melodies, as pure and high as flute song, floated to him in dreams.

Daq rose, and Johar followed. They led their sheep into a round valley, protected from gusts by the rugged branches of pistachio and mulberry trees. "This is where we will shear the herd," said Daq, pulling out rusty shears from his felt bag. "Hold the front feet." Johar helped him flip a ewe to its side, then steadied her while Daq swept up and down with his shears as he held tight to her hind feet. The ewe became docile, as if she liked the strong hold, and by the time one side was done, a pile of curly wool lay in Daq's shawl. Johar helped him flip her over, and Daq repeated the process, his muscled arms flexing under his thick kameez. After each shearing, Johar placed the wool in Daq's shawl and folded it over, securing it with rocks from the wind. Marqa was the only difficult one. She was old, and they had to be careful not to turn her too roughly.

When they were done, Johar asked, "Why are we shearing so early this year?"

"Everything is unsure, little brother," Daq replied as he removed the rocks, rolled his shawl tightly, and strapped the bundle to his pack. "I feel an early winter coming. It's best that Maryam should have the wool early."

An early winter? Everything unsure? If only his father were still alive, thought Johar, he might not feel so chilled by Daq's words.

When the village warlords had swept into Baghlan eight years back in the civil unrest before the Taliban, and just after the Soviets had been defeated, Johar was still a child. There were dreadful battles for power during that time to grab land and leadership that the Soviets had finally given up. Johar's family heard many tales of murders and looting. One day stood out as sharp in Johar's mind as the crack of a Kalashnikov gun.

A Pashtun warlord and his Hizbi Islami crew had rounded up the elders of the village, his father among them, and ordered the women to stay in the courtyard. With the wide end of their guns, the gang pushed the men forward—Johar's father and Uncle Khosal, Maryam's husband; Malik, the tailor; Rashid, the storyteller; and three others. "March! You heard us, you pigs. If you think now that the Soviets are gone that your Jamiati Islami party will rule this town, think twice. You belong with the worms."

Later, Daq, who knew some Pashto, had translated their words. Johar's family spoke Dari, but Johar knew from the harshness of their tone that something bad was happening. He ran to his father's side and clung to his shawl until one of the men pried him away.

Then, speaking in broken Dari, that warlord had turned to Daq, only ten. "You, boy. Hold your brother back unless you want him hurt." Daq's skin was damp with sweat and the color drained from his cheeks. Johar prayed his brother would not be mad enough to fight these men. If Daq obeyed quietly, maybe they would let his father go.

Daq pulled Johar back, and as their father passed he brushed their foreheads with his leathery hand. "My sons," he murmured, tears clouding his eyes, "may Allah protect you." In his father's tormented face there was no clue as to what Johar and Daq should do. The mujahidin thugs beat him on.

Daq, clutching Johar's hand, pursued them up the steep mountain path. The brothers stood there helplessly as the soldiers lined up the village men along a dusty ridge.

"No!" Johar cried out. He broke away from Daq and ran for his father, but they were too far away. The soldiers went mechanically down the row—*ping, crack, crack*—until every last man had fallen forward, eyeballs staring, teeth biting the red dirt where sheep had grazed that unholy morning.

Shouts snapped Johar back to the present.

Daq waved from up ahead on the path. "Little brother! Are you dreaming of flowers and birds again?" When Johar drew near, Daq's face lit up in a forgiving smile. "Come," he said. "The sheep will want one last grazing."

belongings

San Francisco,
September 6, 2001

Waiting by her bedroom window for Victor to leave, Dawn glanced impatiently at the fog as it rolled in from the Pacific. Inhaling the sea air, she tried to find a hint of sun peeking from the haze. Dawn wouldn't get trapped in melodrama. Jude's head might be swirling with emotion, but hers was screwed on tightly, with a no-tamper top, thanks to the hardball life at Epiphany. When she finally heard the dull thud of the door and saw Victor shuffle down Santa Marisa, she felt the slightest twinge of guilt. Then a rush of excitement pulsed through her. Jude had talked Pax's musician friends into giving them a ride east! She'd have to hurry to meet them in the Mission in half an hour. Dawn checked her pack a third and final time. In it was her flute and sheet music, the award for musicianship that she'd won last year at Urban, her disc player, some CDs, a book she'd taken from the group home with her roomies' farewell inscriptions, clothes, an extra pair of shoes, and a rain parka. She counted her chore and allowance money: four hundred in bills that she was saving to buy a Gemeinhardt, the best flute made. Where could she store it? Cash should be stashed in multiple places so that if she was robbed she wouldn't lose it all. Dawn pushed one wad inside her sock, another bunch in her bra, and the rest into her hip pocket.

She wandered into Louise's office, on the first floor, looking for paper to write a note. No crumpled papers or dirty teacups for Louise; her desk was immaculate. Dawn's eyes wandered to a bank of photos on the wall. Here was Louise in her glory, saving the world: Louise hugging a flood victim, Louise giving a typhoid shot to a Peruvian patient, Louise helping dig out a family's injured collie in the San Francisco quake. Then there was a happy one of Victor and Louise from an earlier time. They were sitting on the beach with his arm encircling her. *I won't make you unhappy anymore,* thought Dawn. Her eyes moved to another photo, set off from the others. It was a photo taken on Dawn's second day at the house on Santa Marisa Place. In it Louise was smiling stiffly, her arm swung around a staring Dawn. *Why the hell do I look so blank?* She spotted a stack of *Family Circle* magazines on a side table by Louise's desk and tried to stifle an unpleasant stirring. *Why does it have to end up like this?* Dawn was tempted to climb into one of the easy chairs and sleep, but she refused to wimp out now.

There had been a moment yesterday when her resolve faltered. New York City might be too big, too far. But how many options did she really have? Victor hadn't wanted her in the first place. Louise had wanted her, but why? As some vile experiment in raising a cracked-up kid? Dawn needed a mother who didn't stare at her like she was some third-world refugee. Besides, her real mom was out there, maybe even in New York. And if it came to it, Dawn would rather live on the street than go back to a group home for another depressing three years.

When her birth mother left, Dawn supposed, it must have been for a good reason. You didn't just leave your little girl with strangers for kicks. Someday Dawn would find her, and then she'd know why. Blood was thicker than water; that's what everyone said. It was the mystical bond that would draw them together, and when they looked at each other for the first time it would be like cauterizing a torn vein. Blond hair cascading down, red lips, the scent of powder, and heels that clicked were all Dawn could remember of her mother. It was as if the memory section of Dawn's brain had short-circuited. She'd been five when she went to Epiphany House. That was old enough to recall something! If her mother's face was clear in her mind, why couldn't she remember her mother talking, some events? Dawn would give anything for just one lousy memory of a birthday party.

She continued to drift through Louise's office. Her gaze fixed on the satellite phone. If she took it and she got desperate, it could be sold for lots of money. Pushing away a wave of guilt, Dawn stuffed the phone in her pack, which was now so full it wouldn't snap until she sat on it. Dawn searched the hall closet for a sleeping bag and strapped that to the pack. With the bag it was a struggle to lift the bundle onto her back.

Now for the note. Back in Louise's office, Dawn stood for a moment by the corner-section of shelf where Victor had his books. She would need to keep him from wondering where she was until she could call with an excuse. No doubt he'd be relieved to have her gone. Dawn tore off a page from Louise's memo pad and wrote:

Victor—

I am invited to Jude's country house up in Sacramento for the weekend. His parents are letting me stay in the Haight tonight. They'll take me to school Friday morning. I'll call you.

—Dawn

Dawn went to the kitchen and loaded a grocery bag with apples, crackers, half a loaf of bread, and the rest of the cheddar cheese. She added two sets of silverware, a can opener, and a thermos of water. She even remembered to get soap and a washcloth from the front powder room. She had no clue when her next bath might be.

When her pockets and the grocery bag were full, Dawn thought of one more thing and ran up to get it. The garnet ring. It was Dawn's birthstone and had become a good-luck charm at music recitals.

She stared at the crimson jewel. Dawn pictured Louise's eager face as Dawn had opened the ring box last year. Then she recalled how just a couple of days later she and Victor had gazed out of the airport window and watched Louise's plane get smaller and smaller, carrying Louise to tornado victims in Texas. It wasn't that Dawn begrudged the victims of calamity, but there was something just too easy about giving a ring.

She blinked to clear the stinging in her eyes and hoisted the pack onto her shoulders. Dawn slipped the ring on her finger and walked out of the crud-colored house, slamming the door behind her.

chaikhana

Baghlan, Afghanistan,
September 9, 2001

Johar and Daq unrolled their pattus and knelt side by side
as the sun dropped from its perch and dusk's chill cooled
the rocky soil.

Johar bowed, raised, and then bowed his head in the
prayer ritual called the namaz. His thick black hair curled
in waves around his woven skullcap. When he finished his
prayer for protection, he whispered a few extras. "Allah, let
our sheep survive the winter snows. Bless Daq. Help him
hold his temper. Bless little Bija and Aunt Maryam. Allah,
help me to quiet the rumblings in my stomach so that our
rice stores last until spring." Marqa licked salt from Johar's
toes. "Bless sweet Marqa too."

Daq and Johar rolled their pattus and led the sheep
down through the narrow paths, past the rusted Soviet tank

whose red Cyrillic lettering glowed in the dark orange light, marking the halfway point to home

Turbaned shepherds filed by, followed by a woman balancing a jug on her head. Johar knew from the three rips at the hem of her blue burqa that it was his neighbor, Zolar. She would get into trouble with the Taliban if she was caught walking outside without a male relative, but none in these rebellious hills would tell. Zolar was a widow and needed drinking water like anyone else. The brothers lowered their eyes as she passed.

When they reached their mud hut Johar counted the sheep while Daq prodded them—twelve in all—through the gate and inside the high stone enclosure. One never knew when a thief or starving farmer would creep over the wall at night for a taste of even these bony sheep.

Poor Marqa was getting lame, although she could still produce wool and even a jug of milk now and then. Marqa's last yearling carried a lamb in her own belly. The yearling was so thin that Johar worried she would die before giving birth, so he often searched the passes for extra handfuls of grass to feed her. Johar hurried in to help Daq hide the wool they'd sheared today. Soon they would face a long winter. The Afghanis they received for this would see them through the snowy months if they were prudent, and if luti did not rob them on their way home from market. For now, the wool was safe in a deep crevice dug into the dirt floor.

"I'm stopping at the chaikhana on the way to Aunt Maryam's," Daq announced. He tightened his checkered turban as they walked toward town. Already it was evening, and although Johar feared the street for its thugs and bandits, his biggest fear was the Taliban. One could be thrown in jail for the slightest provocation—a glance at a woman, or even owning a child's doll.

"We must hurry to Maryam's," Johar protested. "Must you see that traitor?"

"What traitor?" Daq grabbed Johar by his shalwar. "I trust you're not referring to Naji." Daq's eyes were as hard as agates.

"Naji's words are crazy," Johar retorted when Daq released his garment. "He is trying to brainwash you."

"Then go to Aunt Maryam's alone," Daq replied. "You're not cut out for the chaikhana anyway. You belong in a woman's house, watching children."

"I belong in the field. I'm as good a shepherd as they come, and you know it," said Johar, presenting a strong front even though Daq's words had cut him. It was true that he loved to tell Bija stories as she sat on his lap with her mouth agape, but so what? Daq would tell Johar, "You are like a fool who speaks in poetic riddles, or a young girl who moons over her wedding." Riddles? Pah! Poetry formed the moral and spiritual base of rule, from the ancient tribal leaders to the caliphs and pirs. Maryam had taught him this. Verse documented events—the history of mystics practicing in the desert, of nine hundred scholars studying in the court of Mahmud of Ghazny, of the workings of the overland spice trade. Johar would become a teacher and hand down what he had learned. Someday Daq would understand.

"I'm coming," Johar said firmly, hurrying to catch up. They passed through a checkpoint, and two Talibs who asked where they were going. Satisfied that the boys held no forbidden goods, the men let them pass.

The dirt road widened. People on foot and on donkeys

made their way toward the bazaar. Merchants called out their wares from roadside stalls. Johar saw dented pots and pans, chipped bowls, a tarnished samovar. The brothers walked on past ragged sections of walls and damaged light poles whose protruding wires flapped in the wind. Mostly men roamed these streets, and around thirty-five of them haggled over the most valued goods—naan, potatoes, melons, chai. But, further on, burqa-clad women crouched along the curb with their hands outstretched. Their children, with tangled hair under dirty hijabs, played or sat listlessly by their mothers. As they looked at the lanes of crumbling structures, it wasn't hard to see that Afghanistan had been at war for an exhausting twenty years.

Soon Johar and Daq were at the chaikhana. They strode up to its mud-brick walls and entered. The pungent odor of sweat and kebabs hit Johar's nose. The place was filled with men eating and smoking, their guns resting at their sides. This was one of the places where all men mixed, even though there were Taliban spies.

Afghanistan was made up of clans. Pashtuns stood in the majority and aimed to keep it that way. The Taliban had risen from the most conservative element of the rural Pashtun tribe, which had its spiritual center in the southwest town of Kandahar. Tajiks held many businesses in the northeast. Massoud, the great Alliance general who was fighting against the Taliban, was a Tajik from the Pansjir. Hazaras grouped in the central villages of Bamiyan and were rumored to hail from the legendary invading armies of Genghis Khan. Hazaras, with their strongly Asian features and Shi'a way of worship, were the Taliban's special scapegoats. Most Afghanis were Sunni Muslims. The Shiites had been persecuted almost since the inception of

Islam, when they insisted that all imams following the Prophet Mohammed must be direct descendants, while the Sunni branch believed that caliphs should be elected, not conferred by heredity.

Daq's old friend Zul called them over to sit on a patterned rug. Zul was a Tajik from Baghram, like Johar and Daq. He was tall and spoke with a lisp through the wide space where his two front teeth had once been. Bearlike Farooq, the Hazara carpet seller's son, was there as well, and to his left sat Naji, a black-turbaned Pashtun.

Naji had attended school in the early years, until his father pulled him away to work in the family fields. The fields had long since burned from the drought and Naji had vanished for a long while, returning suddenly only last month. Etched into his left cheek was a long scar, which Naji claimed was a badge of honor from fighting off an armed bandit. *Just another one of Naji's many conceits,* thought Johar whenever he heard the tale.

When they were younger, they had all played together in the hills around Baghlan, tag and mansur—a game shooting pucks across a board made slick with powdered chickpeas. But since the local commanders had locked teeth like jackals over who would lay claim to each village, and the ethnically divisive Taliban had risen, Pashtun, Tajik, and Hazara had become suspicious of one another. Despite this, these boys, now young men, clung to their old friendships.

"Chai?" Zul asked. Daq and Johar nodded. Zul poured black-leaf chai from a steaming Russian samovar in the center of the patterned rug. He handed a cup to Daq and passed another to Johar, who clutched it between his cold hands to warm them.

"Kebabs?" asked the proprietor, who had come along

with a handful of meat on metal skewers. Johar watched hungrily as Farooq bought one and bit in, the greasy juice dribbling down his chin.

Johar's belly rumbled mercilessly. He could've eaten six kebabs, but he didn't have any money.

Daq put his hand in his pocket and pulled out only a single coin. "No kebabs today," he mumbled.

Naji pulled a handful of Afghani from his vest pocket and threw them grandly on the table. "Four kebabs for these two!" he said to the proprietor. The man returned with meat on blackened skewers. "Eat," Naji said, laughing.

"Thanks," Daq replied between bites.

Johar ate one kebab quickly. He hadn't allowed himself any precious meat in days. He wrapped the other and slipped it in his pocket.

Naji leaned in close, massaging his long scar. "Daq, if you became a Taliban warrior, you'd have more coins in your pocket."

"But our sheep—"

"Your sheep will be fine," Naji said. "Think about it." Naji lowered his voice conspiratorially. "A lucky few of our Taliban soldiers trained at the Arab camps."

"Arab camps?" asked Farooq, noisily slurping his chai.

"The Al Qaeda camps in Kandahar," Naji replied. "I studied at one for several weeks. Their soldiers gave me these." He lifted his feet to reveal black leather boots. Daq touched them with reverence. Johar and Daq both wore cracked sandals on their feet. "You see?" Naji sat back, looking proud.

Zul's brows furrowed in a black arc. "It is pathetic how the Pashtun Taliban pander to the Arabs who flock in from Egypt and Saudi lands. Just because these outsiders have

Taliban backing, they act as if they own our towns." Zul was a Tajik who stood squarely behind Massoud's resistance.

"Watch whom you're talking to," said Naji. He slapped his cup down, sloshing chai on the carpet. "I am Pashtun and a Talib."

"Of course," said Daq. "But you are different." His tone hardened. "A Pashtun warlord from Hizbi Islami killed my father."

Naji nodded solemnly. "Allah bless him, my brother. But all Pashtuns are not the same. Besides, there were many clans in the Hizbi Islami. You can't blame one man's cruelty on the whole group. Now again we have a common enemy. Tajik and Pashtun must band together, like the Taliban have with Al Qaeda, whose Arab fighters are simply trying to help them keep peace."

Band together? Keep peace? Johar was confused. The Taliban were waging a bitter fight against General Massoud's Tajik-led Alliance for control of the northern provinces at this very moment. "Which new enemy?" he asked.

"The Americans, who else?" growled Naji. "They got what they wanted when they came here to arm our mujahidin against the Soviets—Communism was squashed. Instead of helping us rebuild, they left Afghanistan in ruins—kherab!" Naji stabbed a stray piece of lamb with his skewer.

"Huh?" Johar frowned.

"Is this confusing you?" asked Zul.

Johar shook his head. "No, but the American part—I don't get it." Poetry was clear, but politics ... well, he'd never fully understood the entire chain of events.

"The Soviets invaded back in '79," Zul explained.

"When that happened, the Americans sent in troops to help stop the spread of communism. They supplied munitions and helped turn our Afghan mujahidin into skilled fighters."

Daq cut in. "They invited Arabs from the Middle East and Pakistani fighters to help as well. In 1989 we finally drove out the Roussi dogs." Everyone chortled.

"The Americans couldn't wait to leave," snorted Naji. "And they left a real mess. Our local commanders took up the slack. They had to, because the villages were in ruin. They drew up factions, fought a hellish civil war."

"You can't blame the fighting in the villages on the Americans," said Zul. "It was the fault of the greedy commanders—the crazed mujahidin factions who burned entire fields of wheat, raped women, switched sides on a whim."

Johar turned to Daq and said, "One of those commanders was our father's killer." Daq nodded. Even Farooq was quiet; he paused in his loud chewing.

"It got worse," said Zul. "Arab fighters kept pouring in. They took advantage of our weakness to set up training camps against the West, their new enemy of Islam."

"Tell the whole story, Zul," hissed Naji. "America broke their promise to rebuild. We would have been better off without them. When the Taliban gained control in '92, Afghans cheered. Finally we had a strong government to stop the rampage."

Johar said, "I guess everyone has their own selfish agenda."

"Self*less* agenda is more like it." Naji said, and spat on the floor. "America crept in like a whore who takes a man's money and leaves him the gift of syphilis. They taught our women indecent ways of dress and brought us only television and godless music."

"I saw an American television program once, at my uncle's compound," Johar said. "I laughed so hard, I almost started crying. It was pretty clever."

"Which one was it?" asked Farooq eagerly as he picked up another skewer. "I saw *Back to the Future*. Was it *Back to the Future*?"

"That's a film, not TV," Zul replied, whistling through the gap in his teeth. "As far as films, *Titanic* was the finest."

"You see, Daq, my friend?" Naji shook his head in disgust. "Corrupted minds."

"It's good the Taliban enforce limits," Daq agreed. Even Johar admitted that since the Taliban had overtaken the local commanders, people weren't as quick to rob in broad daylight, but fear was one thing, morality another.

"You forget that the Taliban blasted the ancient Buddhas off the mountain face in Bamiyan," said Farooq.

"They're determined to erase any hint of a religion before Islam," said Zul. "And they lop off the hands of schoolboys caught shooting one lousy syringe of heroin," he added. "How ironic that it's made from the poppies they themselves smuggle, even as they officially ban its production. My cousin Omar has a cursed time eating with his right hand gone." Naji seemed furious but remained silent.

"Meanwhile they lounge inside their compounds," Farooq added, "and smoke their hookahs with two able hands." He took an imaginary puff on a hookah and rolled his eyes as his fleshy cheeks ballooned with air.

Everyone laughed but Naji. "All lies," Naji mumbled. "Just wait."

Farooq continued, his tone growing angry, "Our

Hazara sisters are forced to marry Taliban commanders, and our mothers must now beg on the roads. It is shameful." Forgotten juice dribbled down his chin.

"Women have no business working anyway," Naji replied. "The Taliban have brought purity back into Islam and men back to the mosque."

Zul pounded his fist on the floor. "If you think these hypocrites will transform into saints, think again. Impossible, my brothers, not even with magical charms." Zul was the one who most often stood up to Naji.

Johar was afraid of Naji but could restrain himself no longer. "Zul is right! Underneath their fancy talk and their new army they're still luti. The only difference is that they steal lives, not money."

Naji chuckled. "Brainboy speaks! But his words are ill-advised, my friends. Remember that there is rumor of war against those westerners who swooped in to feed, then swooped out like bats in the night. Any man who is not trained–"

"So what's it like to train in Kandahar?" Daq cut in. He sounded so eager that Johar was alarmed.

Naji straightened his turban, then stroked his scar. "We learned about modern weaponry, how to mix poison chemicals, how to fight the kafirs."

Johar wanted to yell, *Then I'm an unbeliever, a kafir, because I don't believe in an Islam that would aspire to kill entire tribes.* But he didn't dare, for Naji's mad eyes frightened him. Did these fanatics really believe all outsiders unworthy of life? Johar longed to take his brother out of here. Next thing he knew, Daq would be volunteering to become a soldier. Johar must try to put sense into his head. "The Taliban beat my aunt at the fountain for lifting her veil to drink," he blurted.

"She deserved it," Naji replied.

"Hey!" Daq started.

"Maybe she didn't," Naji added quickly, then rapped Daq on the back. "You would make a fine soldier. What do you say, old friend?" As Daq hesitated, Naji added, "Your brother can play soldier too—bang, bang!" Naji made his fingers into a gun and laughed. "That is, unless he'd rather hide with his aunt and her child."

"Leave my brother out of this." Daq warned, raising his voice.

Johar tipped his head toward the door as a signal to go, but Daq ignored him.

"Men, settle down," Farooq said. "We are old buddies. Let's have another kebab." He patted his generous belly.

Johar got up to leave. "Daq? Are you coming?"

Daq hesitated, glancing from Naji to Johar. He shook his head. "Go home before curfew, brother. I'll see you later." Daq leaned toward Johar and in a softer tone he added, "Try not to worry." He turned back to his friends.

But Johar *was* worried, and rankled by this hateful talk. If America was the new enemy, then what about a free life, what about its many colors of people, what about his uncle Tilo working in Western lands? As Johar left, he thought of the English words his aunt had taught him: *danger, war, traitor.* But other words too—*consider* and *speak.* Johar breathed out the cold that bit his nostrils, wrapped his pattu close, and scurried down the desolate streets to his aunt's house.

east

Crossing the United States,
September 6 to 9, 2001

Dawn watched the tall guy, Bryce, as he leaned on the battered sedan and arched his fingers until his knuckles cracked. There was an extra-long fingernail on his pinky and tattoos on his fingers. The shorter guy, Kaypo, had a red Afro and multiple earrings. They looked more like drug burnouts than musicians.

Bryce the Burnout snapped the trunk open. "Pack it in."

The Chevy's fender was crunched in like a soda can, but Dawn noticed the car was equipped with a CD player. She dug out a CD, threw her pack in back, and slid in.

Jude grinned balefully and whispered, "You actually talked me into it!" He must have been leery of Burnout too, because whispering wasn't his style.

"Amazing, huh?" Dawn tried to imagine no school for

the rest of the year. With both uneasiness and elation, she pictured her classmates gossiping about their disappearance.

Kaypo barreled into the passenger seat. Burnout gunned the motor, and Dawn heard a dull scraping as they inched down Market and over the Bay Bridge. She checked her watch. Victor would be in his lab, fiddling with beakers. Louise would be seeing the day's last patient at the ICRC clinic in Peshawar. Dawn would start her life.

"So." Kaypo peered at Dawn in the rearview mirror. "How old are you, anyway?"

Dawn weighed whether or not it was safe to reveal vital stats. He was gazing at her as if deciding whether or not to put on the moves. Lots of guys ogled her long blond hair and lanky body. But he was nicer than the driver. "I'm sixteen," she answered.

"That's cool." The kid lit an overstuffed blunt and dragged deeply, which launched him into a coughing fit. He offered a hit to his cohort, then passed the blunt back to Jude. "What do you think of our ride?" he gasped.

Jude passed the joint to Dawn. "It's fabulous," he lied. Dawn knew Jude couldn't handle weed, and it made her paranoid. She faked a hit and passed it.

Red Fro lit a cigarette and switched the radio to classic Led Zeppelin. "You must admit," he said as he exhaled, "this junker has one helluva sound system."

"Yeah, crank that sucker good and loud," ordered Burnout, tapping his fingers on the steering wheel. Dawn noticed his finger tattoos spelled out *N-O-O-S-E*.

"Bryce here plays lead," Kaypo yelled over the din. "I play bass. Our bud in Newark plays percussion."

"I'm a musician too," said Dawn. "I play the flute."

"Flute in a rock band is pansy-ass," ranted Burnout.

Dawn chose not to comment. Instead she asked, "Do you ever play with Pax?"

The kid's Afro bounced as he nodded. "Jude's brother? Yup. Helluva guitarist."

"Fair assessment," Jude said proudly.

"Pax is formulaic," groused Burnout. "Pat in his delivery." He extracted a cigarette from his pocket and lit up, waving the thing around in his skeletal fingers like a neon concert wand. "You know—the standard Pearl Jam and Metallica licks."

"I'll bet you've never gigged with him in a New York club," Jude snapped.

"Nope, not me," Burnout answered, as if it were beneath him.

"I did once, and I'd jump at another chance," answered Red Fro. "It was a helluva concert. Good money compared to the clubs in Newark."

The Chevy chugged up and around mountain curves, and the scraping sound grew to an insistent rasp. Dawn felt dizzy from the heavy smoke and the general excitement of leaving. Some reassuring music would help. "Hey, guys, ever listen to Rampal?"

"Who's Rampal?" asked Burnout.

Dawn held out her CD. "Someone good. Can we put it on?"

Red Fro shrugged. "Sure." He slid it into the disc player.

The flute melody reminded Dawn of seaweed-scented waves rolling over sand. She realized how rigid her shoulders had become and took meditative breaths.

"Get this arty-fart junk off," ordered Burnout. "Is this the schmaltz that you play on the flute? It's worse than hearing flute in a rock band! Classical gives me the hives."

"Sorry," Jude mouthed.

"It's not your fault," Dawn mouthed back to Jude.

Burnout pulled a CD from his overhead visor and switched the music to heavy metal. "You ride with me, you listen to the good stuff, like Noose." He rapped aggressively on the wheel, finger tattoos seesawing like player-piano keys.

As the air thickened with another round of smoke Dawn turned to Jude, who was scrunched in the corner rubbing his eyes. She knew he was wilting. "We'll be okay, Jude." Dawn held out her thermos. "Want some water?"

• • •

Dawn and Jude made up rules of survival. No more mention of Pax's band because it sparked jealousy. No mention of Dawn's music because that invited scathing put-downs. Earphones were a must. Crack a window at all times to air out noxious weed and nicotine fumes. Joke to break tension. She and Jude did silent imitations of their captors, slouching low so they couldn't be seen in the rearview mirror.

For the next couple of days, whenever the guys slipped into taverns for beer breaks, Dawn and Jude sat outside and took in the air of the dusty plains. Dawn played her flute. Jude danced his spacey jig. Cattle farmers ducking in for a brew would break out in grins. And Dawn developed the minor obsession of glancing at her watch every few hours to calculate the time in Peshawar and then in San Francisco. For instance, at 6:30 p.m. Dawn's time, in Peshawar it would be almost morning and Louise would be sleeping at ICRC headquarters. Back at the house on Santa Marisa, Victor would be shuffling into the kitchen for dinner. He would have discovered her note. What bittersweet relief to be far from him. Victor wouldn't bother calling her until Dawn was a no-show on Sunday night. She'd cross that bridge later.

The best times were when Burnout finally agreed to let Dawn drive. She'd recently gotten her license, and cruising on a three-lane in the dead of night was cool. While the guys snored in the back, Dawn and Jude sat in front, played the music they wanted, and talked way into the night.

"Why did you decide to finally make the break and run with me?" Dawn asked Jude one night when heavy clouds opened to a downpour.

"Edith came east to make her mark at seventeen. Pax ran to Manhattan at nineteen. You can't start too early these days."

"I mean besides that." Dawn's persistence matched the pounding rain.

"Does there necessarily have to be a 'besides that'?"

She'd never had the nerve to ask but found it now. "Do you like girls?"

"What does that have to do with anything?"

"Have you ever had a girlfriend?"

Jude was quiet for a long while. "I guess I'm not interested."

That answered a question Dawn had wanted to ask for a while. "Ever have a boyfriend?"

"I had a crush on my drama teacher at camp," Jude muttered, "But that's as far as it went. A teacher dating a camper was a no-no."

"That must have been frustrating."

"Very. None of it's easy. My parents don't even know yet."

Dawn said, "You're a catch no matter what."

"Thanks."

Dawn stared at truck taillights. "Jude, is there something wrong with me?"

"Like what?" She felt his eyes on her, curious.

"Remember teasing me when I was the only one not crying during *Cast Away*?"

"Well, yeah."

"Do I seem cold? *Blank?*" Her cheeks got hot. "Do you feel sorry for me? Is that why you're my friend?"

"You're quiet, observant." Jude let out a low sigh. "You're a sensitive artiste."

But she knew that wasn't it. That didn't explain why she felt like a chunk of wood while others got emotional. "People scare me," she said. "And it's not like I don't have feelings. I just can't get them out."

"Why not?"

"I'm not sure." She paused and looked out at the dark landscape racing by. "I guess we both have our challenges cut out for us."

They were quiet for a while, then Dawn started to hum. She sang Jude the lyrics to some of her earliest flute songs, "Home on the Range" and "Rock Candy Mountain." They were both sad songs about wandering, dreaming of home. "Everyone's looking for that perfect place," Dawn said, "which probably doesn't exist." She sighed, remembering Jude's house: its warmth, the smell of Edith's oil paints, and a bowl of oranges and plums set on the mahogany side table like something out of a Renaissance interior. "You're lucky to have a nice family, Jude."

"You have a family," Jude replied. "Just a different kind."

Memories of almost-strangers overwhelmed Dawn—

Victor's lazy contempt, the DiGiornos' mildewed ranch house, that first foster mother's Hansel and Gretel oven. "It's not the same, Jude." She gazed into his eyes. "I guess in the early days Epiphany had its moments. I got used to the routine: the watery oatmeal, the boring teachers, the revolving parade of social workers. The *institution* was in my blood. Some of the kids were nice too—Sadie played sax like Coltrane, and Little Mo, from Oakland, kept us laughing." Dawn shrugged. "That's where I first learned flute. Playing music distracted me from a lot of awful stuff that hit my friends head-on. Hey, I'll bet my real mom's a musician too."

Jude was watching the wipers swish away the rain. "Wouldn't that be something."

"Yeah." Dawn paused. "Later, Epiphany got really bad. We all found families, but they never worked out. I kept hoping that my mother would walk in and take me away."

"A group home would've destroyed me. Don't know how you got through it."

"Me neither. She's out there—I just know it, Jude."

"Have you ever looked for her?"

"Online, yeah. I spent months looking for a Laurel Sweet. Contacted every online adoption service. Absolutely nothing. She must have changed her name."

"Don't give up," Jude said softly.

"No way." But Dawn sank into the car seat.

Their nighttime conversations were intense. But the daytime views from the window were spectacular. They passed eerie red cliffs in Utah and the Badlands in South Dakota with ancient rock formations reminding Dawn of Mars or of rock-candy mountains. Dawn had never been east of Sacramento, and the landscape belted out stubborn beauty like those folk songs. Later, over the cornfields of

Kansas, the sky was so thick with blue that it could have been sliced like turquoise cake.

• • •

Toward the end of the trip, everyone grew vicious. They had driven through industrial sections of Ohio and were now on the highway north of D.C. The sour pollution matched the foul vibes polluting the sedan.

"I can't wait to take a shower," Jude said. "My shirt is absolutely stuck to me."

"Yeah, you stink like moldy onions," Burnout complained.

"Well, you smell like a urinal," Jude retorted.

"I kind of like roughing it," Dawn admitted.

"You ain't roughing it, you're getting the presidential treatment," said Burnout.

Jude rolled his eyes. "You mean POW treatment."

"I'm itching for a steak and fries." Red Fro rubbed his jelly belly.

"You're getting fat as a rhinoceros," Burnout shot back.

Dawn was sick of them all, and especially of Jude's whining. He whined about leg cramps and his wrinkled silk shirts and sleep deprivation.

"What's wrong with a warm sleeping bag?" she asked.

"It sucks, that's what. I can't wait until we get to Pax's and can sleep in a real bed."

"Maybe we shouldn't even stay there," replied Dawn. "If we stay somewhere else, no one could track us down."

"You've got to be kidding!"

"No, I'm not." She was worried about Victor telling Louise what she had done. Dawn drowned everything out with her headphones for the last five hours of the trip.

In Jersey, Burnout left the highway, pulled onto a shabby street, and parked.

Dawn took off her headphones. "Where are we?"

"Kaypo and I are staying in Newark," replied Burnout. "Your ride ends here."

"What?" exclaimed Jude.

"PATH train into Manhattan," said Red Fro as he shook hands. "It's been real."

•   •   •

In an exhausted but exhilarated daze, Dawn and Jude shot under the Hudson River in the PATH tunnel toward their dreamland, Manhattan, then rode an escalator up and out of the station into a seemingly endless marble concourse.

Jude scanned the signs. "We're in the World Trade Center!"

They wandered out onto the streets of Tribeca. "Look." Jude pointed back to where they'd been. "It goes up forever."

"It's taller than on TV," Dawn exclaimed. "The Transamerica Building doesn't even come close." She cupped her eyes and arched her neck skyward. The vastness of the steel-latticed building made her feel tiny, yet as if she could soar right up alongside it and into the sky. "It's like a mythical castle."

Jude bowed. "I pledge to be milady's footservant in her castle."

Dawn curtsied grandly. "Many thanks, milord."

They watched fancy people slip into seriously capitalistic limos and dash around the sidewalks to pop in and out of dark bars.

An image of Louise clambering into an ICRC jeep in the desert came into Dawn's mind, followed by one of Louise chucking her hiking boots for heels and mincing down the marble concourse of a skyscraper with briefcase in hand. The images made Dawn giggle. It was weird how she had suddenly thought of Louise. Dawn's eyes focused on the empty sidewalk. "Jude?" she called as she spun around. "Jude?" she called again. How would she find Pax's apartment without him? Her throat caught in a half-scream, then held. *"Jude!"* There he was, across the street asking someone for directions. He motioned Dawn back into the concourse. She heaved an enormous sigh.

"We have to go back in here, Dawn," Jude shouted from the steps, which led back into the Trade Center. "Number six train."

●　　　●　　　●

"This street reminds me of the Mission," Dawn remarked as they left the subway and crossed Third Avenue onto St. Marks. It pulsed with art and music types, street hustlers and vendors hawking hats, scarves, and earrings.

"I told you you'd like New York." Jude's eyes scanned a dreadlocked kid who strutted by with a spaniel festooned in a red bandana. "Half these people are musicians or actors. This is going to be so sweet."

Dawn was stoked by the iridescence of St. Marks at night: its tinseled jewelry, awnings lined with blinking lights, the interior of St. Mark's Comics, with rack after rack of gaudy displays. Music and conversation poured onto the street from restaurants and falafel houses. Dawn's ears latched onto a Middle Eastern beat, which jogged her into a vision of Louise tending to a sick child under a Red Cross tent. Dawn forced the image away, refusing to lend it space in her head. "How far are we from Avenue A?" she asked. Jude was the guide.

"Next block." Worry crossed his face. "I hope Pax is OK with this."

"I thought you said Pax would be happy to see you, no questions asked." They squeezed by two restaurants whose outside tables competed for space on the sidewalk.

"Oh, Pax will be fine. It's just his roommate, Sander." Jude's hand went up in a dismissive wave and he grinned. "We'll have to charm him, Dawn." Jude launched into his spacey jig, the pack bouncing on his rounded back.

"Stop it," she laughed. But Jude's antics didn't prevent Dawn's muscles from clenching tighter as they rounded the corner of Avenue A and her eyes rested on two bedraggled kids hunched in a doorway. Their vacant eyes stared past Dawn.

"Excuse me," Jude demanded.

One came half-alive. "Yo, we need to get to Jersey. Can you help us out?"

Jude tossed a quarter into the guy's outstretched hand, which was met with a distracted nod. Jude leaned over them to ring Pax's doorbell.

They heard pounding footsteps. The door swung open, and the two drifters shifted off the doorstep. "Buzzer's broken," said Pax as he tried to catch his breath. He had unruly black hair and untied Skechers and was tall but hunched like Jude. It seemed to take him a few beats to realize who they were. "Jude?" Pax's stare grew angry. "What are you doing here? The parents have been calling for two days!" Dawn averted her gaze to the bank of mailboxes. "You didn't do something loopy like run away, did you?"

Jude seemed to shrink under his brother's gaze. "Well, yeah, um, we did, Pax. I thought you'd think it was a good idea. You know, *you* ran away."

"Don't bring what *I* did into this," Pax retorted. "You can't stay here, end of story. What will I say when the parents are all over me? Huh?"

Jude's voice was bolder, indignant. "You don't have to answer for me, Pax, I'm perfectly capable. But hey, at least have some manners and invite us in for coffee."

"How did you get here, anyway?"

"We got a ride from your friends Bryce and Kaypo."

"Friends! Bryce is so burned out on drugs that no club will hire him, and Kaypo? He's such an *herb*." A goofy grin spread over Pax's face. "Okay. Fair enough, dude, you deal with the parental factor. It *is* cool to see you, just a huge surprise."

Jude introduced Dawn, and they trundled up four flights into a cramped apartment smelling of sandalwood, a psychedelic rainbow shag rug on the floor. Jude had a shag back in Frisco. Dawn wondered if a preference for scuzzy long-haired rugs ran in Jude's family's genes.

"It's gorgeous," Jude gushed as he examined posters and embroidered pillows.

Dawn spotted electric guitars, wah-wah pedals, amplifiers, and a DJ console. The array of instruments awed her. *Professional musicians.* The words trilled in her mind like an Ian Anderson flute riff.

"Our band, Paxmania, is playing tonight," Pax said. "I play guitar, and Sander here writes our lyrics and plays percussion."

A guy moved into the room as a lion might, feet stroking the carpet, blond mane streaming around his face.

Pax was just Jude's brother, Burnout and Red Fro were losers, but Sander was not only insanely cute, he was the real deal—a working rock musician.

Messy emotions began to branch through Dawn. She stared straight ahead at the instruments, willing herself to calm down.

"Hey," said Sander. He padded over to his drum set and pattered out a drum fill.

Keep your head down, Dawn thought, *or he'll see right into you.*

Sander flipped back his hair and glanced at Jude. "So you're Pax's brother, I've heard lots about you. You want to be an actor, right?" Jude smiled, nodding.

Then Sander turned to Dawn, who was twisting her garnet ring around and around. "So what are *you* into, Dawn?"

I'm into running. She turned that holy mother of a ring as if her life depended on it. "I'm into music."

firebrand

Baghlan, Afghanistan,
September 9, 2001

Aunt Maryam ushered Johar in. Peering out nervously from under her burqa, she quickly closed the door.

"What is it?" Johar asked. Maryam's movements were usually calm and deliberate.

"While I was away this afternoon, speaking with a student's mother, Ramila said two men came to the door, asking questions." Aunt Maryam's assistant, Ramila, was a girl who had studied longer than the others and knew the lessons: poetry, Quran, math, and, most forbidden, English. She lived nearby, so she often stayed late to share in the evening prayers, eat, and keep his aunt company.

"What questions did they ask?" Johar removed his pattu and put it on the mat bordering the mud-brick wall.

"How long have I lived here? Why were girls coming to my house? Where was my husband?" Aunt Maryam checked to make sure the curtains were closed, then removed her burqa, letting it fall, wrinkled, in a corner near where Bija slept on a square of carpet. His aunt's brown eyes were sallow and puffy with worry in contrast to the vivid blue of the lapis lazuli earrings her brother, Tilo, had given her before he'd gone to England. She kept them on even to sleep.

"Were they Taliban?" asked Johar.

"Who else?"

"What did Ramila tell them?" Johar asked anxiously.

"She told them my husband was a cloth merchant on the road to Herat. She said the girls helped me with washing and cleaning." Aunt Maryam laughed bitterly. "Lovely lies, eh?"

Johar sighed. "At least they didn't torture the truth from her."

"Not this time." She walked toward the back room. "Some chai is in order."

When Johar and his brother were younger, before the Taliban, Aunt Maryam never hid her village school. Children would flock from Baghlan and the nearby villages. They would sit in eager rows on the carpet as they listened to the morning lessons. Maryam had a decent blackboard and chalk then, and even the English textbooks Tilo had brought quietly in from England. "You must learn to read Dari, but also to speak English, the modern language of the world." She had pronounced the word *English* slowly so that her students, who called it Ingleesi, could hear its common usage. But that was then.

His aunt returned with steamy chai, and little Bija stirred from her nap. She burst into hungry tears.

Johar bent down and lifted her in his arms. "Hello, my jewel."

Bija's tears stopped. "Jor! You're here!" she screeched in Dari, then settled into his lap. Johar searched his pocket for the flask of milk he'd managed to coax from Marqa.

"My milk!" Bija grabbed it greedily and drank. Johar put the kebab he'd saved from the chaikhana on a plate of rice that Maryam laid down.

"What a lovely feast!" she cried, and joined him on the carpet.

Johar smiled and stroked Bija's forehead. She was three years old and growing fast. Aunt Maryam had her hands full trying to teach the older girls while Bija played. "Where is Ramila now?" Johar asked.

"Her brother picked her up. She said she would try to stop by later to drop off vegetables from the bazaar."

"Have you eaten today?" Johar asked, worried as he watched Aunt Maryam take delicate nibbles to draw out the meal.

"A bit of rice," she answered. Johar and Daq tried to bring her food, but it was painfully clear that a visit every few days was not enough. As difficult as it was to have the family separated like this, the brothers needed the hillside compound for shepherding, and Maryam had to live in Baghlan in order to teach.

"Soon we'll have a real feast," Aunt Maryam said wistfully.

"Yes! When all this is over," Johar answered, "we'll have mounds of gabli pilau and a barrel of keshmesh."

"I'll make samosas," added Maryam. "Samosas with yogurt and mint."

"Picked from the finest gardens in all of the country," Johar added.

"Samosas are yummy!" Bija shouted.

"Inshallah, someday." Maryam sighed.

Johar glanced around the room. It was almost bare except for a faded carpet over the dirt floor, the mat bordering the wall, and a square of Persian fabric with gold and turquoise designs tacked to one of the walls. Under the window stood a row of flowering plants in Russian porcelain that his aunt watered fastidiously. Johar saw these objects—the rug, a piece of fabric, plants—but in his mind's eye he saw additional objects, more precious than her wall hanging and her porcelain, hidden like prayers. Schoolbooks and weaving supplies were stuffed under tiles, behind a false wall, in a mud sinkhole under a water gourd, sewn inside the bottom of old prayer carpets. Like the burqa, the head-to-toe covering that kept his aunt's face a secret, she was an expert at veiling her existence as teacher and weaver. It was as if each person lived in opposite worlds at once: conforming in the apparent world, but nursing a rebellious fire behind closed doors.

Bija tugged at Johar's tunic, shaking him from his reverie. "Tell me a poem."

Johar cleared his throat. "Let me see . . . I'm thinking of a Rumi poem.

"My worst habit is I get so tired of winter
I become a torture to those I'm with.
If you're not here, nothing grows.
I lack clarity. My words
Tangle and knot up.
How to cure bad water? Send it back to the river.
How to cure bad habits? Send me back to you."

Bija clapped her hands. "More poems," she demanded. "That was lovely, Johar." His aunt touched his arm.

"But it's almost curfew. Amniyat nist! You'd better be going."

"You're right." Johar rose reluctantly. He kissed Bija and his aunt on each cheek. "See you in three days, then?"

"Yes," she answered. "Salaam. Bring Daq too." She covered herself with her burqa before opening the door. "Johar, one more thing."

"Yes?"

"If anything happens to me—" She paused. "Do you remember the family plan to meet at Suryast?"

"The camp in Peshawar that your friend went to when she ran from the mujahidin."

"That's right. If the situation gets worse, we must do what we can to remain safe." She paused. "You promised to care for Bija if she needs it."

Johar nodded. "I know."

"Thank you." She peered out into the street. "Be careful. Do not wander from the main road, Johar. Taliban." Worry returned to her brown eyes.

Worry filled him too as he hurried down the dark road to his hut. The angry words in the chaikhana replayed in his mind. *Taliban this, Taliban that. Arab foreigners here to fight our American enemy.* Aunt Maryam and Uncle Tilo had taught him that the Western lands were woven with many colors: brown, yellow, red and white—with many Muslims as well. Yet Johar had heard people here say that *all* in the West mistrusted Islam. That didn't make sense—brown, yellow, red, and white were bound to have different opinions. Underneath all this mistrust, fear must lurk. Fear existed on all sides, for sure. If Allah had created the world, then surely he'd created the infidels, nonbelievers, as well. Only a madman would create a world doomed to fatal division. And wasn't Allah just and pure?

● ● ●

Johar was startled from sleep when Daq stumbled into the room, set out his quilt, and unearthed his radio. Strains of the Talib-run Radio Shariat crackled forth. The announcer ranted down a list of commandments: no kite flying, no musical instruments, no laughter in the streets. There was static as Daq switched the dials. He was always searching for a station that offered more than lectures. It was frightening how fast the Taliban had risen from a small group of rural clerics and Pashtun farmers to the power they were now. They had seized almost all the stations around Baghlan for their shariat broadcasts. There were only a handful of stations up north still free to play music.

General Massoud's Alliance army, made up of Uzbeks and Hazaras, but mostly Tajiks like Johar, had staved off the Taliban's encroachment in the northern fronts around Taloqan and Mazar-i-Sharif. Johar prayed that the Alliance would force the Taliban south until they were far past *his* town, then even further south, past the capital, Kabul. Until then Johar felt that every day might be his last.

But the Taliban continued their ruthless push north. In a few years even General Massoud's warriors would not be strong enough to stop the Taliban from seizing the whole of Afghanistan.

Johar heard more static and slips of voices. Finally the melody of *tanbur* and *rubab* danced through the house, and his brother sighed beside him. Johar missed Daq these days. Even though his body was next to Johar's, his mind was worlds away.

After some silence Daq spoke, as if he could read Johar's thoughts. "A soldier came to the chaikhana with startling news. General Massoud is near death."

"Massoud near death!" Johar's insides tightened. This was tragic! If Massoud died, the north would fall in days, and a Taliban stranglehold on the entire country would be ensured. Massoud was hope. Massoud was life, the future. Johar felt sick. "How did it happen?"

"They say he was hit by an imposter reporter with a television camera that hid an explosive," Daq replied. "They say it was an Al Qaeda spy helping the Taliban."

"Al Qaeda?"

"The Arab fighters who came here from other countries," Daq explained. "The warriors whom Naji trained with in Kandahar."

"Why are they here? They don't belong on our soil," Johar exclaimed. "They fill up our bazaars and chaikhanas. They push the townsfolk around. And what will become of the Alliance?" Johar was overcome by a sense of doom.

"They're here to help fight the West, but what do you care?" Daq snarled. "You are not rushing to join their cause. Let the Taliban take over. They know how to keep order. They would have stopped the mob who killed our father. If I became a soldier, it would not be for the Alliance. It would be for the Taliban."

"But you are Tajik. Tajiks fight with the Alliance."

"It's complex. What do you know of it? All you know is weaving and poetry."

Johar was silent after that. He was frightened of his brother's hatred and new allegiances. Their tension reminded him of lines from Rabi'a's last poem, which she wrote on the wall with her own blood: *I knew not when I rode the high-blooded steed, the harder I pulled its reins the less it would heed.*

"How was Aunt Maryam?" Daq asked finally, in a more docile tone.

"She's worried. Men came to her door today asking about her students," Johar replied. The merry flute countered his anxious mood.

"And what did she say to them?"

"Ramila answered. She told them her students were helping her with chores. But what is to stop them from bothering her again? They must suspect something."

"She should stop her teaching," Daq remarked.

The tanbur reached a high pitch, and its notes stirred Johar's anger. "How can you suggest something so wrong? Teaching is her life. Life doesn't stop because we're living under tyrants."

Daq snapped off his radio. "Tyrants? Naji's not a tyrant. He says the Taliban will bring money and jobs into Baghlan, build Afghanistan into a true Muslim state."

"Naji has stolen your mind. Go fight, then, and leave me to the sheep."

"Maybe I will. Don't try to follow, because you'll never make a good soldier."

Johar heard thumping. He froze as noise from outside the stone enclosure sifted in: men's voices speaking in urgent whispers. It was way past curfew, and the roads should be empty. Johar's stomach clenched. He heard Daq scramble to hide his radio. They both knew it was a jail sentence if the radio was discovered.

"Hide, Johar," Daq ordered.

"What about you?"

"I said hide!"

Now voices were inside the courtyard and pounding on the latched door. Johar should face these intruders by Daq's side; after all, wasn't his brother protecting him, even now? Yet every drop of Johar's blood quivered with the urge for invisibility.

The pounding again, and Daq's stern command: "Johar, do what I say. *Now!*" Johar raced into the storeroom and squirmed into a hole beneath the floor for water jugs. He scrambled to pull a prayer rug over the hole.

"Open up!" a voice demanded.

Johar sensed Daq's hesitation. "Open up, or I'll break this door down," the man shouted again.

Daq's footsteps plodded heavily toward the door. Someone kicked the door once, then twice. Johar heard Daq unlatch the lock.

"Time to fight!" Johar heard a familiar voice but dared not peek out. "Tell him, Farooq." *Farooq?* He would never break into their house! And Farooq would not fight voluntarily, even if it filled his stomach in winter, even if it meant new boots.

Johar heard a sharp slap, and Farooq let out a grunt. Someone was hitting him.

"Tell him," the voice ordered again. Where had he heard that voice? At the chaikhana. It was *Naji's*!

"We're going to join the Taliban army." Farooq choked out the words.

"What is this?" demanded Daq. "Coming to my house in the middle of the night? For what? We'll talk tomorrow in the chaikhana. Go now. I have not yet made up my mind." Daq's tone was indignant.

"I've made up your mind for you," Naji replied sharply.

"Get off. Stop! Put that gun away!" Daq's voice was fearful now. Johar was filled with a nightmare image of a Kalashnikov pointed straight at his brother's temple, and his mind flew to the day eight years back when his father was forced up the sheep hill. He could almost smell the warlord's acrid sweat and hear the snap of the guns. Johar couldn't just hide. He climbed from the hole and crept toward the door that led to the outer room, taking care that his steps were silent.

"Now. Collect your pack and hurry," Naji yelled. "Or else I will end it here!"

"Bastard!" The English curse catapulted from Daq's mouth. Naji wouldn't understand but would hear hatred in the tone.

Johar peered around the wall. Naji's gun was rammed right against his brother's ear. Johar's insides burned as if pierced by firebrands. "No!" Johar bellowed.

"What did you say?" Naji turned to Farooq, fury on his face. Johar hid again behind the wall.

Farooq's voice shook. "I was starting to say, 'No, curses do you no good, Daq.'"

"Hmph," Naji grumbled.

Johar saw Naji inch Daq to the door, his gun now on Daq's back. Farooq lagged behind a step. If Johar could grab a log, if he could only gather the nerve to strike Naji . . . Johar crept toward the logs near the smoldering fire.

Farooq's head spun around, and his eyes locked with Johar's for one precious moment. He waved frantically for Johar to retreat. "Hide," Farooq mouthed.

Somehow Johar lost his nerve and scrambled back into the hole. He cursed himself under his breath. The footsteps stopped, turned, then shuffled perilously close. Johar kept still but feared his breaths were as loud as crow caws.

As if he sensed Johar's proximity, Naji blurted, "Where

is that brother of yours? He won't do as a soldier, but we'll bring him along as our cook."

"My brother's not here. He went out," Daq replied.

"Out so late? You said yourself it's past curfew," Naji replied. "You're lying." Johar heard the crashing of objects, maybe his mother's wooden trunk. He prayed Naji would not find the radio.

Daq spoke once more, "You were my friend. Don't you believe me?"

"Friends, yes," Naji murmured.

"Then believe me. Johar went to care for our ailing aunt in the village," insisted Daq. "Leave him alone. You're right, he's not fit for the life of a soldier."

Naji snickered.

Johar heard footsteps retreating once more. He heard groans, the thump of the door, then footsteps fading. Curled like an infant in the crawl space, Johar thought, *Daq is right. I'm not a soldier, and not even a man.* He hated himself then for not having shouted, "If you take Daq, you take me as well!" Would he see his brother again?

Johar heard the sound of crackling. As he shoved the rugs aside, he was blinded by black smoke. They'd set the house on fire!

driftwood

New York City,
September 10, 2001

"But I don't know how. I've never improvised before," protested Dawn. She was scrunched on her sleeping bag in the storage room, which had been hastily transformed into Dawn and Jude's crash pad. Despite her nervousness with Sander leaning close, the air buzzed with excitement.

"When I was your age I didn't have much confidence," he said. "You've got to start somewhere and build up." Sander waved her toward the door. "Come on! Five-minute improv. I'll coach you. Hey, you said you were into music."

"But really," Dawn began, "I'm not sure. . . ." She felt shy with Jude off to an open call for an extra in the musical *Rent*.

"No excuses." Sander took her hand and gently pulled her up. Dawn followed him out to the practice area, where

Pax was already rehearsing, his fingers racing up and down his Stratocaster in manic riffs.

Sander picked up an electric flute, plugged it into an amp, and handed it to Dawn. "I borrowed this from a guy in BronxBox. Practice on it till you get your sea legs."

"Thanks!" Dawn had never tried one before. She spread her lower lip over the mouthpiece and tried a few notes. Walls of amplified sound rose up.

"Dude, let's go," grumbled Pax.

"We're going to play a song I wrote," Sander explained to Dawn.

"Cool! But how do you . . . you know—improvise?"

"Inject yourself into the mood," said Sander, settling onto his seat and rattling out a fill. "Then oil your bones and belt it out." She nodded dumbly.

Pax began the melody, then Sander leaped in on snare. Sander's song rocked—it was a heady mix of Alanis Morissette meets Incubus meets Thelonious Monk.

Dawn, almost swooning as she stood next to Sander, honed in on the song's essence, and tried hard to imitate, but her syncopation was stiff and her tone was flat.

"You're off-key!" protested Pax. How did his fingers know just where to fly?

Dawn was trying, she really was, but after so many years of reading music how was she supposed to improvise just like that?

Sander kept grinning at her and patiently laying down the beat.

Dawn's fingers stumbled over themselves, and her mind froze with the unfamiliar tension of creating novel runs while attempting to match the key and the pace. She could hear the flute screech. It was awful! The band stopped dead.

"You're like stone," Pax grumbled. "Relax! We're not going to bite."

Dawn would have punched Pax if she hadn't wanted to punch herself even more. "I'm trying to," she said.

"That's your problem," Pax shot back. "You're trying too hard."

"Paxman, cut her a break," Sander insisted, and turned to Dawn. "When you force the riff, it sounds canned. Take it slow, Dawn. Don't rush it." Sander's gravelly voice sent charges down her back. "Have fun with it like a kid with a toy, you know?" He tapped on the snare. "Here's something easy. Pax, let's play 'Siesta.' "

Pax rolled his eyes but laid down the guitar track. Dawn picked up the flute and listened. It was a lazy, summer theme, a butterfly theme spun around from flower to flower. OK, she could picture it, and began to play.

"Not bad," Sander said. "Oh yeah," he sang as he swung his shoulders.

She was good. She was hot! Even Pax started to dip his hips.

The door burst open. Two girls—a brunette and a honey blonde—threw themselves onto the couch. "Hi, guys," they cooed. "What's up for later?"

"Hey," Sander said. "We're going to a BronxBox jam. Want to hang here until we're done?"

"Sure." They both started to giggle like groupies.

Dawn's mind went fuzzy when the women stared at her. Sander didn't seem to notice, and the guys started up again. She tried to pick up the thread but rambled off the beat. "Um, sorry," she mumbled.

"This is a drag," Pax complained. "I'm taking a break." He lifted the guitar strap over his shoulder, laid the instrument on its stand, flopped onto the couch, and lit a cigarette. Then he took a drag, tapped it on the edge of the ashtray, and chuckled to himself on the exhale. *So, the big-shot guitarist was laughing at the incompetent flutist, huh? Well, to hell with Pax!* Dawn was far from a beginner. The women started to whisper. *What now?* Dawn wondered as she stood there like a bonehead.

Sander slid his drumsticks into one of the metal ridges along the side of his bass drum. "Girls," Sander said, gesturing toward Dawn, "This is a friend of Pax's brother." They offered a distracted hello.

Their hair's prettier than mine, Dawn thought bitterly. She said hi, then fumbled around the furniture and shut herself in her room, her cheeks hot with shame. What had made her think she could jam with someone like Sander? Pax was right; she was inept.

"Is she joining your band?" Dawn could hear one of the girls ask.

The other one piped up, "She's *staying* here?"

Sander's response was so muted that Dawn couldn't make out his words. She flopped on her sleeping bag as the band resumed. The apartment door slammed shut, and the music stopped. "Hey, Jude, how'd it go?" she heard Pax ask.

"Just terrific," Jude snapped. Dawn could tell he was upset.

"Good to hear it," said Pax. "Oh, by the way, Edith and Tom called, all yelling and stuff. Call them back. I can't cover for you again, dude."

"I'll call them, I'll call them," Jude grumbled. Dawn heard footsteps approach, and the door swung open. Jude trudged in looking bummed, and crumpled onto the rug.

"So what happened?" Dawn asked, distracted from her gloom.

"It was beyond demoralizing," Jude muttered. "They cut me off after three freaking lines, and you should've heard how lousy some of those wannabes were. I was good, Dawn, I was *so* good!" He raked his hair in despair.

"Of course you're good, Jude." Inwardly Dawn cringed, thinking of how squeaky Jude's voice got when he was nervous. "They don't recognize talent when it's staring them in the eyeballs," she said, her voice gentle as she leaned toward her friend. "Let's go out walking. Forget those jerks. You'll land something soon."

"You think so?" Jude's face lit up. "Yeah, those bozos were clueless."

Dawn and Jude set out to discover the island with serious determination. They footed it from the hinterlands of Avenue A across St. Marks with its jewelry vendors and art students, west to the Hudson River piers, and up to the midtown skyscrapers. The city was packed with every kind of person imaginable, and some of them even seemed friendly. Though cabs buzzed around like mad hornets, the city was brighter and safer than she'd always assumed from watching edgy shows like *NYPD Blue*. Dawn and Jude reached Forty-second Street and ducked into stores displaying rows of I ❤ NY T-shirts, Yankees hats, postcards of the World Trade Center towers, and statuettes of Miss Liberty.

Back on the street, Dawn and Jude flowed with the tourists, all searching for the spiritual heart of Broadway in the billboards and flashy news blips moving in lit-up bands around buildings. Dawn pointed to a subway entrance, and they hopped a train downtown to Tribeca. They wandered along Greenwich Street past loading docks and trendy lofts, and passed twenty-something couples who pushed strollers of whining children into a park called Washington Market. Dawn and Jude followed them in and climbed with the toddlers on monkey bars. After that, Dawn talked Jude into buying a fire-engine-red silk shirt in a boutique—"to get noticed the next time you audition."

As they meandered further downtown and back inside the Trade Center concourse Dawn's energy ebbed. In this place where she'd first set foot in Manhattan, the loneliness of her arrival hit her full on—the tension of driving east with Burnout, the terror when she'd lost Jude for those seconds on the concourse. She thought of today's humiliating jam session, of Jude's dismal audition. They rode the escalators aimlessly. *What am I doing here?* she wondered. All the earlier exuberance of the afternoon now seemed forced.

"I'm going to meditate," Jude said. "Want to join me?"

Dawn felt an urgency to connect with something steady. "Give me a minute, Jude. I need to make a call."

"Sure." His voice sounded unsettled too.

She watched Jude sit on a bench and raise his head toward the arched line of windows as she leaned into the phone partition to block out noise. Dawn pulled the SIM card from her pocket and dialed.

After a few seconds she felt her resolve falter. What was she going to *say*? She should hang up now, while she still could.

Louise's scolding words from their last battle popped into her mind like a computer virus: *Who do you think you are, Miss Rude?*

I don't know who I think I am, Dawn thought. *Certainly I'm not as important as a starving refugee.* Dawn's neck muscles stiffened. She glanced out of the phone booth to the cold marble concourse spreading in all directions. Then her finger went to the button that would cut off the call.

"Hello?" Louise's voice vibrated inside Dawn. "Hello?" The voice was solid. Dawn's reply withered in her throat. *"Hello?"* Louise repeated persistently. Seconds passed. Sweat broke out on the back of Dawn's neck.

"Dawn? Is this you?" Dawn heard the stern tone, and something in her shifted. All feeling, from her brain to her ankles, cooled like a canary left by an open window. She hung up.

run

Baghlan, Afghanistan,
September 9, 2001

Johar pushed through the carpet layers. *Khub ast!* he thought frantically. Flames were curling around the door to the front room. He was almost to the storage room door. "Am I such a coward, Allah," he said aloud as he stepped into the blazing front room, "that you wish me dead?" Johar strained his eyes for shapes. On a square of over-turned bedding, flames jumped. Around the circle of logs on the hearth a fire danced. Smoke poured from the ceiling bricks. He took a hurried breath in and out. The hairs inside his nose scorched. *If I burn,* thought Johar numbly, *Bija and Aunt Maryam will have no family. No food.*

"I'm braver than you think!" he yelled to the fire as he tripped through the smoke to search for his pack. It was lodged in the crevice under the floor with the singed wool.

Johar stuffed it full, then shot through the door to the sheep paddock, escaping flames hotter than the hellish sands of Rigestan.

"Come," Johar commanded his sheep. He lured them from the stone enclosure behind the house, prodding the skittish ones along the path and toward his neighbor's house as they bleated with terror. "Zolar!" He beat on her door until she opened it.

"My brother," Johar cried. "They took my brother, and now the men may be headed for my aunt Maryam's!"

Zolar wept at the sight of Johar's house in flames. She was thankful for the sheep he gave her, and so moved by his worry for Bija and Maryam that she offered him her donkey. "Protect what you can. My beast will get you to your aunt's faster than on foot."

Johar uttered grateful thanks, took one last look at his burning hut, and flew like a free-tailed bat to town.

He guided the donkey onto a back path, praying he would not run into guards. Where would Naji take Daq, and what did these Pashtun Taliban want with a Tajik like Daq, anyway? It would be absurd for Daq to fight against the Alliance—against his own Tajik tribe in the north. And Farooq was not as tough as Daq—Farooq's would be a swift decline. These thoughts drove Johar to Maryam's, more fearful than ever for her safety.

Spotting men up ahead, across from Maryam's hut, Johar took cover behind an old Soviet rocket that had pierced the hill like an ogre's arrow. His breath came in sharp stabs. In the darkness it was impossible to tell whether the men were Taliban or not. They prattled on. While Johar was devising an alternative route he heard the rumblings of a truck, and the men drove away.

Maryam's door was open. Johar leaped off the donkey and tied it to a post. He trembled as he eased in the door. Neither Maryam nor Bija was anywhere in sight, but the house! The house had been torn apart! Fabric was ripped from the wall. The flower pots and dishes lay in shards. Books had been trampled. The samovar was gone from its perch. What had they done with his family? Kidnapped them? Or, pray not, murdered them?

Johar shuddered with a rising hysteria as he scrambled into the courtyard and around the village lanes. "Bija! Maryam!" he called, splitting apart the silence. Oil lanterns lit behind curtains, and faces peered out.

"Johar!" a woman's voice called from a nearby shed. "Johar, is that you?"

The burqa-clad figure was hazy in the dark. As he hurried toward her, he saw that she stood a head shorter than Maryam. "Who are you?" Johar asked.

"Shh." The woman pulled him inside. "It's Ramila."

"Ramila, what happened? Where did they go?"

"Soldiers took your aunt." Ramila's eyes, through the burqa's opening, had a stunned look. "They're searching for you too, Johar. You must leave!"

"But my aunt, my cousin—" A catch in Johar's throat would not let him continue.

"Come." Ramila lit an oil lamp and motioned Johar to a corner where a sleeping child lay curled on a quilt, stalk doll in hand.

"Bija!" Johar leaned over and hugged his little cousin. "Jazakullah, Ramila."

"I was taking her to help me sort the vegetables when the soldiers came for your aunt," said Ramila. "Before they could capture us too, we ran and hid here." She knelt down next to Bija and stroked her head. "I gave her my old doll to calm her." Ramila gazed at him. "I can keep her with me, Johar, until it's safe for your return."

Johar couldn't concentrate on Ramila's words. As glad as he was to see Bija's tiny chest rising and falling, he knew Maryam might be in great trouble. If only he knew where she was. If only he'd been with her, she would not have been alone when soldiers came.

Bija was waking. Johar swept her up in his pattu. "Ramila, was there any clue as to where the soldiers would take my aunt?"

"No, Johar. But I heard them inquire of your whereabouts when they came near the shed. The soldiers will be back for you. You must go!" Ramila gathered supplies and pushed them into his hands.

Johar hesitated. "I must find my aunt."

"They will hold her in jail for a time, but they won't kill her. Go before the soldiers carry you off," she insisted.

Johar remembered the old plan, the family plan they'd hoped they'd never have to follow. "When you see Maryam, tell her we will ride south, over the Pakistani border, to the camp where her friend once went—the camp Suryast in Pakistan—where Bija can be safe. Tell her we'll wait for her there. Tell her I love her."

Ramila held her arms out. "I can look after Bija."

"Bija must come with me," Johar answered. "I promised my aunt."

"Are you sure?"

He nodded. No one would harm his cousin. He would make sure of it.

Ramila lowered her arms to her sides. "Asalaam alaikum. Safe travels, Johar."

"Alaikum asalaam, Ramila."

Bija clung to his shoulders as he ran back to Maryam's. Johar had memorized each of her hiding places, and went to them now: gathering the spindle behind the false wall, the knitting needles stuck inside straw, the wool in a false ceiling, a trampled Rabi'a book from under the floor. He moved them to his own hiding places: an extra pouch in his pack, a pocket under his pattu, the inside hems of the quilt. The donkey would carry only the essentials, for he could not bring attention to the cargo.

Johar hurried down a deserted path toward the temple of Sorkh Kowtal. He knew this winding trail well. That old crater hole had been his playground; this ruined hut had been a fairy-tale bazaar where he'd sold imaginary crafts to his friends. Mixed with his fear was a powerful nostalgia for these things of his past, which he might not see again. If he made it tonight to the southern trade road leading to Charikar, he would feel safer. Johar quieted Bija's hungry fussing with a heel of bread that Ramila had given him, and pressed her close to warm her.

As the hovels on the outskirts of Baghlan receded and bushes gave way to camel thorn, Johar imagined he heard his father's murmur from the fog-laden sky: "Follow the dried riverbed if need be, *and speak up*." Speak up? The poetry of the dead was sometimes murky, as the heavens were tonight.

"Speak up," a voice demanded from the clearing. Johar jerked to attention. Bija began to howl.

In his confusion Johar had led them to a checkpoint guard. "Foul, foul hell," he hissed under his breath.

"I said halt! What business has kept you past curfew?" ordered a black-turbaned Talib, emerging from the shadows. His small eyes were set inward, like knots on trees. "Why are you travelling the roads so late? Where are you from and what is your destination?" Johar had a momentary urge to spur his donkey on, but yielded when the guard raised his Kalashnikov toward Johar, and two other men stepped from the shadows. Johar draped the pattu over Bija to conceal her.

"I'm from Baghlan, sahib. I travel to see my uncle in Charikar." Not exactly a truth, but the first story Johar's panicked mind could summon. His uncle Tilo *had* lived in Charikar but was far from there now.

"Jor." Bija tugged on Johar's shalwar, restless. "Play." Johar's heart pounded as he raised the pattu higher to muffle her words.

The guard lowered the machine gun to his side and strode close. "Turn back. We cannot guarantee your safety." Curious, the younger guards followed closely behind.

Johar breathed slowly—in, out, in—as if by calming himself he could make the men lose interest. "I'll be fine," Johar assured the beady-eyed guard. He snapped the donkey's reins to go. Bija poked him in the side, and he jerked with discomfort.

The man raised his gun once more. "I said halt! Dismount." He leveled it to Johar's brow. Johar understood then that it wasn't a matter of ensuring his safety at all. The old guard's eyes fixed on the lump that was Bija. "Smuggling, eh?" His knotted eyes grew shiny with interest as he drew close to Johar, who now stood beside the donkey. Johar gripped Bija, still under the pattu, close to his chest. The others leaned in, suddenly interested at the prospect of smuggled goods.

What if they take Bija? worried Johar. If he'd had the

nerve to own a gun like other boys, Johar could have blown these bullies to dust.

The guard, smelling of grilled meat, grabbed Johar's pattu and yanked it open.

"A child!" The man spat on the ground, then began to rifle through Johar's clothing. Bija yelped and clung to her cousin, her doll clutched in one hand, the cloth of Johar's vest in the other.

The younger guards left to interrogate an incoming group at the checkpoint. The beady-eyed man began to search one side of the donkey's pack. Johar prayed the man would not feel the wool sewn into the borders of the quilts. The guard unearthed a pan, Ramila's keshmesh, and some bread. "This is all?" he asked. Johar nodded.

Then the man moved to the other side of the donkey. He reached into the folds of the saddle pack and pulled out Johar's English dictionary and the Rabi'a book. This was bad, very bad! The guard thumbed through both with a frown. "Nothing else, eh? Then what are these books? These are not Quran. This poetry, this Ingleesi, is good for a jail sentence!" He hurled the books to the ground.

Bija began to whimper. She balled her free hand into a fist and held it in front of her eyes, as if to protect herself from the guard's sharp tone.

The man's gaze settled on Bija. "Yes, good for a jail sentence along with that doll." He ripped the stalk doll from Bija's fingers and crushed it under his heel. Bija howled as if he'd plunged a scimitar through her chest. "No images of people will be tolerated. It was *decreed*."

Johar knew then that the beady-eyed guard would snatch Bija and torture him without a flicker of remorse. What would happen after? Johar could hardly bear to think. He would rot in prison much longer than a woman, even a teacher, and Aunt Maryam might never know what had become of them. Johar's mind snapped precariously from one dark imagining to another as the younger guards argued with a new arrival at the checkpoint.

The guard began to bind Johar's hands.

Johar spoke loudly, urgently, to project over Bija's weeping. "Sahib, I may have *one* thing for you—if you let us pass."

"Eh?" The guard's eyes shone with greed. He loosened the strap. "What is it, boy? Quickly, now."

Johar unrolled the waistband of his kameez. "Your feet will be cold soon. Snow is coming to this pass, no?"

"Snow, yes." The guard picked up an oil lantern. He screwed up his eyes in the dim glow to examine the objects Johar held. "Boy, what is it?"

"Socks. For you."

"Bah! You expect to bribe your way with these rags?" The guard grabbed them. "Go now," he grumbled, motioning forward with the lantern. "Be off with you, and don't come back here."

"Many thanks, sahib." Johar spurred the donkey to action just in time to avoid the younger Talibs, who had finished their other interrogations and now approached.

Johar hurried the donkey down the road, murky except for star haze softening the fog on a hut here, a bit of brush there. Bija mourned her doll and continued to cry hopeless tears for the next hour.

There were few on the path this late. The occasional truck rumbled by with goods for the bazaars. Lone men with heavy eyes limped by, bundles and rifles hanging from their shoulders, and a family passed on two donkeys, both loaded with piles of blankets and sleeping children.

Bija finally cried herself to sleep. Johar kissed her dirt-stained face and wrapped her tighter against the chill. Far from the town and in the stony pit of night, he heard hyena howls and the scurrying of weasels. Johar kept on past his endurance. He must create as much distance as possible between himself and those who hunted him. Where was his brother now, and would Daq worry about Johar, as Johar had about him? At least Daq was strong and could take care of himself. Aunt Maryam's welfare worried Johar more. Would she be let free to travel south through the Khyber Pass to Camp Suryast? Would Daq? Camp Suryast was rumored to be huge. Even if by some miracle they all made it there, it would be like three lizards searching for one another in a desert.

Khushal's poem sifted like a breeze through the sagging canopies of Johar's despair: *I parted with them at Khwarrah with sad heart. Love's troubles are like fire, Khush-hal, what though the flame be hidden, its smoke is seen.*

Johar prevailed almost until dawn, when he tied the donkey to a tree and dropped beside it. He and Bija went to sleep in quilts by its base as the wind fluttered the leaves above.

Johar dreamed they were passengers in a truck piled with ripe melons, grapes, speckled plums, and pomegranates. Grape juice dripped down Bija's chin as she gobbled. Johar stuffed melon in his mouth and was laughing, laughing, laughing.

He awoke with a start. Sweat beaded his pounding head. He cupped his hand to shade his eyes from the sun and heard Bija's sharp cries of thirst and hunger: "Aab! Naan!" His belly ached for the same. He would need twice the food to feed his cousin. How would he ever survive?

Bija's cries mixed with a woman's guttural moans. Johar

spun around. In his exhaustion last night they had dropped without regard. The fluttering last night was a sea of flags in a makeshift graveyard. Each flag stood to honor a dead person. The plane tree under which they had slept was covered by devotional tacks–every tack denoted a prayer. The woman was hunched over a freshly dug grave, and she rocked back and forth, clutching her head as she moaned. Her child, a girl in a dusty hijab, slightly older than Bija, worked at digging a hole near her mother, all the while reciting a singsong verse between watery coughs.

Bija paused from her tears to observe the girl, then swung back around and pulled on Johar's sleeve. "Naan, Jor!"

Johar retrieved their modest food bag and offered Bija a piece of bread with one precious dab of honey. Bija chewed it hungrily. The mourner's child got up and ran to Johar's side, coughing. She stared at the bread with black-currant eyes. Johar placed a piece in her hands as well.

After morning ablutions, Johar dotted another piece of bread with honey and savored it with the tiny bites he'd seen Aunt Maryam take. He leaned back, not yet ready to journey on, and turned his face to the sky. Such a blue it was, a lapis blue like Maryam's earrings. A sheer light filtered onto the mountains ahead, lending them the delicacy of pastel parchment.

Bija's face poked into his as she leaned on his crossed legs. "Jor, doll," she murmured miserably. She had not forgotten.

Johar stumbled up and dusted himself off. He searched for objects in the sand, while the woman's low moaning duetted with Bija's high cries. Johar cracked off dry twigs from a shrub and made a stick figure. Next he rescued a bit of torn flag from the sand and with it fashioned a skirt. He tied the skirt with a strand of mulberry-hued wool he fetched from his pack.

When Bija looked up from wiping tears on their quilt, she gasped with surprise as he held out her gift. "Dolly!" she shouted. Bija ran to the girl in the dusty hijab and showed it off proudly. Johar was already crafting another one for her.

As the girls chuckled and squealed with their dolls, the mother paused from her mourning to raise her head. Johar couldn't see the curve of her mouth under her burqa, but he knew she smiled from the way her dark eyes crinkled through the eye grating.

He leaned back once more, gazing at the flags, ragged in the wind, and imagined that this was a day after all wars were over, when the land was safe and brother was not torn from brother. He could almost imagine it here, in this humble place of death where souls were honored by a bouquet of flags set lovingly in the sand.

hit

New York,
September 11, 2001

Lucky's Coffee on Sixth Avenue and Eighteenth Street was a reliable spot for Dawn and Jude to set up shop. People went in grouchy, then paraded out with coffee and a bagel in their bellies, apparently guilty enough that they'd eaten and the street kids hadn't to throw money their way. Dawn made sure to be friendly with all the vendors, and they welcomed the crowds that her music attracted. If Dawn and Jude worked all morning, they could each pocket around twenty-five dollars. The hat was set up on the pavement with Dawn's sign propped in front—Need Money for Food—that she had drawn with Sander's purple markers and taped to the cardboard back of her award for musicianship.

Usually Dawn's morning medley was Ian Anderson's fast-paced "Thick as a Brick," some breathy Radiohead, the vibrant Telemann. When she played she would slip into an altered state, caught in the music's passion, her body supple yet straight, her eyes directed toward the sky. Jude would dance his spacey jig, all elastic arms and slithering body mirroring her flute's crescendos and dips like the snake in a charmer's lure. His long hair would thrash around his charismatic smile.

Most days the routine attracted quite a crowd, but this morning everyone seemed lazy and distracted. Indian summer infused the senses. The day was a sunlit seventy degrees, the kind of air that made Dawn think of apples, school binders, and summer's last swim. It also didn't help that Jude looked too darn middle-class with his silk shirt and new denims to pass for a panhandler. Dawn warned him not to wear the fancy outfits. She had on her ripped tie-dye and patched jeans. The last thing they wanted to do was advertise that they had a bit of cash and a roof over their heads.

Besides, that roof was iffy at best. Ever since the ill-fated jam session Pax had developed a seriously superior attitude toward Dawn. Not to mention that Sander's hot looks and musical expertise still made her nervous. But what really panicked her was that it was only a matter of time before Edith and Tom figured out where Dawn and Jude were. And when they found out, they'd tell Victor.

Dawn was playing the last stanza of the Telemann when *kongg!*—something like a sonic boom shuddered through the street. She bit her tongue in a reflexive startle. Her eardrums felt as if they'd imploded. The blast trembled window glass and ricocheted off brick walls. "What was that?" asked Dawn as the crowd suddenly dispersed.

"Who knows?" Jude replied, snatching up the hat and

stuffing the cash in his pockets. They paused on the pavement to listen for more booms. Dawn noticed that traffic seemed to tangle and pedestrians were starting to dash around on the sidewalks.

"People are acting weird," said Dawn. "What do you think happened? Where did that noise came from?"

"Dunno. Maybe a semi crashed down on Fifth." They'd walked this area, boning up on street names.

"Must've been severe." She pulled apart the flute's three sections and placed them in her case. "Let's check it out." People started to shout and scatter up the street. "What the hell's going on?" Dawn asked Jude as they hurried along Sixth Avenue and turned east on Fourteenth Street toward Fifth.

"It could be a drug bust," Jude replied as two police cars sped past, their roof lights spinning red.

As they walked past jeans and electronics stores, street vendors and a Starbucks, workers began to spill from offices onto sidewalks. More sirens shrilled. "This is way too huge for a drug bust," Dawn remarked.

"Someone must have gotten murdered," said Jude.

"Well, it sure stinks." An odor like charcoal starter began to sour the air.

At the corner of Fourteenth and Fifth a lady was ranting, "It hit! It hit!" She pointed southward into the sky. An old woman at the bus stop stared downtown too, mumbling, "Omigod, omigod, omigod!"

Dawn and Jude looked up to where the lady was pointing. "Jude, a building's on fire." Smoke billowed from behind a brick apartment building.

"Where?" he asked, craning his neck.

"Wait." Dawn shifted her gaze to the left, past the brick

building. "One of the World Trade Center towers is on fire!"

"No way." Then Jude saw it too—a cord of furious black unwinding into the robin's-egg blue sky.

Everyone was shouting and talking at once, crisscrossing paths and skittering like ants. Traffic jammed to a standstill. All eyes focused on the twin towers.

"Come on!" Dawn started to jog, and Jude followed. They made a break down Fifth, past a bowling alley, a deli, a Citibank branch, and a bookstore. Dawn ran steadily downtown, as if by running toward the towers, the image would become less bizarre, controllable somehow. Surely firefighters would have it under control before long. Finally she stopped at the corner of Fifth and Eleventh Street. She and Jude stood with a large crowd, watching the tower burn.

"Did the pilot fly into the tower by accident or on purpose?" a kid asked a traffic cop.

"Honey, I don't know," she answered. "If it was an accident, it was *some* accident." She began to mutter what sounded like a prayer.

"You think a pilot hit the building on purpose?" Jude's voice cracked. "You've got to be psychotic to fly a plane smack into a building."

The cop shook her head. "Honey, you ain't kidding."

"It looks like it took out a huge section," Dawn said. She shuddered. How many people would that mean, and what about the floors above?

"This is too awful," Jude said quietly.

They started walking again. Ambulances and fire engines blared. Their wail warped into audio trails as the rescue cars raced past. A couple in a Subaru clung to each other. College kids huddled in front of the arch by Washington Square Park. Other groups of stunned people hovered by the opened doors of vehicles parked in the middle of sidewalks. Crowds moved in a steady stream. Their faces were drawn and fearful. Dawn overheard bits of conversation.

"Those people won't make it out."

"Doesn't Larry work near the top of the tower?" A heavy man in a blue suit asked the woman next to him.

"Yes. What floor's he on?"

"Hundred and something." The man fumbled for his cell phone and dialed. "Can't get through. I'm getting a strange busy signal. Much too fast."

"The cell phone antennas were on one of those towers," cried the gray-suited lady.

"Yes. Some of them," the man replied grimly. He re-dialed. Everyone who had a cell phone was dialing, but it looked like hardly anyone was getting through.

Jude nudged Dawn. "Hey, that guy got through." A man walking past was weeping and yelling into his cell at the same time.

"I should call my parents," Jude murmured.

Time seemed to warp. It seemed prolonged, excruciating. Seconds ticked by. Dawn thought of Louise in the desert. "Stop burning," she begged under her breath.

"My husband works in the north tower," a woman sobbed as she limped up the middle of the street with one high heel off and her nose streaming. "My husband!"

I've got to help her, thought Dawn, but she felt useless. She wished she could run after the woman, give her something to stop her pain. "My sneakers," blurted Dawn, and she started to remove them.

"Huh?" Jude turned to her, confused.

86

"I'm going to give—" Dawn started to explain, but when she held up her sneakers she saw another person already handing the woman shoes. Jude nodded silently.

Apartment windows were flung open. Someone cranked a car radio to full volume. "One of the World Trade Center towers has been hit. It is unclear whether this is an accident or the work of terrorists," said the radio announcer.

"Terrorists!" Dawn looked again to the towers, craning her neck to see them through the smoke. She spotted a silver object. "Jude," she shouted, her breath coming in stabs, "look at that plane." She shook his arm. "Another plane's flying too close!"

"Oh, God, I see it," Jude whispered as they watched another jet streak in from the west. It careened straight into the second tower and tore a parking-lot-sized gash into the building's wall. What remained of the wall burst into orange fireballs. "The tower's exploding!" Jude yelled. He grabbed Dawn's arm and shook it. "Who's doing this?" he cried. "Did you see that plane just fly into that fucking tower?" Jude yelled hysterically. "Is this some kind of war?"

"War. This isn't real, it can't be," murmured Dawn. Jude's spindly fingers on her arm kept her from screaming, from hurrying to Sander's, grabbing her flute, and running up to the George Washington Bridge and clear out of Manhattan.

They were many blocks away, but they could still smell the acrid reek of burning fuel and plastic. It stung Dawn's nostrils. People covered their mouths with scarves and jackets. A construction worker passed out painter's masks. An old man was hacking.

"No accident," Dawn murmured. Horror vibrated to her core. She imagined the passengers as the jet made contact with the wall. The workers must've been at their desks, switching on their monitors, sipping their first coffee, she thought. All those networked computers were melting into plastic soup. People must have been trapped in those boiling rooms with no air. There was no way they could have escaped below a floor of solid fire.

The vision was like some sicko movie poster—Satan takes Manhattan. Hell is here. The last image of the plane wouldn't leave Dawn's mind. It was stuck on replay: *crash*—rewind—*crash*—rewind—*crash*. She felt blistered and dizzy, and Jude was coming in and out of her awareness. Then, abruptly, she felt like a voyeur—the most lurid, revolting kind of lowlife scum, to stand there and gawk. If this was war, the island would close up. If it was war, the city could be bombed. *It can't happen here,* she thought, and then, with a curdling terror, she realized that yes, it certainly could.

"I've got to get out of here," Jude said, as if he'd read her mind. "I need to go back to my brother's." She nodded.

A slow rumble seemed to rise from the ground, like a train careening off the tracks or a torpid thunderclap.

Jude grasped Dawn's shoulders. He pressed his face into her neck and sobbed. "I need to go home."

Dawn thought numbly, *What do I do?* "We'll be OK," she said softly, and put her arms around him in a timid embrace. He pressed in further as Dawn focused in on one of the towers' latticed columns. Like a sky-high accordion, and with a low and dreadful rumble, it folded down on itself, floor after floor after floor.

•   •   •

Jude had his head on her shoulder for a longtime afterward and Dawn felt him shaking. When he raised himself, his eyes were red. She felt yellowed, brittle, torn like a damaged piece of music parchment. They stood there, mute, for what seemed like forever. Other people stood motionless, as if the whole city had frozen in place.

Jude broke the silence. "I've got to get out of here. Let's go." She nodded. On the way back they noticed lines snaking out of delis. People emerged with armfuls of bottled water, bags full of cereal boxes. It reminded Dawn of those faded black-and-white photos of the Depression, when throngs of the hungry waited in lines for handouts.

"Should we get some milk?" she asked. "The stores may close."

"Yeah, we'd better," Jude muttered.

It was a challenge to find a deli with any basic foods left. It was almost noon when they took their place at the end of a line that stretched out onto the pavement.

"The second tower has fallen. Again, the second tower has fallen!" the grocery radio blared while they were inside and waiting to pay. All the customers became silent, listening. "A third plane has hit the Pentagon," the announcer continued, "and a fourth plane has crashed in Pennsylvania, possibly en route to the White House. Officials are following active leads—that the tragedies might be the work of terrorists, like those who bombed the Navy ship USS *Cole* last year. It's too early to say definitively." Dawn and Jude were too stunned to utter a word. The order of the world seemed fatally skewed. Bread, milk, and some cans of beans were concrete things—objects to count on. They paid for two loaves of bread, milk, and a bag full of canned food.

Back outside on St. Marks, the air was thick with soot. Dawn's throat throbbed. Military-looking jets streaked by overhead, their deafening rumble offering a flimsy illusion of safety.

They were almost back at Sander's apartment when

Jude started pleading with Dawn. "Let's hitchhike home. It's dangerous here. What if they bomb Manhattan? My parents will be so worried. What if—"

"No one knows who did this," she reasoned. "Whoever they are, they're probably done, but if they're not, what's to say that Manhattan will be the only place hit? San Francisco could be next." Dawn had considered leaving, but just for a moment. Now she needed to say something— anything—to keep Jude in New York. She didn't want to be alone.

They trudged up the stairwell and flung open the door. Jude wearily stumbled into the bedroom, hurled himself into his sleeping bag, and passed out.

Dawn dumped the food in the fridge, cans and all. She paused in Sander's bedroom doorway. He was still asleep. She gazed at his hair, spread out like a sheaf of golden wheat, and took a few steps into the room. An urge swelled in her to crawl under Sander's blanket, but instead she returned to the living room, flopped down on the shaggy rug, and stared into space. A thousand horrible images filled her mind. At the same time Dawn thought of her birth mother, Laurel Sweet, the blond mystery, then of plain, brown-shoed Louise. Would it matter to either of them if she died today?

north stairs

New York,
September 11, 2001

It had been hours since she'd left the apartment. Dawn wandered the streets. As she paced to the West Village, then back east, the scene at Sander's played in her memory. He had woken up, and in fumbling words she had described the disaster to him. They had sat on the rug, and she'd wavered between panic and an overwhelming urge to jump into his lap like a kid. His breath had smelled of warm milk, and his eyes had been hazel pools of warmth. Her ribs had moved in and out like those of a cornered mouse.

"You're safe now. Stop trembling," he had whispered.

She had felt like such a nerdy baby, suddenly missing her school and her room and how pure the sun had been last week as it played along the Pacific. Tears pricked her eyes, but her clenched muscles held them in place.

Sander's TV was busted, so he turned on the radio. The announcer said that paramedics were waiting in front of hospitals for the injured to be brought in, but there were few incoming survivors. He reported that crowds were starting to congregate downtown for impromptu memorials in Tompkins Square Park and Union Square.

The ringing of the telephone made them both jump.

While Sander talked to Pax on the phone, Dawn got up and peeked into the storage closet. Jude was curled in his sleeping bag, completely zonked. Sander's voice droned along with the news. Dawn tore a piece of musical notation paper from a pad on the coffee table and wrote: *Going out for a while—Dawn.* She left the note by the stereo, grabbed her pack, and hurried out into the street.

Having walked around for hours, Dawn now dawdled by the phones. *I'll call Jude and Sander soon,* she decided as she overheard people weeping to their families. Flyers with the numbers of the emergency information lines that had been set up had been taped to the sides of the partitions. When it was her turn to use the phone, Dawn called all the numbers and asked about Laurel Sweet. No one by that name was registered in a hospital or anywhere else. "I don't know why I thought she was here," she muttered. She called Sander's, but the phone kept ringing. After that, she walked back west and studied the crowds in front of St. Vincent's Hospital who waited to donate blood or follow clues to their injured and lost. She asked the person in charge if more blood donations were needed, but he said no, they had enough. Dawn paused near the line. There was something comforting about the group quietly waiting to help.

The sun began to set in the smoky sky. Dawn was nauseous from the toxic fumes that rolled up the streets from the south. She couldn't grasp the enormity of six thousand estimated missing or dead, or shake the eerie images she'd seen on a store's TV. Layers of white debris appeared to cover the whole of downtown like a dry snow. "Crowds are gathering," she repeated like a mantra as she again walked east and approached Union Square. She climbed the stairs at the north end. Candles illuminated the entire park! *Six thousand candles for six thousand missing.* She drifted with waves of people to a stone monument of Abraham Lincoln where hundreds of origami cranes wound together in a pyramid, taped to the statue's boots. A torrent of papers fluttered around Lincoln's granite base.

On each paper an image screamed, *Look at me!* Faces beamed from graduation photos and wedding pictures. Proud fathers held babies. Hundreds of photos of missing husbands, wives, sisters, lovers, and friends.

In the World Trade Center they must have been making their first phone calls of the day, Dawn thought. Trading Snapple and Shell and Microsoft, buying stocks of Martha Stewart and spring water, discussing the latest hot tickets. There were probably workers from every country in that building exchanging rubles, yen, dinars, rials, pesos, rupees, euros.

She lingered in front of one photo: a lady in front of a Christmas tree, who held out a present. The type read: *Please help me find my mom! Gail Kalinska has brown eyes, a narrow face, is 5' 7" tall. She was last seen wearing a black skirt, pink knit top, and a necklace with a heart-shaped amethyst. Any information please call Nona Kalinska.*

Dawn wondered if the woman's necklace had been a gift. It horrified her to think that amid the crushed metal few bodies would be found. That amethyst necklace might be the only thing left to identify someone's mom.

Drumbeats sounded, a woodblock filling in the beats— *te-kang, te-kang.* Dawn followed the sound to a group of kids hunkered down on a picnic table—some had matted dreadlocks, others long, straight hair and jeans. *They're my age,* Dawn realized, without turning her head to meet their eyes.

I have my flute. It's in my pack. I'll take it out, she thought, but decided against it. She wouldn't know how to approach them.

Across from the musicians a square mat of candles, about two feet by three feet covered the walkway. The candles, red, blue, and white, formed a flag. Teenagers, silent and focused, crouched around it and replaced spent candles with new ones.

One of them motioned her over. "Candle?"

"Thanks." She took the candle and crouched tentatively along the outer rim. In the dark, the undulating flames were hypnotizing. Dawn had never considered herself a patriot. Waving the flag and pledging allegiance were so forced. But who had attacked, and why? *Whoever flew planes into buildings full of American workers must hate us a lot.* She gazed back at the kids. There were all sorts of different ones sitting vigil. Soft tears rolled down their cheeks. Dawn's eyes were dry as sand. Her left eyelid twitched, and she scratched it roughly with the nylon of her jacket, scraping the soft flesh above her eyebrow.

Dawn felt as if she were floating above the candles. She wanted someone to pull her down—to connect with someone. Maybe she could talk to the boy with the key chain dangling from his jeans. He was next to her now, lighting a red candle and placing it in the striped pattern. Or maybe the weeping girl who sat cross-legged to her left would reach out a hand. Dawn wondered if you could be taught how to connect. She sure needed lessons. It seemed to her as if there were invisible strings that bound other people, but she never felt them. Even with Jude the string was so loose.

Louise had been bad at it too, as far as Dawn could tell. If Louise knew where Dawn was, she'd freak. Dawn wondered where Louise had been when the towers fell. It was almost morning in Pakistan. Had she heard about the tragedy?

Dawn lit the blue candle with matches that a quiet girl handed her. She tried to think of a prayer or poem—just one phrase to give meaning to the blue candle—but Dawn was too aware of the others. Their prayers were more important.

She thrust a hand in her pocket and traced around the edge of the SIM card Louise had given her. Taking out the satellite phone would attract too much attention. She got up and stumbled through the crowds to a phone across the street. She'd dealt with Victor yesterday, leaving him two messages while he was still at work. In the first, she said she'd gone to Seattle with a friend, that she needed time alone. In the second she told him not to come looking and not to tell Louise. The more Dawn thought about Victor's hateful demand—*send her back before she ruins us*—the more menacing he seemed.

Dawn's heart hammered as she picked up the receiver. *I'll just see if Louise is okay.* She'd heard on the radio that camps in Afghanistan had trained Arab terrorists and that there might be a connection between these camps and the World Trade Center strike. Maybe Louise was hurt. Maybe terrorists had raided the Red Cross camp. Maybe terrorists had killed her because she was American! *Get off this paranoid track,* Dawn warned herself. She dialed the number. *It's not because I need to.* She immediately heard a rapid busy signal. She recalled what the suited man had said earlier about the damaged phone lines. Service would probably be spotty for days.

Should I go back to Sander's? Jude would want her there, but his parents had probably tracked him down by now. The apartment seemed light-years away, and she had a powerful urge to stay on the street. But if she stayed out, where would she sleep? Dawn felt tense as she trudged along Fourteenth Street past the CD megastore, its oversized posters of musicians smiling supremely unaware from each window.

Her feet drove her downtown, closer and closer to where the towers had fallen, where loss was most palpable. It was strange how she felt disconnected from people yet was so aware of their pain.

Dawn pleaded her way past a police officer and then tried to persuade another one at the final checkpoint. "I live here, sir—up on Vesey." "No, I won't go into the building." "All right, all right, I'll leave if you say so." She had almost given up when she saw her chance. The overwhelmed officer was dealing with two hysterical guys who were begging to get to Reade Street to find their dogs. While the officer had his back turned Dawn slipped through the opening in the makeshift gate. She hid behind the corner of a building, then stumbled along eerily silent lanes littered with bone-colored powder, papers, mismatched shoes, and smashed cars. Through the acrid haze, police lights swirled. Holding her jacket over her nose to block out the fumes, Dawn found the limestone steps of a church–St. Peter's. She lurched down the aisle to a set of red candles and knelt down, her eyes watering from their heat. There were buttons in front of each candle. She pushed one. It lit.

It must be near midnight, she thought, and looked around. There was a lone man in the back, his gray head bowed. No one was watching. She pressed a button, and a second flame rose. "For the people," she murmured, lighting another. "For my mother out there somewhere." And another: "I hope Louise isn't hurt." She lit the last one. "God, keep me safe." With that Dawn crept back down the aisle, sneaked up the wooden stairway to the balcony, and slid under a bench for the night.

luti

Charikar, Afghanistan,
mid-September 2001

Johar and Bija labored up the hills of Parvan province toward Charikar—a city perched on the mighty peaks of the
Panjshir. Zolar's donkey trudged bravely on from dawn until late in the day, through snow and winds that cracked lips
and bit through the weave of their meager attire. Bija's
coughs grew frequent. Still, it was hard to keep her from
wanting to jump off the donkey to play, or to distract her
from asking for Maryam.

"We'll see your mother soon," Johar repeated over and
over. He was weak with exhaustion and disgusted by his
own resentment at being saddled with a child. It might
have been wiser to leave his cousin with Ramila after all.

"But when is soon?" Bija would persist.

It could be months . . . or never. He did not answer.

By the time they reached Charikar they had been on the road for at least four days. Johar was desperate for rest, and his thighs burned from saddle sores. Their food had dwindled to bread heels and a dozen stale walnuts, and the old donkey wouldn't hold up unless he was watered. Johar guided the beast through narrow streets toward the village bazaar. As he circled around a loud clump of boys, he overheard them bragging about run-ins with Taliban soldiers.

"I outran the fat lout," said one. "They're too slow on their feet to take Charikar."

"Right!" said another boy. "Let them fire all the rockets they want from up on the hill, but they'll get nowhere. I threw a stone at a bazaar spy, then hid so fast he thought it was a ghost from the otherworld." They burst into laughter.

A third boy, taking notice of Johar, shouted amiably enough, "Where's your gun? Why do you travel on the road with no gun?" When Johar didn't answer, the boy pointed a finger at him and released a pretend trigger. "B-b-bam! B-b-bam!"

"Shouldn't you be off fighting, not tending toddlers?" the boy added, apparently irritated by Johar's silence.

Johar ignored him. The group broke out in snickers, made bold by their numbers.

Bija drew a finger up to shoot them. "Boom!" she fired back. "Bija is not a baby." *So, even Bija is better at defending our honor than I am,* thought Johar. Even total strangers could make him feel unworthy. He prodded the tired donkey to a faster pace.

The market bustled with merchants hawking carpets, bicycle parts, sandals, soap, and pans. Charikar, despite curfews and checkpoints, had a surprising wealth of goods. Johar traded a hat he had knitted for rice and a bag of keshmesh. He and Bija were luckier than most. Some families had nothing to trade and lurked on the fringes of the bazaar, bellies empty, waiting for handouts.

Johar couldn't resist spending the last precious Afghanis hidden in the heel of his sock on a branch of Charikar's luscious grapes, which launched Bija into delighted squeals between coughs. As they devoured the grapes, Johar and his cousin gawked at the rows of burlap sacks, split open to reveal wheat, walnuts, cherries, and apricots. He had been to bazaars such as this since childhood, but days of hunger made it seem as if he'd never laid eyes on such splendor.

"Colors, Jor!" Bija, wide-eyed, pointed to wooden bowls displaying curries, fennel, cardamom, and other spices. Their golden hues contrasted with the overcast sky.

"Bowls!" Bija cried. Johar nodded, slowing his gait to match hers, as they made their way to the pottery stall. He admired the merchant's bowls and cups—Charikar was famous for them—and remembered that when he was a child his uncle Tilo had brought such a bowl to his mother, who'd kept it far from Johar's reach. What had become of Tilo? The last his aunt heard, Tilo was teaching in London. For all Johar knew, his uncle might have made it to America by now. London, America—places as remote as ranches he'd seen in those fantastic cowboy movies years back.

A man in a gray turban held a contraband transistor radio at the end of the pottery booth. The crowd of men around him shook their heads. Kalashnikovs clanked against one another, and the air snapped with tension. *Better leave,* thought Johar, unnerved by the simmering anger. As he turned to go, a Talib voice broke through the radio's static. "Praise Allah, the infidels have been struck in their American homeland!" The crowd buzzed.

Johar leaned over to a wiry man whose ear was affixed to the radio. "Sahib, can you tell me what happened?"

"Pilots flew planes into American buildings," the man replied. "The buildings burned and then fell! Thousands died."

The Charikar grapes that had tasted like nectar moments ago stuck now in Johar's gullet. His hand gripped Bija's tightly as he pictured domed mosques caving in and worshipers crushed by giant minarets whose marble columns snapped like twigs. "But why?" he asked. The man did not reply.

"The infidels have been punished for their sins," blared the radio.

"Sins?" Johar tapped another man's arm. "Who flew these planes?"

A muscled man spun around. "They say it was Al Qaeda pilots; some say they crashed the planes on purpose. They say it was the Al Qaeda Arabs who train in Kandahar."

Kandahar! They trained in Johar's own country? Naji had bragged about training there with a few lucky Talibs. Was this the new jihad against the West that Naji had spoken of—the one for America's broken promises? If so, then it was true that Taliban and Al Qaeda worked as one. *Khub ast*, thought Johar, *then even Daq could be trained to fly such a plane.* Johar's skin crawled at the thought.

Bija yanked on Johar's kameez. "More grapes, Jor." Johar gave her the last handful. She was blissfully unaware.

"Such craziness!" A jade-eyed man like those from the forests of Nuristan turned toward Johar. "The Taliban have ranted such lunacy since they first seized the radio broadcasts. We Nuristanis know that they make up many lies."

His eyes narrowed with suspicion. "Who knows, my friend, if this event is their imagined fairy tale, eh?"

Johar nodded. Nuristanis were fiercely independent. They had been the last tribe to convert to Islam. Their women wore bold colors, and some refused to wear the burqa. People called them wild, but Johar knew they spoke their truth without regard for others' beliefs. If it was a lie, it would be so much easier to accept. Bija tugged at Johar's sleeve again. He swept her up and kissed her forehead. It was impossible to imagine any man so evil as to fly into buildings full of people! *Inshallah, make it not true.* But if it was, what then?

"Don't speak too loudly, sahib," the wiry man warned the Nuristani. "This place crawls with fanatics. A Talib has ears like a donkey, my brother," he chuckled.

"I'll not be a slave to the Taliban or any other scoundrel," spat the Nuristani. "I challenge them to fight me." He shot his hands skyward. "Free to the death!"

Two swarthy men emerged from the crowd and began to argue with the Nuristani.

Alarmed by the rising commotion, Johar and Bija veered around the swarm and toward their donkey, tied near a truck filled with cauliflower. Johar grabbed one, resisting the urge to grab an armful. Days were still warm, but evenings brought a frost-nipped dusk, maybe snow, and Kabul, the next town on their journey to Camp Suryast, was at least a two days' ride. They must depart now.

Johar heard the call of the muezzin to prayer and gazed longingly at the mosque. Like a celestial Charikar bowl, its turquoise dome rose from the hill overlooking the market. Girls were not allowed in the mosque, not even tiny Bija. For a moment Johar thought of hiding her in his pattu in order to pray. But her coughs would disturb the worshipers, so he said his prayers where they stood.

Caring for a toddler was a challenge. One needed the endurance of a camel and the raw strength of a lion—how had Aunt Maryam ever managed? Johar's heart ached. He'd let Maryam down by not trying harder to find out where the Taliban had taken her. Bija was his last chance to make up for past mistakes. No matter what, he must carry her to safety.

Johar fastened their goods to the saddle pack and hoisted Bija, coughing and fussy, onto the beast. For the next few hours, as they traveled on the road south and Bija slept, Johar's mind was ablaze with nightmarish thoughts. What had happened in Charikar? There had been a maelstrom of people, impassioned voices, and brawls. There had been news of American palaces on fire, destroyed as in ancient tales of Genghis Khan, cities conquered and cities lost. When would the insane hatred end—hatred of Shiites, of Christians, Jews, and Muslims? And what about America's biased neglect and Islam's unseeing fury against America? *Maybe,* thought Johar sadly, *it won't end until the last man has killed his twin.* They passed travelers on the road: one-legged men, children whose worm-infested bellies were as bloated as the throats of toads. It was a long procession of sorrow. Johar felt that Allah must cry with bitterness at his own creation.

For the next two nights he and Bija took rest where they could—with a group of vagabonds in a protected valley, and near a well where he filled his jug. Johar's stomach churned from its silted water. He wasn't sure whether it was from the cold or from dirty water that Bija's body grew hot with fever, but her cough, which had been mild, seemed to creep deep into her lungs. Bija had no more energy for play. She clutched her doll and with listless eyes slumped against him.

In the rose quartz light of dawn, as Bija slept fitfully, Johar removed the wool that was spindled from the quilts and other places, and knit, the wooden needles clacking like a woodpecker's bill. Hats were born from his hands— one with geometric patterns radiating from the crown, a spiderweb design, another skullcap of mulberry-hued strands. He wound them around his belt or pulled the socks in layers over his feet. These were his currency, and easier to conceal as finished products.

As he worked he recalled his childhood wonder in learning the trade. "Nephew, watch me and learn," his aunt would say as she took strands of wool between thumb and forefinger. She would twist them until they lengthened into one long string, then spin that strand onto a wooden spindle. Johar would copy her. When many spindles were done they would set out gourds filled with dyes: mountain blue, pomegranate red, mulberry, mustard. After the spindles were dry, they would set to knitting. These pleasant memories were disturbed by worry for the future, and Johar tried to imagine his father's voice, and his mother's songs. But they were silent, maybe frightened from a sky through which planes flew into buildings.

On the eighth morning of their trek to Kabul, before Bija stirred, Johar knelt on his pattu and bent his head toward Mecca, for morning namaz. As a breeze tickled his neck, a Farrukhi poem came to him:

> *"Stored in its sleeve, the wind, it seems, fine powdered musk unfolds,*

Whilst the garden, in its bosom, shining buds like puppets
   hold.
The narcissus a bright necklace, set with shining gems has on,
And the red syringa wears in its ear rubies from Badakhshan."

He spoke out loud, and that was how the bandit found him. "Money!" demanded the luti, thrusting a switchblade at Johar's belly.

Johar jerked in fright, then cursed himself that he had not so much as a stick with which to hit the thief. "Sahib, I've no—"

"Give me food, then," hissed the luti.

Johar moved slowly so it wouldn't seem as if he were escaping. He didn't want to aggravate the thief. With silent pleas for Bija to sleep on, he moved his hand cautiously into his pocket and pulled out a skullcap. "I've just made it. It's all I have." He tried to conceal his shaking.

"Play games with me, will you?" The thief bent down and with a sweep of his arm sliced clear through Johar's pattu. "Your neck is next."

"No games," said Johar. "This will fetch you Afghanis if you sell it in the bazaar."

The luti cackled scornfully but grabbed the cap nevertheless, and closed his blade. "Keep still!" he commanded, and scrambled over to Johar's donkey.

Bija began to stir. While Johar ran to her on trembling legs, the luti stole the donkey, the quilts, and all the provisions, and vanished as swiftly as a jackal. Bija was woozy with fever. "Where's our donkey?" she asked.

"The donkey got away," Johar whispered, hiding his panic. He staggered to the road with Bija clinging to his back and cursed the dust as they trudged on southward.

"Jor, how soon will we get to Suryast?" Bija asked wearily.

"Soon, little jewel. Soon." But Johar knew better. Without a donkey it could take them days even to reach Kabul. Camp Suryast seemed as far as the distant shores of America.

The few vehicles that passed were mostly Taliban, with one fancy Western-style van carrying some Arab soldiers. Most travelers passed on foot.

Finally, as the sun began to bake through Johar's shalwar and redden Bija's cheeks, another truck, different from the others, rumbled toward them. This one had colorful sides that sparkled like flint, and it tinkled with bells.

Johar waved, and the truck slowed to a stop. Sequined scenes of mountains with grazing sheep adorned its sides. The driver motioned them in. Souls like them—sojourners and refugees, trekking south to heaven knew what—sprawled every which way in the back of the truck like a mound of pungent melons. It was the custom to give travelers a lift, but this driver, whoever he was, seemed exceptionally generous.

"Where are you headed?" one man asked Johar.

"To Camp Suryast in Peshawar."

"Ah, my brother is there," said another, nodding. "And my neighbor's family lives in a camp farther south. We are all running."

"Where are you headed?" Johar asked the first.

"To Karachi, to the gun bazaar. We must protect ourselves. General Massoud is dead. There is rumor of more war to come." Johar stayed quiet after that. He had nothing to say about guns. And news of Massoud's death made him despondent. Besides, Bija was burning with fever.

When the men stopped the truck for a break, Johar pleaded with the driver, a Pashtun from Kabul with a handsome nose and oddly impeccable garments.

"Sahib, I will do any bidding," Johar explained. "I can clean, cook, knit, and weave. It's a matter of survival. My cousin is terribly sick; you can hear it in her lungs."

"Any bidding?" The Pashtun gazed at Johar with interest.

"Yes, sahib." *Almost anything,* thought Johar, *but I'll remain on guard.*

"Thank you, Allah be praised," murmured Johar when the Pashtun took pity and brought them to his place near the radio station in Kabul. It was an elegant compound with three rooms and a courtyard full of flowers. The dashing Pashtun, with his kohl-rimmed eyes and curiously dainty manners, fed them pilau with—grateful heavens— lamb! He offered Bija chai with comfrey, which eased her spluttering.

The man, named Aman, accepted Johar's gift of wool socks and laid out a quilt in his spare room.

"I've been looking for a houseboy," said Aman. "My days are too busy."

"You will not regret it," Johar answered, and thanked Aman as if he were a prophet. Aman went into the other room and turned out the oil lantern. Johar listened to the man's steady breathing, then fell into a dreamless sleep, with Bija enfolded in his arms, laboring for her breath.

kabul

Kabul, Afghanistan,
late September 2001

The next morning Aman announced to Johar, "You say you're good with your hands. Do the women's work, for I have no wife." He ordered Johar to hem the frayed seams of his tunics, darn his woolens, and cook his meals. Later that day Aman brought back wool from the bazaar, saying, "Make me a blanket, boy, then keep some wool for yourself." Aman seemed oddly feminine, and Johar still felt wary. He had heard tales of how some Pashtun men kept boys for their pleasure. But Aman was only polite and generous, and the temporary comfort of his home was a blessing. Johar and Bija had a cozy room and meals on a clean platter. Johar especially liked going outside to the garden to cover the roses with rags for winter safekeeping.

And there was no city with as magnificent a reputation

as Kabul! As a boy he had pored over faded photographs in Aunt Maryam's books. Decades ago Kabul's Dilkusha Palace had burst with flowers and bubbled with the water of marble fountains. Invading tribes had brought with them a new religion, Islam, in the seventh century, and the country was converted in waves. Soon after, some of the most magnificent places of worship were built, like Kabul's blue-tiled Sherpur Mosque. Many invaders later, and long after British rule ended in 1919, Maryam said that women and girls had walked boldly in Kabul. Johar was stunned by her photo book showing ladies traipsing down streets without the hijab, in Western dress and heels. The captions read, "The 1960s were a period of peace and relative security." Maryam told him that during that time, King Zahir Shah ruled, and Kabul was a popular destination for westerners seeking out Sufi wisdom and the rugged beauty of Asia. She said that progressive schools were the pride of the city. But all too soon after that, the king was deposed by his own cousin, who was against modernization. A weak Marxist government followed, and the Soviets saw their chance to invade and import communism. For the next ten years conflict beat Afghanistan's buildings and pocked its roads. Then the Taliban came to power and shrouded the women. Afghanistan's was a tragic history, in dire need of some happier chapters thought Johar.

On the second afternoon when chores were done, with Bija fast asleep in a cloth slung around Johar's back, Johar and Aman wandered down Kabul's winding streets. Pieces of walls rose up like ghostly spires. Kinsmen shuffled by, their eyes sunken with fear and hunger. When Johar saw those eyes, fear burned through him too. Arab soldiers in a Toyota truck sent dust up in clouds, and a bedraggled man hacked and spat as he rumbled behind their truck in his shopworn ghadis. Kabulis lived in a ravaged city, yet signs of life and beauty remained. Plane trees still lent their shade along alleyways. And on the outskirts of town, fields of mud huts still encircled the city. "One day we must rebuild this place," Johar said.

"Inshallah, we can only hope." Aman pointed to the Talib-run radio station four buildings down. "I work over there."

"For Radio Shariat?" Panic rifled through Johar. Who was this Aman, really?

"Yes." Aman sounded proud, but guilty too. An engineer could pay for a compound such as his? What other things did Aman do?

Johar's words stumbled out. "You work for the Taliban, but you are not . . . ?"

"I'm not. But yes, I work for them." Aman sighed. "Everyone has their price."

•   •   •

"All the way from Delhi," Aman bragged about the chai he steeped for Bija. "I have comfreys, mints, and black chais, the finest Hindu cure-alls."

As Bija drank, she pinched her nose with stubby fingers and her eyelids fluttered. "I'm better," she announced later that day. How Johar wanted to believe Bija was cured! Her breath still rasped, but the fever was down and enough energy had returned for her to sit in the courtyard and build a dirt palace for her doll.

Despite Aman's affiliations, there was no doubting he was kind. Though Johar was only a servant, Aman told them stories after the evening meal. "Have you heard the one about the caliph and his camel?" Aman asked. "What about the story of Iqbar and Aqbar, the feuding mullahs from Khost?" His kohl-lined eyes twinkled, and every tale would end in gales of laughter. Johar recited poetry while Aman swayed with pleasure and Bija twirled her doll around like a dancing dervish. Johar worked quickly on Aman's blanket, but he also managed to spindle the loose wool, knit hats and hoard them in a borrowed pack. This journey was not over. Soon they must move on.

The third night Aman hosted the Taliban. Johar shrank with fear from the black-turbaned men who crowded into Aman's for dinner. The thieves who had seized the radio stations and the cities were brushing right up against his sleeve! It wasn't fair that the poor begged for stale rice while these men had robust bellies and clean robes.

He served the men mutton soup and samosas with leeks, then chai from Aman's silver samovar. Bija had been put to bed early, so as not to disturb the conversation. What Johar overheard disturbed him greatly.

"A proper servant boy. I'd like one of those for myself!" one man said. "Can I borrow him?" Laughter all around.

"The boy is inspired with his hands," Aman bragged as the men clacked over the feast.

"Just like a little wifey," another noted. Their roars of amusement turned Johar's cheeks crimson, and it was all he could do to hold back an insult.

Later, as the men settled on the mats after the meal, the talk became serious.

"Word is that the Americans are planning to bomb the Al Qaeda camps," one announced. "They say there is proof it was Al Qaeda who flew those planes into the American towers." So it was true what the men had said in Charikar, about buildings falling. And true the Arabs in Kandahar had been the pilots. Bombs! If Americans bombed Kandahar, they might bomb Kabul. A sickening dread shot through Johar. He and Bija were not safe even here. How many days until bombs fell?

"What proof do these Americans have?" asked a gray-bearded Talib.

"They have not shown the proof because they have none. It's all hearsay." A barrel-chested man took a pull on his hookah, and peach-tinged haze filled the air. "They claim that the Al Qaeda Arabs in Kandahar are behind it. The Americans say we Taliban are next if we do not throw out our Qaeda guests. *Big bosses,* the Americans!" The Talib puffed out his chest in mockery. "They forget that it was they who lured the Arabs here and gave them money to fight against the Russians. A convenient memory lapse."

Aman spoke next. "Whoever led those people to our country is not the point now. If the Arabs in Kandahar are responsible for bloodshed, shouldn't we force them to leave? We are *not* Arabs—we are *Afghans*. It was not Afghans who flew those killing planes. If they stay, we will be un-justly blamed and American bombs will fall on our people." Aman's handsome face creased with worry. "Since Genghis Khan men have invaded our land—Mongols, British, Russians, Arabs, soon maybe even Americans. How many more years of war can we endure?"

Johar glanced from Aman to the irate faces of the Taliban. *Allah help us if the Americans invade,* he thought, *for their army is the most powerful in the world.* Aunt Maryam might be killed, and the people of Baghlan too. He busied himself pouring another round of chai so he didn't miss a word, even though he didn't want to believe what they were saying.

"Why should we cater to America? Al Qaeda is our ally. They've given us money and helped protect our businesses," shouted a man with a furrowed brow. "Al Qaeda helped us kill Massoud: a device in a television camera—ingenious!"

The Taliban were definitely in cahoots with Al Qaeda! And they had assassinated the great Alliance general Massoud. Johar felt cold. His grip on the samovar tightened. If only Massoud were alive, Johar would not be fleeing. If only Massoud's Alliance had overrun the Taliban, Daq would not have been captured.

"But why?" persisted Aman. "Why did Al Qaeda want to kill Americans who were not even soldiers?"

"Is your mind ill, sahib?" Graybeard muttered disapprovingly. "It is clearly in disrepair tonight."

"Why does a mouse like to see a dead vulture?" asked Barrel Chest. "Qaeda's jihad is for interference in our affairs, for Americans' obsession in controlling the oilfields in Muslim lands, for the humiliation westerners have brought on us."

Barrel Chest went on. "They install their puppet leaders in Islamic lands, dictators who oppress the people. Remember the shah of Iran?" A murmur went up. "And Hussein—there was a time when they were shaking his hand in order to quell the Iranian uprisings. Later, when he didn't follow their every order they decided he was the enemy. They switch directions as quickly as the wind." *They're not the only ones,* thought Johar, remembering the local commanders of the mujahidin.

The man with the dark brows said, "America has no understanding of Islam. They see our men as dogs." The men buzzed in agreement.

Johar busied himself clearing cups so that they would

not notice his disgust. Maryam had insisted that Johar think as an individual. The American government might be corrupt, but to blame all of its citizens—that was just too easy. No government was innocent. Afghan commanders took bribes and sold opium poppies on the black market. These Taliban weren't dogs, but they passed judgment in the lazy rule of the pack.

"And what about our Muslim brothers in Palestine?" roared Barrel Chest. "Little boys throwing rocks at metal tanks are shot and killed. It's not a fair fight when only one side has the tanks." The men nodded together, their black turbans rising and falling.

Johar saw Aman's mouth curve down in a frown and open, ready to argue, but then he fell silent. Even in his disgust, Johar considered their points. There were injustices. And it was true the West was at odds with Islam. Aunt Maryam had spoken of how westerners thought Muslims were religious fanatics, simple carpet sellers, or bloodthirsty banshees—

But violence seemed only to lead to more violence. What had been accomplished by the murder of his father and mother? Johar was glad he had never joined an army, even General Massoud's. Johar had to speak. "Can't you all see? Killing hundreds of westerners will only strengthen their prejudice against Islam." Aman's mouth dropped open, then curled into a faint smile, but the clamor from the Taliban was furious. The dirty cups trembled in Johar's hand.

Barrel Chest turned to Aman. "Teach your impudent servant a lesson!"

"I'd beat him if I were you." Graybeard paused to scowl at Johar before hobbling out the door.

No matter that the suicide pilots were Arab, not Afghan—westerners would send their bombs here to kill. Daq might be on the front lines by now. Johar pictured Daq fighting in a stranger's army and was filled with despair. His brother's life could end in a hail of explosives as easily as a candle extinguished by a sigh.

Later that night, when Aman gave Johar gifts of kohl to line his eyes and bright polish for his nails, Johar felt only a nostalgic affection for him. He had already decided to leave Kabul. "Aman, you must flee," he urged. "Kabul will not be spared!"

"It is my home, dear Johar. I cannot leave it."

Johar dared not tell Aman his plans.

The moment his friend's breathing was even in the next room, Johar scooped up Bija and crept out. He apologized silently for stealing the donkey and a satchel of provisions. *Bless my friend,* he prayed. *Keep him safe.*

Johar led their beast toward the outskirts of Aman's neighborhood. He looked up at the night sky and imagined the ominous outlines of American warplanes against the moon. How soon would this sky glow from the butchery of bombs? Clutching Bija, he rode into darkness.

squat

Up on the balcony of St. Peter's, Dawn set up the sat phone and dialed.

She'd barely uttered hello when Jude burst out with questions. "Where were you? What happened? Why didn't you come back last night?"

"I tried to call, but you were out."

"Oh, yeah? Did you leave a message?"

"Jude, if you really want to know, something drew me outside. I just couldn't sit around with everything going on, and the longer I stayed out, the more I got swept into it. The memorial at Union Square was incredible."

"That's nice." Jude's tone was bitter. "Sander was asking about you, and I couldn't even tell him anything. We both went out searching for you."

"I'm sorry. Are you okay?"

"I guess. Pax must have taken my parents' call while Sander and I went out. Edith was crying and asking if Pax knew where I was. He was beyond furious for having to lie for me again. So I had to call them. I tried the number ten times before it went through."

"You spoke to them?" Dawn's heart leaped to her throat.

"Not directly. I left them a message."

"Have they called back?" Dawn already felt the terror of being alone.

"No. I used Sander's friend's cell phone so they couldn't track me down. I told them I was fine, that I was somewhere in Michigan, and that I needed my space. I said I'd be back soon." Jude's voice wavered as if he were on the verge of tears. "I don't know how much longer I can string them along, Dawn."

"I know," Dawn said softly. "But . . . Michigan?"

Jude chuckled sourly. "That's where my drama teacher from camp lives." He paused. "I've been worried about you. Where are you?"

"I'm staying at St. Peter's Church. Last night I had to sneak into the area south of Canal Street, but I peeked out this morning and they're building a barrier just beyond the church. It's as close as I could get."

"*What?* What are you thinking? That's crazy. Come back to the apartment."

"Come down and stay at the church with me, Jude."

His tone sharpened. "I'm just not interested in studying for the ministry."

"You don't have to be so flip."

"Well, don't be such a martyr."

"I'll call you later." Dawn hung up.

•   •   •

Jude was unpredictable. If he freaked and spoke to Edith, their whole plan would be ruined. Even if he didn't spill the beans, Pax would. No way she was going back to Victor. She had to find somewhere else to stay. She stepped outside the church, and acrid smoke caught in her chest. In the gutter she saw evidence of lives—scorched resumés, a business card and a flattened keychain. The area was crawling with National Guard soldiers, cops, and workers erecting a plywood fence just past St. Peter's. A guard came over and suggested she move on. Before she turned to go, she took a long look over the fence at the metal pile and recalled the wonder of her first night in New York—the magical towers, their clean marble concourse. Now, metal poles and tree-sized columns veered at lunatic angles, some eight stories high. A large federal building stood, but its windows had exploded out of their blackened frames. *So this is what war looks like.*

Dawn wandered uptown to Union Square. All the fences were plastered with posters, and so many candles had been lit on the courtyard that they formed a waxen sea. Scrolls of brown paper were rolled out with messages written in dozens of languages. A peace sign was painted on the left flank of George Washington's metal horse. On the grass, bouquets of lilies dedicated to a fire brigade were arranged in a coffin shape. A horde of difficult emotions—pity, loneliness, and grief—pressed up against Dawn's throat. She had to play to release them. Dawn crept behind a hedge, took out her flute, gathered her nerve, and trilled out the first pure notes of a serenade while folks walked back and forth in front of the hedge.

A guy about her age came toward her and sat on the

grass. He took off his backpack and set it beside him. "That's pretty music," he said.

"Thanks." Dawn replied. She continued to play, gazing straight ahead.

"It's, like, haunting," said the kid. "What is it?"

Dawn felt the familiar clenching of muscles. "It's Dvořák's serenade for flute." She went on playing, waiting for the guy to get impatient and move on. When the song ended and he didn't leave, Dawn felt panicky. *What now?* she wondered, putting her flute in her lap. She could try to talk to him, but she couldn't think of the right question—any question. Why was it always so hard with anyone but Jude?

The kid beat her to it. "Where are you staying?"

Do I look that down and out? she wondered. Without meeting his eyes, she murmured, "Nowhere, really. I'm a refugee, I guess."

He told her about C Squat, an abandoned tenement on Avenue C where lots of runaways holed up. C Squat seemed like a good solution. If she and Jude stayed there, no one could track them down. They wouldn't have to deal with Pax, and Jude wouldn't be as tempted to run back to his mother. Dawn thanked the kid. *Don't be so uptight,* she scolded herself as she walked to the squat. *Some people actually want to help you.*

A Goth guy draped in a black shawl sort of ran C Squat. He said, "You can stay in my friend's room, but only until he gets back from Santa Fe." The room stank of mildewed mattress, and she had to clasp back the black polyester curtains with her hair scrunchies so a slice of sun could peek through. But after a vigorous sweep and the old boot-stomp on no less than five monstrous roaches, she settled in.

Two days later it seemed the right time to call Jude and

tell him the good news. He answered on the third ring. Dawn didn't go into detail or delve into the scary bits—her sweaty insomnia, how each ambulance siren convinced her the city was under new attack, how alone she felt. "C Squat is good," she said. "Come stay there with me. There are lots of cool kids, and your parents won't find you."

"I don't know," he said. "Is there hot running water and a shower?"

"Communal bathrooms," Dawn answered. She kept her mouth shut about the black polyester curtains, the mildewed mattress, the bare lightbulbs, and the roaches.

Jude's tone was cool. "Honey, I need a mirror and a private john."

"Come on, Jude. It's fun to rough it. Remember our ride east?" Dawn hummed some lines from "Rock Candy Mountain."

"Let's face it, that was hell on wheels, and the squat sounds like grunge city. If I were you, I'd lose the hobo fantasy and come back. I miss the way you entertain me."

Dawn's giddiness fizzled to flat. Jude had seemed less nice ever since they'd left San Francisco, but maybe she was being too sensitive. "Come for a visit, then." Maybe if Jude saw it, he'd change his mind.

"Okay, just for a visit," he promised.

Dawn folded up the sat phone. She got out her flute, propped her music on the dusty sill, and began the mournful Grieg. Her music poured up the rickety staircase, out onto the tar roof, and through the unusually somber streets of her new neighborhood.

camp suryast
Outskirts of Peshawar, Pakistan, early October 2001

Far past Kabul, Johar and Bija had seen the smoke from distant rocket fire in the city, and Johar could sense the sickening onslaught of war. After 430 kilometers and what seemed like months (but was closer to three weeks), Johar stood, heavy with exhaustion yet relieved, on Camp Suryast's northern ridge. He surveyed the mirage of tents undulating in the afternoon heat. It was a canvas city pitched unsteadily on poles and fringed by hastily dug mud caves with tarpaulin roofs baked to cracking. The camp stretched into the horizon.

Riding closer on Aman's donkey, Johar and Bija saw the refugees. Wizened men stared vacantly, children bit nubs of fingernails, babies' sticklike limbs splayed from their mother's arms, and boys leaped over a ditch that reeked of human waste. Aunt Maryam's friend had come back from this place? It seemed a spot where all roads ended. As Johar continued to look, the dread that he'd felt since he left Kabul agitated to toxic levels, and he fought the urge to scream. He clenched his fists around the reins and began riding toward a wooden building that seemed like an office.

It was Suryast's main office. Johar dismounted, lifted Bija up and onto the ground, and tied the donkey to a post. After an eternity in line, a Pakistani aid worker tipped his head in greeting. "Your business, boy?"

"My name is Johar. My cousin here is Bija. We fled the Taliban and the rumor of war. We ask for shelter here in Suryast."

"Bad bombs are coming," Bija whispered, her brown eyes fearful.

"Vikhrim my name," announced the worker. "Many flee and many come here. Over three thousand peoples at Suryast. No tent available."

"What can we do, then?" Johar asked, his voice rising. With no tent, Johar and Bija would have to search for another camp.

"Until application will be approved and more tents, you share tent with other family," Vikhrim answered in clumsy Dari.

At least this man was trying to speak their language. Most Pakistanis spoke Urdu. "Many thanks," Johar replied as he studied Vikhrim's Western pants and odd felt hat that rounded over one side of his head. Johar followed Vikhrim wordlessly, Bija's hand in his, as Vikhrim pushed his way through the throngs. Even a corner in a tent would be merciful splendor.

Dust blew into Bija's eyes. She began to wail as she

rubbed them, which prompted a coughing fit. Her coughs turned to hacking, then retching sounds. Johar steadied Bija's shoulders as she vomited reddish phlegm onto the sand. Her illness had returned with even greater force after leaving Kabul.

"Is there a doctor here?" Johar asked anxiously. "I had hoped my cousin was better, but she is worse than ever."

"Many sick here. There is one medical compound." Vikhrim pointed to the outskirts of the tent city. "But lines stretch around the camp. See the red mark on the white wooden building past the tents?"

"I see." Johar nodded as he kicked sand over Bija's blood-flecked mess. She lifted her palms, begging Johar to pick her up. He swept her up and under his arm.

"Many have disease." Vikhrim waved toward the cacophony of voices and bodies, the circle of waifs shadowing them. "Ration tickets scarce. Little food. Aid workers promised wheat to Suryast, but delivery delayed by American bombs. First they bomb and then bring food. Can you imagine?" Vikhrim raised his hands in exasperation.

I can, thought Johar, pained at the memory of the droning jets that had appeared overhead some time after they'd left Kabul. Later the yellow packages had fallen from the sky and onto the road like golden kites. Johar had first suspected they were land mines; the Russians had dropped tiny mines years back. He'd heard stories of children who had picked them up, thinking that they were toys. But these yellow packages had English writing–*Humanitarian Daily Ration*–and pictures of people eating. Food! Johar had been hesitant, but hunger overcame fear when he'd poked a package with a stick and it hadn't exploded. He and Bija had ripped the plastic and gobbled up a sticky mess of peanut-flavored glop with raisins. What odd food the Americans ate. They managed to pick up one other before the rest were grabbed.

"Tent number one-oh-two," Vikhrim announced as they reached a tent larger than most. Its number was printed in faded ink on the canvas flap. "Wait here." He lifted the flap and stepped inside. While Johar helped Bija wipe her nose and drink water from their flask he overheard what sounded like a heated argument from inside the tent.

They sat on a nearby ridge and waited for Vikhrim to emerge. Curious bands of children stared from a distance. Johar stroked Bija's feverish head and thought of Aunt Maryam. If she was lucky, the Taliban would have freed her from prison. If she wasn't lucky . . . Johar didn't dare imagine that now. And Daq, did he fight with the Taliban? Was he injured, or worse? If by some miracle Daq had escaped, Johar prayed he would remember the emergency family plan to meet at Suryast. Johar must write letters as soon as he managed to procure paper. The hardest part of having the family split was the not knowing. Would Johar never know? The pieces might be thrown so far that their perfect puzzle curves would never again fit together as one.

Vikhrim's sun-baked face finally poked through the tent flaps, and he motioned for them to join him.

Inside the tent, an aged man with a snowy beard sat in a corner clacking prayer beads through his fingers. "Johar, meet Wahir," Vikhrim said. Johar said hello, and the old man grunted. Two boys crouched in front of Wahir by the cooking fire, warming a pot of rice. One was a boy of six or so, and next to him a boy about Johar's age.

Vikhrim pointed to the large boy. "Johar, this is

Romel." Romel continued to stoke the dung coals without looking up. His scowl seemed to say *Go back to where you came from.*

"And this is Romel's small brother, Zabit." Zabit's grin was guarded as he poked a stubby finger over gums where two front teeth had been.

"I am grateful to you for allowing us to stay," Johar murmured.

"It wasn't our choice," Romel blurted. "You'll have to get your own food. We've not enough food to feed our own."

"You must apply for ration booklet." Vikhrim explained. He adjusted his slanted hat and skittered from the tent.

Johar and Bija faced the old man and his sons. "What did Vikhrim mean by the ration booklet?" Johar asked the old man, Wahir.

Wahir eyeballed Johar as if he were a fool. "No wheat without ration tickets. Apply at the compound for tickets. It takes many days."

"But what will my cousin and I eat until then?" Johar asked, alarmed.

"Drink from your tears and eat your despair," laughed Wahir bitterly. Romel chuckled along with him.

"I have some nuts." Zabit removed the fingers from his mouth and shoved them in his pocket, producing two walnuts. "But I need them."

"Share," Bija cried sharply. The last of their keshmesh had been eaten a day ago, and Johar knew she was famished. Bija approached Zabit, who popped the walnuts back into his pocket. She started to howl, which sent her into another coughing fit.

Wahir paused from his beads. "What's wrong with the girl? Her lips are blue."

"My cousin has a bad cough."

"There is a doctor by the western edge of the camp," Wahir mumbled, resuming his bead clacking.

"An American," snorted Romel as he stuffed a mound of rice in his mouth.

"Thank you for telling me." Johar piled his bags in a corner near the door. "We will not take up much room."

"No, you won't," agreed Romel, stretching his feet toward Johar's bags. Zabit stared wide-eyed at Bija's blue-tinged face.

The sound of Zabit and Romel gobbling their rice made Johar's mouth water. What would they do for food? He must get his cousin to the doctor, but if she could eat a bite first, it would do her good. Johar pulled a hat—the one with the sunburst design—from his pack and held it out. "Would this do in return for a handful of rice?"

Romel's eyes gleamed with interest, but he held back. "I said we do not have enough. Didn't you hear me the first time?"

Wahir's beads fell silent. "Give them a fistful, boy."

Romel scowled as he slapped a clump onto the plastic cloth near Johar's feet and grabbed Johar's hat. Bija scrambled over and stuffed in a mouthful. As she chewed, she began to cough again, but this time she couldn't stop and with each cough her lungs produced a wretched gurgling.

Was she breathing? Her eyes were wide, but she didn't seem to see him. Johar couldn't let her choke to death! He scooped her up, hurried her outside and tied her to the donkey's saddle. He mounted and raced the beast toward Suryast's western edge, to the building with the red mark.

What a disaster! thought Johar. The line of sick people stretched over the ridge into the fading sun—maybe thirty people deep—just as Vikhrim had warned. Bija's eyes rolled back to show the white parts. Her breaths were barely audible. Bija might die if they waited in line. She needed help now! Every nerve in Johar's body strained to ride faster. The donkey clambered along the cracked plain, sending up clouds of dust. Finally they reached the front of the line. Johar leaped down, untied Bija, and pulled her into his arms.

He pounded fiercely on the flimsy wooden door. "My cousin is dying!"

"My son is sick too," yelled an angry man, "and we've waited for hours to get up to the doctor's door." He pushed Johar away, but Johar swerved around him and pounded harder on the door.

"What are you doing, you selfish boor?" demanded a one-legged man behind the first. He hopped on one foot as he brandished his cane. "I've waited all morning in the wretched sun to get a leg."

"American doctor, please help! She's dying!" Johar yelled in English through the open window.

The door swung open. A man with cloud-colored hair around a pink face emerged. Behind him was a woman in owlish spectacles, also with pale skin. "What's the trouble, Nils?" the woman asked the man.

The pink-cheeked man began speaking to Johar in Dari. "What is the trouble?"

"I'll show you trouble!" screeched the one-legged man. He smashed Johar on the back with his cane. "The boy jumped the line." Johar winced in pain but held his place.

"Stop!" Nils grabbed the cane. "Patience," he shouted,

127

prodding the man back into the angry crowd. Nils stationed himself between Johar and the throng like a human shield.

The spectacled woman approached. She began to examine Bija, peering down Bija's throat and listening to her chest with a metal stethoscope. "Rales," she muttered.

"Can you help my cousin?" Johar begged in English. "She cannot breathe!"

The woman raised her eyes to his, startled by Johar's words. She turned and opened the door. "Bring her in."

The crowd roared. "Thrash that boy! He cut in."

"Just because the boy speaks Ingleesi."

Speaking in Dari, Nils attempted to calm the crowd. "Your turn will come. We will see you all."

Johar's heart pounded as the woman took Bija in her arms and carried her into the compound. She laid Bija on a metal table, stuck an instrument down her throat in a concentrated motion, then pulled it out. Johar came over and helped to hold Bija steady. She shuddered and coughed, then began to breathe—breaths that beat like hummingbird wings. Bija was still alive! The doctor rubbed the instrument along a glass slide, then removed some blood with a needle.

"This medicine will treat her infection." The woman said. She rubbed a patch of Bija's skin with a piece of cotton, then poked another needle into her arm.

Johar sighed deeply. The din of the crowd, which had faded in those awful moments, returned in a swell outside the window. "Will she live?" he asked in English.

With sturdy hands the woman set Bija on a cot by the wall. "We hope so." She removed her glasses. Her eyes and the strands of hair that peeked from her scarf were both the slate color of goat's wool. "Your cousin is one sick little girl with an extremely high fever. I suspect that she has bacterial pneumonia. Do you understand?"

"Yes. Understand."

"How is it that you know such good English?" The woman motioned him to a folding chair. Her owlish eyes pierced his.

"I learned from my aunt. She is schoolteacher near Baghlan." Johar loosened his fists. He'd been clenching them so tightly, the nails had cut notches in his flesh.

"But even for a teacher to know such good English!" The doctor crossed her arms and leaned into the table.

"Aunt's brother is in England. He give us books."

"Aha!" The woman smiled, her stern features softening. "My name is Dr. Louise Garland. What's your name?"

Johar blushed and looked down. He wasn't used to speaking with foreigners, even though she was a doctor. "Johar. Name of cousin is Bija."

"Call me Dr. Garland. This may sound rather sudden, but—" Her next words made Johar look up suddenly to return her gaze. "We are in desperate need of translators here at the clinic. Nils, my nurse and translator, will leave for Kabul in a few days. We are severely understaffed. You see, I am from America, and I speak no Dari."

"You want *me* for translator?" Johar glanced at Bija, who was sleeping. "Can we get ration tickets and wheat? We hungry."

"I'll make sure you get ration tickets, and I could pay you something. If you want it, the job is yours." Dr. Garland straightened up and began to busy herself putting instruments in order. "I will speak to the main office right away."

"When I to begin work?" Johar asked.

"Tomorrow morning. Nils will show you how to work the phones, help with the patients, send e-mail."

E-mail. Someone said they had computers with e-mail in the library in Kabul. Things were happening so fast. "And my cousin?"

"She will need more shots tomorrow. In the meantime, watch her carefully."

"So. It is serious, this pneumonia?"

Dr. Garland nodded.

Johar would watch his cousin as carefully as a mama lynx watched over her young. He must keep her alive. Johar was relieved and anxious all at once. One day and four words—*the job is yours*—had propelled him from despair to hope.

weight

New York,
early October 2001

Dawn couldn't talk Jude into staying at the squat, but he did visit. He even hit it off with the Goth guy, who'd also come to New York to act. The three of them would often sit on the stoop and yak—about school, why they'd run off, and what they wanted out of life—while they watched Puerto Rican moms push strollers up the avenue. Dawn visited Sander's only when Jude was with her. She was leery of Pax and intimidated by Sander's groupie girls. Meanwhile, Jude played phone tag with his parents, telling them he was okay, promising to come home soon.

Jude and Dawn continued their routine of playing flute and dancing spacey jigs for food money, then eating lunch in Union Square. She pleaded with him several times to come down to ground zero with her. He'd declined each time, but one morning she talked him into it. They sat on the insurance company steps, across from St. Peter's and three blocks from the site. The ledge of this building was as close as they could get to the craters of the twin towers, which were obscured behind the plywood fence. Sitting across from the church, they could just make out the ruined steel beams above the fence, huge as mountains, tipping precariously out of tortured steel abutments. Beyond that were the dinosaur cranes, twisting and digging in front of office buildings whose windows had imploded. Constant smoke plumed upward.

Jude sulked and paced. "Why did I let you talk me into this?" he complained. Even though they had made up, something had changed between them since the day after the tragedy. Jude recited lines from the play he'd starred in last year as he paced on the stairs next to the ledge. "A day unlike any other. A day, my love, for the undertaker."

"Quiet, Jude!" Dawn yelled. "What's the matter with you? It's not some off-Broadway farce here. Show some respect for the dead." Jude's theatrics drowned out the weight—the dense, tragic weight that begged to be felt.

"But it's *so* depressing," he moaned.

"Give me a few more minutes, please." For Dawn, the nights at C Squat and the days on this ledge had been an odd comfort. She'd stared obsessively at onlookers as tears streamed down their faces. How could they flow so freely? Hers were frozen deep inside. When people wanted to stop crying, could they just will themselves to stop? How could you dam up a waterfall?

Jude stretched up as far as he could on the stairs, craning his neck. "It's just that it's so horrible, Dawn. It goes on forever; and the smoke—"

Dawn took out her flute and cleaned it with the chamois square. "What are they doing in there today?"

He leaped off the stairs and climbed onto a fence perpendicular to the site gate, teetering slightly before finding his balance. "Loading a flatbed with beams. Spraying water on the fire. Drinking coffee." Dawn noticed a National Guard soldier posted at the makeshift gate, eyeing Jude warily. "I can't deal with Armageddon, Dawn."

"Fine," Dawn sighed, "I'll come down by myself from now on." She pressed the flute to her bottom lip, cleared her scratchy throat, and played a drawn-out G. She purred it up to B, D, then a high E and lingered there. On her exhale she felt something: a gentle push, a whisper, a sudden breeze.

Something seemed to echo. Her eyes were drawn to the opening in the gate, past the guard where the sun glinted off a jagged shard of the latticed tower. Two seagulls floated through the rubble. Dawn turned to Jude. "You say something?"

"Negative." Jude leaped down and winked at the guard, who quickly shifted his gaze. "I'm out of here, girlfriend. This place is haunted. Are you coming?"

Dawn didn't answer. Maybe St. Peter's arches across the street had produced the echo. She played a soft G. The note spread out until the church walls absorbed it. No echo. Dawn yanked apart the flute pieces and flung them in the case. "Jude, you're so impatient. Should we just go to our other spot for some extra money?" They began to walk up Hudson Street.

"I can't," Jude muttered. "I've got something to tell you." Jude's face had turned pasty. He looked guilty.

"What is it?"

Jude stopped and faced her. "You know I'm on your side and you're like my best friend in the whole world and all that stuff. . . ." He slouched like a mutt that had just wet the carpet.

"Well, yeah."

"I'm going home, Dawn."

"You mean to Pax and Sander's?"

"No, Dawn. Back to San Francisco."

"You can't! I mean–" Dawn laughed nervously. "What about us–my music and your acting and–"

"It's over. For now, anyway." Jude shook his head.

"Hey, I'm sorry I decided to live at C Squat," Dawn blurted out. "It wasn't because of you. It was something I had to do. We'll hang out more. Make it fun and–"

"It's not about that, Dawn," Jude cut in. "I'm going home in a few days. My parents sent me a plane ticket. Don't worry. I didn't tell them you were here, but you could still go back. Call Victor. He'd fly you back."

She would be alone again. Abandoned. That thing she'd felt so many times before was spreading inside Dawn–her insides getting cold and stiff, like hamburger meat in the freezer, so hard you could hit the block on the stove with all your might and it wouldn't break. But some parts stayed soft and raw.

Jude had that look of pity on his face. "I'm not like you, Dawn."

The biting parts inside her flamed up, furious. "What's that supposed to mean? That I'm some kind of street trash? Just because you come from a good family where your mom and dad love you and stand by you and indulge your every whim doesn't mean you're a better person than I am. Shit, if I had all that stuff, I never would have run off to

no

134

New York. I'd be studying flute and thanking my lucky stars every day I had parents like yours. And I wouldn't be such a prick. You were so into your own selfish pain at the Trade Center site. What about the people who actually had to *die*?"

"Yeah," Jude mumbled. "You don't believe me, but I feel bad for them."

Dawn watched tears pool over Jude's lids and run down his sunken cheeks. Her own eyes burned with dry loathing. "You might feel bad for them," she said, "but you feel much worse for yourself."

"So you think I'm a selfish, spoiled wimp. What about you, huh? You connect with this big tragedy, but when there's a real person in front of you, you're a total ice queen."

"Says the drama queen."

"At least I connect with people. I guess for you, actually *talking* to people is too damn messy." Jude brushed his tears with his silk cuffs. "Are you really sad, or do you just get off on being dark and moody? Maybe you're the one who's addicted to drama."

"Well, you're addicted to superficiality." Dawn pointed to Jude's new studded jeans and silk shirt. "How can you go on a shopping spree after a tragedy like this? I used to think you were a kindred spirit. I guess it was wishful thinking."

He shook his head. "Look, I'm just not cut out for this. My parents are freaking hysterical." He reached out to touch her arm. She shook it off. "Whatever," he mumbled.

"Yeah, whatever." Dawn turned and shot across Canal Street. Car horns blared at her and a bike messenger squealed to a halt, cursing her out. She hurried through the cobbled streets of Soho, around semis unloading, past furniture stores, and across Houston as the light clicked to yellow. Jude had been disrespectful at the site. *And what about me?* she wondered. *Am I there for the right reason?* One thing was for sure—Jude was a spoiled mama's boy, so good riddance to him.

When she reached Union Square, Dawn went behind the hedge and tried to catch her breath. She had run too fast. Panic rifled through her. With Jude gone, there would be no one to help her laugh it off. Things would be so much more serious now. She set up the satellite phone and dialed. It rang and rang and rang. *What am I thinking?* No one had ever been there for her—her birth mom, the DiGiornos, Louise. Dawn's finger went up to cut the connection.

"Hello?" Dawn jumped. It was a young man's voice with a heavy accent.

"Uh—uh, hello," Dawn stammered.

"What can I do for you, miss?"

"Who *are* you?" Dawn asked curtly.

"My name is Johar. May I help you?"

"Is Louise there?"

"Who?"

"Dr. Garland."

"Dr. Garland away from clinic at this moment. May I give her message?"

Dawn ignored his question. "Do you work with Dr. Garland? Is she all right?"

"I work as translator. I speak with Dr. Garland every day. She OK."

"Did you talk to her today?"

"Yes, I speak. Are you daughter?"

"Um—"

"Dr. Garland says she has daughter who may be calling.

Must worry too, about mother." He paused. "Hard to have mother all way over here."

Who was this guy? She shouldn't tell him anything. For all she knew, he could be a terrorist! Dawn hung up and slumped to the ground. She stared at the tattered notices and drawings along the fences. It didn't take long for hope to sink into grief.

socks, hats, guns

Suryast, Pakistan,
early October 2001

Dear Maryam—
   When I could not find you or Daq, I took
Bija and carried her to the camp we had
often spoken of. The man in charge will show
you to us. Have you heard from Daq? Please
send word that you are all right. We pray
every moment for your safety.
—Your devoted nephew

Johar dared not say how sick Bija had been, dared not
mention Suryast, the Taliban's capture of Daq, or that they
might be searching for Johar as well, for who knew into
which hands this letter might fall? At least Maryam would
know him by his handwriting. More news of American

bombings spread through the camp within hours. Kabul had been hit, as Johar knew it would be. He felt ill when they said a bomb had struck the radio station where Aman worked. The airfield near Baghlan was also hit. Even here, above Suryast, there was a constant drone of warplanes and distant smoke from mortars.

Nils, the ICRC nurse from Switzerland, promised to carry Johar's letter to Baghlan on his way north. Johar provided directions to Maryam's compound and Ramila's as well. Maybe she would have news of his aunt. With a kiss to the paper, Johar thanked Nils and placed the note in his hand.

• • •

With Nils gone, Johar plunged into clinic tasks with vigor. He rehearsed the lines "May I help you?" and "What can I do for you?" in order to answer Nils's phone properly. Dr. Garland taught Johar which medicines treated which illness. She demonstrated procedures for common ailments like amoebic dysentery, cholera, jaundice, malnutrition, loss of limbs, pneumonia, and infection. Nils had given him rudimentary lessons on a computer and a lesson in e-mail. Johar was finally learning how to use things he'd always thought so modern and fast.

The bulk of the work was translating for Suryast's constant flow of patients. He worked alongside Dr. Garland, though he was timid about working intimately with a foreign woman. Nonetheless, Johar gave it his all.

The first patient was a girl as thin as camel thorn, whose cheekbones pushed through pallid cheeks. Johar translated Dr. Garland's question into Dari. "How long since your daughter has had fruits or vegetables?" he asked the young girl's mother.

"Since before we left Kandahar. A month or so, maybe longer," she replied.

Dr. Garland examined her swollen, bleeding gums, while Johar translated the mother's words back into English. The doctor went to the cabinet, took out a bottle of white pills, and handed one to the child. "Tell her mother this is vitamin C, which will help cure her malnutrition. Tell the girl to place the pill on the back of her throat and tip her head as she swallows." Johar instructed the girl while the doctor gave her water and demonstrated the necessary motions. It took many times of trying, for the child was weak and kept choking on the pill.

Next was a man who had fled Afghanistan with his grandson. In the trek from Khost blisters had formed on his knee stump where the wooden leg had rubbed it raw.

While Dr. Garland applied disinfectant and a bandage, Johar listened to the man's tale of escape. He'd awoken at night to a blast that ripped apart his roof. Fleeing to the courtyard, he and his terrified grandson had found his daughter's body, which they wrapped and took with them. Neighbors helped shepherd them out while the sky exploded into trails of greenish flares. American bombs had missed their target, a Taliban compound near the mosque. He buried his daughter outside the village on his way south.

"The walk nearly killed me, but I had to get my grandson to safety," the old man explained as tears dropped onto his shalwar. "He's all I have left." Johar glanced at the boy who sat by the door, and thought of Bija, struggling to recover as she slept at Anqa's, a friend of Dr. Garland's. Johar felt guilty that he had a job and ration tickets, that Bija had such good care, and that he hadn't lost a leg or an arm like so many people at Suryast. Guilt ate at him when he heard crying at night, and when he saw the skeletal bodies of children being carried to the edges of camp for burial it pushed him to work even harder at the clinic.

Dr. Garland and Johar heard many shocking stories. Patients were desperate for treatment, but also to talk. Johar spared Dr. Garland the details. It wasn't her fault that America had sent bombs, just as it wasn't Johar's fault that the Taliban and Al Qaeda had seized Afghanistan. His heart broke as he heard the suffering of his people. Rumi's words whispered in Johar's mind.

Cry out! Don't be stolid and silent
with your pain. Lament! And let the milk
of loving flow into you.
The hard rain and wind
are ways the cloud has
to take care of us.

Dr. Garland had not discussed the tragedy in her own country. Johar wondered what she would say. Instead, she spoke often of her daughter, Dawn, of her flute playing and how she was so talented she would surely earn a living with her music when she grew up. "I miss Dawn. She's about the same age as you, Johar. You'd like her. She's such a strong girl."

Somehow Johar knew it was the girl he had spoken to, even though she hadn't admitted it. He'd almost told this to Dr. Garland, but instinct told him not to. Dawn seemed afraid to leave a message. Johar would stay out of it. If it were his mother, Johar would've offered her poems and blessings, even through a telephone line.

Maybe Dr. Garland wasn't who she seemed to be. Johar searched for a sinister element between her words, for hatred in her eyes, ill will in the awkward way she greeted him, harshness in her steady hands. He came up with no evidence of anything but determined doctoring. He felt nothing but gratitude for her help in saving Bija's life. No matter how many hours into the evening or how long the line of patients, Dr. Garland was solid.

•　　•　　•

Day after day, Romel threatened Johar as a jackal threatens a hare. "So, your cousin got seen by the doctor on the first day. I heard you jumped the clinic line. People were ready to beat you and throw your body in a ditch. I'd like to take part in that. You must think you are as important as the muezzin. Did a magic bird fly a ration booklet into your greedy palms? Seems as likely. I can only imagine what kind of favors you offered Vikhrim, that Pakistani rat. With all your magic, surely you could get yourself another tent. You better find one soon, or I'll finish the job they started in that clinic's line."

Despite feeling guilty, Johar pleaded with Vikhrim to find him a tent. Vikhrim shook his head. "Make do! People who came before you still wait with no tent at all."

Johar was ashamed. He should be able to defend himself without seeking escape, but he couldn't. His dread of conflict had slithered with him to Suryast. It would stalk him endlessly unless he forced himself to change.

Johar took to avoiding Romel. He left before Romel stirred at sunrise. When he walked Bija to Anqa's on the way to the clinic, he wound around the outskirts of camp, far from where Romel and his thuggish buddies gathered.

Romel's old father, Wahib, was no help. He spent his days clacking his beads and babbling nonsense. After his kind words on their first night, he now kept silent no matter how rude Romel's comments became. Only the little one, Zabit, was friendly. With his gap-toothed grin, he played with Bija at dusk whenever bursts of her old energy broke through.

Johar returned from the clinic one night, his head splitting with headache. He put Bija to sleep, then lay down, using his flattened pack for a headrest. There were sounds of weeping, of arguing, of lovemaking from neighboring tents. Johar tried to block out Romel's rank odor and a vague stink of death, which wafted in as he fell into a nightmare of the robber near Charikar. He'd had this dream before, only this time Johar fought back and wrestled the luti to the ground. But the luti prevailed, and at the moment his blade slashed the veins in Johar's throat, Johar startled awake, drenched in sweat.

He reached for the hats and socks inside his pack. "Khub ast, I've been robbed again!" He took a mental inventory: two pairs of socks, four hats, and the knitting needles. Romel's work, no doubt. Johar was such a fool. *Will I ever learn to defend myself?* Johar stayed in the tent later than usual, wondering what to do. He must confront Romel, yet he couldn't prove a thing. But that was his whining coward's voice, and his coward's voice was wrong. When Romel rose and stirred the coals, there was a sneer to his expression.

"Did you take my hats?" Johar asked.

Romel laughed. "What would I want with those silly hats?" His face turned hateful. "I'll tell you one thing—if you don't find another tent, I'll take more than your hats.

Maybe I'll take your little cousin." Romel chuckled with contempt.

"You won't," Johar muttered, and left. Though the donkey was usually left tethered to the tent, this day Johar and Bija rode the donkey to the clinic.

"Why are we riding today, Jor?" Bija asked. "I want to walk!" Since Bija's return to health, her energy again burst forth in wild gusts.

Johar didn't answer her.

They rode past tents, which were so close they touched, until they reached the main office. "Sahib," Johar called to one of Vikhrim's friends from Karachi, who sat smoking. This Pakistani was the kind of leathery bazaar hawk that Johar steered clear of–a salesman who would sell his own mother's jewelry from her wrist. He often came to Suryast looking for young children to do his most difficult hauling of goods. The children were so famished, they would do anything for a few coins. As if the Pakistani sensed Johar's disdain, his lidded eyes scrutinized Johar without rising to greet him.

"You have something for me?" the man asked as he took a draw from his hookah.

"What would you give me for my donkey?" Johar's offhand manner belied his pattering heart.

Bija tugged on Johar's arm. "Jor, let's go. That man is scary."

The man's lids raised like lazy curtains. "What would you want for the beast?" He rose and ambled toward them, like a westerner in one of those American bootlegs that Johar had seen in Baghlan as a child, ready for the shootout at the OK Corral.

It had come to this–his allegiance to peace, to the

power of poetry, gone. A scoundrel like Romel could change Johar's direction as swiftly as wind shifts from east to west. "A gun," Johar answered. "Not too big; no Kalashnikov. Something I can hide in my pack. A simple thing that works."

carneys and birds

New York,
early October 2001

Dawn sat on the steps at Union Square, watching the carnival freaks. It was just weeks after the terrorist disaster, yet there were people selling American flags and postcards of the twin towers, loonies hawking herbal bioterror remedies, and people advertising Web sites that promised to crack terrorist cells through astrology, numerology, and even hair sculpture. This travesty of a memorial had happened in stages, like flowers in a vase that go from pastel blooms on upright stems to Day-Glo mold on gnarled fibers.

Dawn read in the *Times* that the suicide pilots had trained in what the press called Afghan terror camps. This was proof that there was some connection between Afghanistan and the attack on the twin towers. She hoped

Louise was safe over the border in Peshawar, then wondered why she was thinking about Louise so much. Dawn didn't hate her. And no matter what had gone wrong between them, it would be dreadful if she were hurt.

What about the boy who had answered Louise's phone—Johar, was it? He had a warm, kind voice. Dawn doubted he was a terrorist; that was just her stupid paranoia. She'd met a number of International Committee of the Red Cross workers. The ICRC people were always so mild-mannered and liberal. And they surely did thorough background checks.

Dawn's gaze returned to the plaza. She watched a camera operator zoom in for retakes of teary mourners lighting candles. The TV reporters' sound bites seemed rehearsed, disingenuous in relation to the tragedy itself. Hucksters oozed from every state and every borough. Why did tragedy bring out the ogling, warty worst in people?

Some of the activity at the park was still genuine. The day before, Dawn had played in two jam sessions, first with a lively jazz group from Vermont and then with an earnest gospel group. After that, she'd sat on the steps on the park's south side, where the largest crowds mingled, and watched an Indian girl in a head scarf set up a microphone by the subway entrance. The girl had to share the stage with a Korean violin player and a ranting socialist. Dawn found herself rooting for the girl as she explained how the Muslims in her Queens neighborhood were peaceful, how they grieved for America—were Americans. The girl said that the women feared going out of their houses. They were afraid to wear head scarves because people yanked them off and called them terrorists.

The crowd listened respectfully—some even clapped.

But a few shouted, "Go back to the Middle East." You could hardly blame people for hating—so many had died at the hands of an Arab few. Dawn waited for the girl's expression to harden, but she paused patiently until the hecklers simmered down. Some of Louise's co-workers must be Muslim too, and prejudiced against westerners the way some here were against this girl. How would Afghanis or Pakistanis have reacted to American speakers over there?

When Dawn heard the news about the first bombing on Sunday it made her feel sick. The reporter explained that the United States was going to free Afghanis from their Taliban oppressors, who executed people and refused to hand over the Al Qaeda masterminds behind the attack on New York. But war was not a science; innocents got killed right along with murderers. Dawn had learned that much in history class. Afghans would be hurt! What would Johar think of working with an American then?

Dawn rested her elbows on the concrete steps and leaned back. A memory filtered in of a rainy day last autumn. She had been driving with Louise through Oakland on the way to the grocery store, the windows cracked open just enough to keep the glass from fogging, when a silver sports car shot through a red light, swerved around them, and smashed into a pole with a terrifying crash.

Louise sped to the shoulder, placed a call for help on her cell, then grabbed the first aid kit from the glove compartment. "Stay put," she said with steely calm.

Outside the car, a black guy, huge as a wrestler, yelled at Louise. "You crazy bitch. This was your fault!"

Through the fogged-up window Dawn heard Louise staying cool, taking charge. "I'm a doctor. I can help you." Blood streamed down the man's forehead as she helped him under her umbrella. She patched him up. He became docile as a child under her firm touch, her calming words. Louise defused the tension brilliantly that day.

Dawn remembered what Johar had said before he had hung up—*must be hard to have mother all way over here.* There was something so caring about that, and Dawn realized it was true. She went behind the park hedge, set up the sat phone, and dialed.

"Hello. May I help you?"

"Hello. Is this Johar?"

"Yes. And you, Miss Dawn?"

He remembers my voice. "Yes!"

"Sorry, Miss Dawn. Dr. Garland out in camp. Shall I get?"

"Oh, no! Um . . . I'll just speak to you."

"Not talk to mother? Why?" asked Johar.

Dawn scraped zigzags in the dirt with her fingernail. "I don't know." *Because Louise scares me, that's why, because she'd be furious with me.* "Hey, Johar?"

"Yes?"

"What did Louise say about me?" Dawn's insides churned.

"Very good flute player."

"Anything else?"

"You are little bit older than I."

"I'm sixteen. How old are you?"

"I, fifteen." His voice was almost delicate.

"Is everything still OK in Afghanistan, um, I mean in Peshawar? Uh, is Dr. Garland OK?" Dawn stumbled over words. "And are you OK? I mean—"

"Dr. Garland OK, and OK here. My cousin and I came here from Afghanistan."

"Oh, that's good. That's great!" Dawn drew in a long breath. "Tell Louise I called, OK? Tell her I'm fine and I'm glad she's fine. Tell her I'll call soon."

"Yes, Miss Dawn. She say she miss you."

"Really? You're sure?"

"Sure."

"Nice talking to you. I mean, thanks, and, um, talk to you later." She hung up.

•　　　•　　　•

Dawn traveled down to the site early, before the crisp-collared businessmen who had returned to work poured out of the trains, before cabbies inched along Broadway, pressing their horns. She sat on a bench looking out onto Greenwich Street's wide expanse, just a few blocks from the piles of ravaged metal that had come to be called ground zero. She imagined that exhausted workers were still searching for bodies. Dawn pictured them crawling out of the pile and heading home to Staten Island, the Bronx, or the brick apartments of Stuyvesant Town.

She gazed beyond the supermarket, beyond the bright bars of the jungle gym in Washington Market Park and just past the plywood fence, to the funnel of smoke, and the remnants of Building Seven standing several stories high. She gazed further back to the skeleton of the south tower, its broken lattices jutting east. After all these weeks it still seemed as if mere fragments of the metal graveyard had been piled on barges. She slipped her three flute parts to-gether and practiced a B-minor scale.

Dawn's throat was scratchy from the fumes, and she had to keep clearing it as she practiced a trill, another trill, and then began a Mozart sonata, its sweetness trailing up on the breeze. A National Guard soldier, posted at the fence, turned toward her music. The Mozart was buoyant. She hadn't played this unselfconsciously since she was young, before her feelings had gotten stuck.

As Dawn swayed through the sonata's allegro into the adagio, a weight settled on her chest. She tried to shake it by launching into a second sonata, but the pressure grew. As she hit a high B and trilled it, she felt a whoosh of incoming energy, as if birds fluttered underneath her coat. Alarmed, she placed her flute on its case, unzipped her jacket, and examined herself. She'd let herself get grubby, but she saw only her tattered jersey and the bulge of money tucked into her bra. She resumed playing. It was so weird; the pressure—almost as if she could feel the weight of souls trapped in this place. Icy fear branched into her nerves. "I'm out of here," she muttered, yanking apart the flute pieces and plunking them into their case. A few curious storekeepers stared. Dawn hadn't noticed them before. She flung on her pack and hurried for the uptown train.

When she reached Union Square, Dawn crouched between the flower-strewn memorials. *Calm down,* she ordered herself, *or you'll end up in the loony bin.* Jude was sensible not to want to face the horror down at the site. Why was *she* so interested? Was she into self-torture? There was still time to run to Sander's and plead with Jude to forgive her, travel back west with him, and forget about this nightmare city. But what was there back in Frisco? Victor was probably delighted to be rid of her. It was weird to think of him going on with his work as if she'd never existed. She hadn't, except as an annoyance. And if it hadn't been for Louise running off, Dawn wouldn't have left. Jude had a home there, not Dawn.

She jumped up and pushed through the midmorning throngs to the camouflage of the park hedge and set up the phone, praying that Johar would answer and not Louise. Each ring felt like a trumpet blast. *Come on,* Dawn pleaded, her hand spring-loaded, ready to hang up at a second's notice. *Come on . . .*

"Hello, may I help you?" Johar's voice.

"Hi!" Her pulse was racing again. "Johar."

"Yes. Miss Dawn?"

"Yes!"

"Sorry, Miss Dawn. Dr. Garland on rounds. Shall I get?"

"Um, no."

His voice was hesitant. "You angry to mother?"

"It's not quite like that. It's more like she'd be angry with me, Johar."

"Why?"

"You promise to keep a secret?"

"Yes."

"Because I ran away to New York City." Why was she saying all this, revealing to this perfect stranger her whole life? She had to. She just . . . Johar was silent on the other end. Had he hung up? "Hello? Johar?"

"New York City." Johar's voice was a whisper. "What happened in your city? Is true big American buildings fell?"

He knew about the towers! Something in Dawn broke, and a torrent of words spurted out. "Yes, Johar, it was horrible!" she exclaimed. "People ran wild in the streets. It was like the world was ending! Black smoke. Fighter jets streaking back and forth. When you're stuck on a subway that's stopped between stations, I mean stuck in a black hole with no exit and they tell you it's a subway investigation, for all you know your life's about to end in another explosion. I'm afraid to go to sleep. I have these weird nightmares. People are wandering around like zombies searching for lost relatives and friends. The whole city is numb." Dawn paused. "They say the pilots were trained in Afghanistan. I read it wasn't Afghans, but do your people hate us too?"

"Some. Not most." Johar paused. "We try just to live, to get food. Many run from their homes. My cousin Bija and I left from Baghlan when brother taken by Taliban army and aunt taken by their spies. We escape over mountains. Run to this camp. Most do not wish death on any soul. We under war for many years. Afghans are weak, so others grab country for self. American bombs hit Kabul. I afraid my friend Aman killed. Bombs kill invaders, but kill innocents also. All misery." Johar continued in a whisper. "You hurt? Many people hurt?"

"I'm fine. But many people were killed, Johar, thousands of people."

"Sorry," Johar whispered. "Very sorry."

"I'm sorry too. It's all so sad." She wished she could just get the feeling out with words, with crying or even a scream. *It's sad* sounded woefully inadequate. She gathered her courage. "Johar, do you believe in ghosts, spirits?" There, she'd said it. It sounded nuts.

"Spirits, yes."

"You do? You don't think it's all nonsense?"

"Not nonsense. I speak to my father. He spirit, and mother too. Songs of my mother come to me in dreams. Many, many dead here. Afghanistan full of spirits."

"That's so awful."

"Yes, but part of life, this death."

"So I'm not just losing it." Dawn sighed. Confessing her feelings was frightening, but also a relief, like a plunge into a cool spring, and surprisingly easy with no edgy face-to-face.

"Losing it? What mean?" asked Johar.

"Crazy. Because . . . this is going to sound crazy."

"Not crazy."

"OK, not crazy. Well, I went down to the site where the towers fell."

"Yes?"

"And the place . . . It's full of some weird energy."

"Confused spirits, they."

"But how do you know? It's hard to believe. Kind of scary."

"People here. We believe in this. People in your country, not believe in spirits?"

"No. Most people in the U.S., they think ghosts are a silly superstition."

"Ah, superstition of white things dressed in sheets. Like Casper the Friendly Ghost? I see this guy in American film." They both laughed, then Johar went on. "Superstition, or belief, whatever you feel is true for you, no? I believe these spirits, they find a way out."

"Really?" That was way far-fetched, but the terror that had Dawn's neck stiff as a plank fizzled away. "Thanks." She felt light. "Tell Louise I called again. Tell her I'm thinking of her."

"OK."

"And Johar?"

"Yes?"

"Do you mind if I call or e-mail you?" Jude was gone. She was alone. Johar was a way to Louise.

"That would be nice, Miss Dawn. Internet less money, no? ICRC e-mail address, you have?"

"I do," Dawn said, and gave him hers. Now she had reason to venture into one of those trendy cybercafés in the East Village. "And just call me Dawn." She exhaled, sending sparky things through her limbs.

"OK, Dawn. Salaam."

"Salaam, Johar." She didn't know what *salaam* meant, but it was the nicest word she had heard in weeks.

play

New York,
early October 2001

Dawn flipped through her *Songs of the World* book past "Danube Waltz," "Erie Canal," and "Salsa Picante." Here was something that spoke to the gravity of the site—the Irish ballad "Danny Boy." Using her flute case, she propped the opened pages against the insurance company stairs and launched into the first measure. Over by the wooden fence, the National Guard soldier tipped his head her way, the hint of a smile showing. *Good,* Dawn thought, *he's gotten used to me.* Shadows of buses and people walking seemed, in the autumn sunlight, to sway in a ballad too.

Dawn tapped her foot to regulate the tempo. Some notes were high as a pennywhistle, and heads turned as passersby searched for the music's source. One tourist snapped a photo of her. Another man stopped to gesticulate at the smoking steel beyond the walls, his wife nodding in solemn understanding. Dawn imagined herself in a rag-tag military band playing a flute reveille on a bloody battle-field. The song took her to her feet. Was it the energy of performing that had Dawn feeling that peculiar tug again? It was so odd how she belonged here.

"Pretty music." Dawn turned, startled. An old Chinese woman had climbed the stairs. Next to the old woman stood a young man—the old woman's son? He was trying to scrunch a dollar into Dawn's hand.

"Oh, no, no money. Music is free here." Dawn smiled and raised her palm to make her point. It was inappropriate to charge money down here, where the wretched fumes still invaded her lungs. No, she'd save panhandling for a differ-ent neighborhood.

"Please." The young man offered the dollar again, im-ploring. "My mother asks, can you play a Chinese song?" Dawn turned to the old woman. Her eyes held tears.

Dawn felt a flurry of panic. "What's wrong?" she asked.

The man answered. "Her son—my older brother, Lin Wong—was killed here. He worked in an accounting firm." The guy whispered something to his mother in Chinese. Dawn stared at the old woman's tears as they spilled down over her wide cheekbones and onto her plain cotton jacket. The old woman whispered something back to her son, and he continued. "Our family comes from China," he ex-plained. "My brother's body has not yet been recovered."

The old woman held up two photos. "Lin Wong," she said. In the first, her son wore a black suit and modern glasses. In the second, a more youthful Lin Wong sat on a country porch. He beamed proudly, his wide cheekbones echoing those of his mother beside him.

"That one was taken in our village," explained Lin's brother. "My mother thinks if you play for Lin, it might help bring his spirit back to China."

"Me? Play for him?" A pang in Dawn's chest made it hard to speak. Were there actually spirits, as Johar said? It seemed irrational, but Dawn could almost feel them waiting for her music. Maybe it was all in her head, but if she played, it could mean something to this family.

"Can you play something for my brother?" the young man repeated.

"Yes." Dawn's hands trembled as she flipped through her songbook. "I'll try." Again the young man spoke Chinese, and the old woman nodded emphatically. Were there any Chinese songs in here? What would she play if there weren't? Johar had been brave to climb over icy mountains to reach the refugee camp. She imagined herself being brave too. Dawn kept flipping through the book and finally saw a possibility. "Ah, 'Bamboo Pond.' " She propped the book back on the stairs, downturned her lips across the mouthpiece, and attempted a measure.

The melody implored as the old woman's eyes had. The woman leaned toward Dawn, swaying and nodding with eyes closed. Dawn pictured herons on a pond. They ducked into the water, then unfurled their necks in the wind to shake off droplets. She pictured a bamboo forest, like she'd seen in a TV show about China, its tender leaves offering shade. Dawn entwined the notes—sheltering leaves on branches of sound—around the woman and her young son, over to the soldier, and into the air above ground zero. A crowd formed, but Dawn was far, far away now, honoring Lin Wong, whose body had been caught in a crush of metal.

She imagined his soul pictures, like ones from a travel show: China, a village, a house with a friendly porch, and green and blue bicycles resting on its railing. Radio music might be tinkling from the kitchen window. Dawn pictured fields tilled by a wooden plow. She thought of Johar. Their talks had made her feel safer. Warmth flowed into Dawn as the notes of Johar's voice played in her mind: *I see my father in the clouds; I hear my mother's music in dreams.* She finished the last measure and laid the flute down. The old woman took her hand.

"So beautiful," exclaimed the younger son, his eyes moist. "Thank you."

His mother whispered something to her son and he spoke again. "My mother says she feels Lin in your music!"

The old woman pressed Dawn's hand tightly for a moment before letting go.

"I'm so glad to help." Dawn felt herself blush and smiled. She watched the woman and her son walk down Barclay Street. When they disappeared into the throngs near City Hall, Dawn put her flute away and set out for the East Village. It occurred to her that she had some unfinished business.

Her step was purposeful. What would Louise have thought of Dawn's concert today? It was a strange concert— directed outward, for someone else's benefit, not just for Dawn. Louise had always attended school concerts, but Dawn had never acknowledged her presence. Louise had no feel for music, so what could she get out of it? But if her real mother had been there, Dawn had always assumed, she would understand the music. Would Louise have been proud of her today?

Dawn recalled the day the summer before when she'd

stepped on a rusty nail at the beach. Louise's movements had been swift. She'd driven Dawn to the local doctor fast, but not above the speed limit, then sat awkwardly by Dawn's side as the doctor administered a tetanus shot. In the following days Louise had changed Dawn's bandage, her gray hair curtaining forward, eyes keen beneath the owlish glasses. Dawn had let Louise touch her for that. That had been one of the only times. She remembered Louise's cool fingers on her skin as she'd skillfully applied the medicine and pressed firmly on the bandage to make sure it stuck. Louise might be awkward and formal, but Dawn sensed she was a damn good doctor. Had her own mother cared for her as well?

Dawn turned up Third Avenue from Houston and marveled at the chrysanthemums and holly bushes in the Liz Christy garden. Even in these dark days flowers still bloomed. Even in these dark days it was mercifully warm. She opened the gate, wandered in, and picked a few—orange and golden petals past their prime, but still vital. Then she veered up Avenue A, bouncing past Korean greenmarkets, past soap and clothing boutiques, and up to Tenth. She rang the doorbell, her overworked heart pounding hard for the fourth time that day. *Buzzer's still broken,* she thought when she heard feet pounding hard down the stairs.

Sander opened the door. He looked hot in a Weezer T-shirt and ripped jeans. But it wasn't Sander whom Dawn had come to see. She looked at him shyly. "Hi. Is Jude here?"

"You came just in time. He's leaving for the airport in a few minutes." Sander examined her grubby face and clothes. "Where are you staying, anyway?" he asked.

"C Squat." Dawn tried not to stare at him on the way upstairs.

Sander turned, catching her looking. She detected a sly grin, but he covered it. "I've heard bad things about that place," he said, and turned to face her. "You know, you could have just stayed here."

Dawn was still fumbling for a reply when Jude swung open the door and stared at her with a frown. "Hi," she muttered.

"Hello," Jude answered sourly, standing in the doorway to prevent her entrance. Sander nabbed a cold soda from the fridge, padded diplomatically into his room, and closed the door. "What's up?" Jude demanded.

"Um, uh . . ." This wasn't going to be easy. "I'm really sorry, Jude," she began. "I was upset the other day, so I wasn't very nice. Forgive me?" Dawn extracted the mums gingerly from her pack and offered them to him.

Jude hesitated, hands stuffed in his pants pocket.

"Oh, come on. I was a beast, OK?" Dawn admitted.

His face melted into a smile. "Sorry, too. I said some shitty things." He took the bouquet. "Ah, my favorite colors." Jude leaned over and hugged Dawn.

"It's not your fault. I'm just not good with people leaving." Her eyes felt prickly, and she rubbed them, then looked up to meet his gaze. "Your parents need you," she said.

"Yours too," he replied.

"I'm going to call her, Jude, I am." Dawn pictured Louise waiting by the phone. She pictured herself talking to her—connecting.

Just then Pax ran into the apartment. "Get a move on, Jude, the cab's waiting." He noticed Dawn and snickered. "If it's not Miss Snow Queen with her icicle wand."

Dawn hated to think of the crappy things Jude probably had told Pax about her when he was mad.

"Hey." Jude held up his hand. "Spare her the humor."

Pax shrugged, then lifted one of Jude's bags over his gaunt shoulder. "Dude, so fast we change our tune."

Sander's door opened. He emerged with a business card and pushed it into Dawn's hand. "Call my friend Susie. She'd be happy to have you crash with her. She's always looking for folks to feed her cats. She's a reporter and travels for her job."

Was Susie another one of Sander's girlfriends? wondered Dawn. How many girls did he have? She shot a look at Jude, and he winked. Sander's hand cupped Dawn's chin and raised it to meet his catlike eyes. "Hey, you'll like her," Sander said. Dawn's skin tingled where his fingers touched it. "Don't spend another second in that awful squat," he added, "you're too good for that."

Too good! No one had ever told her that before.

"I agree," said Jude.

"And Dawn?" Sander took his hand away to help Jude with yet another bag. He needed an army of doormen, he'd bought so many clothes.

"Yeah?" Dawn twisted her birthstone ring around and around.

"Don't be a stranger."

"I won't," she replied. Sander's voice was kind, like Johar's, but different. Sander's was firm and expert, while Johar's was questioning, exploring. Johar was drawing closer inside her head in some puzzling way.

They all clomped downstairs in a big lump. Jude hugged her again, and she and Sander stood on the corner waving like nerdy kids as Jude was driven off. But without Jude there, Dawn suddenly felt exposed. "Bye, Sander," she said, and jogged down Avenue A as fast as her legs would carry her.

•   •   •

Dawn paid for her coffee and settled into an overstuffed chair at the cybercafé. She logged in and started to type.

Louise—
How are you? I am fine. I have been busy with practice and that is why I am never home. Is it safe over there? Did you get the message I left with your assistant, Johar? Do you ever talk to him about his situation?
Dawn

Dawn felt jumbled up but good. E-mail would keep it slow and prevent them from yelling. She downed her caffeine and set out just as the streetlights came to life.

doubt

Suryast, Pakistan,
mid-October 2001

Johar's fingers brushed the gun where it rested inside his pack. He took his hand out and nervously brushed it on his vest, then clambered into the tent to confront Romel. "Give me my hats and socks, thief!" he shouted.

"I told you, I know nothing about your stupid hats." A shock of coarse hair fell over Romel's sneer as he leaned forward to break apart the coals with a stick.

Johar suppressed an urge to push him into the fire—that would spark a memory! "I'll kill you," he muttered.

Romel rose to his feet and inched toward the tent door. The old man was out. Bija was sleeping at Anqa's. "You're a pathetic coward," Romel shouted, his nostrils flaring. "You wouldn't have the nerve."

Johar grabbed one of Romel's arms and was shocked at

its solidity. He forced himself to close his fingers around the handle of the gun inside his pack. Its cold metal was as repellent as the scales of a poisonous lizard. From inside the pack, Johar jabbed the gun into Romel's stomach. Its sharp outline stretched the fabric taut.

Romel's eyes darted between fear and mirth. "Shoot me and you'll regret it."

Johar's fingers slid from the gun and it dropped inside his pack. He released Romel's arm with his other hand. "Go," he muttered, "You're not worth the bullets."

Romel leaped through the tent flaps, then jogged to a safe distance. Only then did he look back. "Can't even squeeze the trigger. Tell your American doctor what a baby you are." He strode cockily into the warren of tents and disappeared.

Fear, newly freed, swept down Johar's spine. His legs teetered on the path to the clinic, tripping over rough pits he'd avoided before. Why couldn't he finish the matter? Johar tried to shake off the horror of the gun's metallic touch. How could a sane man blast a hole through a belly? The flimsy wooden door clattered on its frame as he entered. He was relieved that Dr. Garland wasn't there yet. She couldn't see him this way—sick with disgrace and seething with rage. If only he could talk to Maryam. She'd always been the person Johar showed his heart to, much more so than to his brother. Then Johar thought of Dawn. She was alone too, and had pleaded to talk with him more. Today he would try.

He hurried to Nils's office, pushed the door shut, and pressed the power button on the laptop. So far Johar had convinced himself there wasn't time to send e-mail; he'd been too busy with patients or on the phone. The data he needed to send had grown into a massive pile. In truth, he couldn't remember all of Nils's coaching for logging on. Instructions in hand, Johar watched anxiously as bright designs popped on-screen and the laptop went through a series of dings and beeps. He clicked into Write Mail, and in the Send To line he typed *dawnmusic@usa.com*.

Before he had a chance to calm down, Johar was struck with a new anxiety. It was one thing to have Dawn phone him under the pretext of asking for Dr. Garland. It was another thing to begin a correspondence. The sharia laws that the Taliban had brought back, and which most had followed in the small villages, forbade Johar to associate with a strange woman. According to the sharia, women were to be strictly protected by the men in their family from outside advances. But Aunt Maryam had said it restricted people unduly, keeping women from accomplishing much. Johar tended to agree. *It's not as if I'm talking to a woman on the street,* he reasoned. *She's just a voice, just—dawn music.*

Johar remembered when he was thirteen, walking with a girl to school. They walked on either side of the road as it widened in Baghlan to two lanes. A truck driver and some shopkeepers stared, then pointed to them after Johar mouthed a few words to her. All bristled with the knowledge that a boy walked *with* a girl, even though they were held apart by the traffic that rumbled between them.

If the village mullah, much less the Ministry to Prohibit Vice, knew he was communicating with this American woman—of family, of war and the agony it brought—surely he'd be punished. But Johar was far from his village in a world beyond boundaries. Laws about who could talk to whom seemed pointless when people's lives were all twisted up. There were more important things to worry about. *She'll laugh at my spelling,* he thought. He sighed and began to clack away with one finger.

```
Dawn—
I think abot you much in New York City. How is
play of flute? Your brave mother is help meny
sik peepul from war. I feel afrayd. I run from
army and run from war, same way you run from
resless sprits. I need ask you qestun now. How
for me to defend from thief? In your contry
how? I no want to be coward but no want to
shoot gun.
Johar
```

The words floated on-screen until he referred to Nils's notes, which said to click Send, then they vanished with a ping. The instant he sent the letter he regretted it. Why had he typed the word *coward*? Now she would know of his shame. His brother, Daq, would've been disgusted. Heat spiderwebbed Johar's cheeks. There was another ping and new words replaced the first. *Your mail has been sent.*

Johar glanced at the poster above the desk—a satellite photo of the world. Green and brown lands connected to lapis seas. Mountains gave way to deserts. If all tribes came from one cradle, there must be people who agreed with Johar—that humans were put here on earth to talk to each other.

Johar was sure of one thing: he couldn't spend one more night in Romel's dreadful tent!

• • •

Work that day inched by like the stagnant flow of the sewage ditch. Each patient had a story worse than the last. There were victims of misguided bombing raids, people with infected pockets of flesh where shrapnel lodged, victims of frostbite from trekking over icy passes in sandals, children sicker than Bija had ever been. Resources were limited. The clinic had the basics—alcohol to sterilize wounds, gauze for bandages. But there were never enough wooden legs, never enough antibiotics, never enough blood for transfusions. Female patients would only allow Johar to translate for them, not help with procedures, so he helped Dr. Garland with the children and the men.

At dusk he locked the office. Where would he and Bija sleep? Romel's tent was out of the question. So was the clinic. Dr. Garland had already helped enough with the job and ration coupons. He must figure this out on his own. Johar prickled with resentment. Bija was a constant worry. If he were alone, he wouldn't need a tent; he would sleep on the sand. He'd be free to read poetry and to roam the Pakistani desert like some wizened nomad. Begrudging little Bija made him feel even guiltier.

Romel was still away when Johar and Bija reached tent #102. She played with Zabit while Johar collected their belongings. The old man, Wahir, paused long enough from his beads to mutter cynically, "Safar-e khosh."

"But why are you leaving?" Zabit's eyes saddened to limpid pools. He and Bija had become playmates, and Zabit had even taken to offering her a walnut if he had extras.

"It is time to move out and give you space," Johar replied. "We will still be at Suryast." He hadn't been sure, but the words helped to decide it. "You'll still see her."

Zabit's eyes brightened. "Where will you move to?"

"To the western edge, near the clinic." Johar spotted Romel strutting toward the tent. "Come, Bija." He pulled her up by the hand. "Hurry!"

● ● ●

Stars that pierced the heavens like fiery tacks would be their tent for now. Johar and Bija wrapped their garments tight around them as they spread their pattus and quilts near the clinic.

"I left my dolly in your office yesterday," Bija whimpered.

"We'd better fetch her." What a perfect excuse to check the computer!

The clinic was dark. Johar groped his way around corners to light the oil lanterns and found Bija's dolly on Dr. Garland's chair. As he bent to pick it up he noticed a photo on the doctor's desk, half hidden behind a stack of memos written in her meticulous script. Dr. Garland was in it, and a girl, a beautiful girl with hair the color of desert sand that waved around her face. This must be Dawn! Her eyes seemed to look out of the photograph into a distant, private place. Johar saw strength in her jaw, sorrow in her eyes and uncertainty in her stance. *She's like me,* he thought.

"Jor, dolly wants to play!" Bija squealed.

"In here," said Johar. "I'll show you something magical." He stepped into Nils's office, switched on the computer, lifted Bija to his lap, and logged onto the Net.

"Jor, the machine lights up!" Bija pointed to the bright shapes on-screen. They both jumped when a male voice boomed from the laptop, "You've got mail."

Dear Johar—
It doesn't do any good to close up and stay

169

quiet. Yes, defend yourself, but with words.
Hey, you journeyed over steep mountains to
Suryast with hardly any food. You carried your
little cousin to safety. But if a thief has a
weapon, I say run! In America there are lots of
crazy criminals. And if you have a gun, a thief
could grab it and use it against you. Have I
answered your question? And Johar, you helped
me be brave. I went to the Trade Center site
and I played flute for a victim's family. I
helped someone else because of you. You are *no*
coward.
Dawn
PS—Write back. I check my e-mail every day.

All the day's misgivings evaporated.

Johar gave Bija a ride on his knee, which set her to giggling. He was surprised that the words of a girl he hardly
knew could quell a doubt that had rumbled in his belly like
curdled sheep's milk—a girl who was connected to him
through a black phone wire, a satellite. Johar clicked Write
Mail. He typed Rumi's words:

Dawn—
    Sometimes I forget compleetly
    wot companyonship is.
    Unconshus and insane, I spill sad
    Energy everywer.
    —This is poem by grat poet. Says wot I feel
You ansered qestun. Thank you for kind words.
Plees rite back.
Johar

With his heart hammering, Johar pressed Send. Then, retracing his steps, he shut off the laptop and the lanterns and locked the clinic door.

Once again they were under the stars. Johar nestled Bija under her quilt with the dolly. Then he began the evening namaz. Still standing, he recited three small verses from the Quran. After that he bent with his fingers spread over his knees and said more blessings, then knelt and touched his nose and then his forehead to the pattu, whispering "Allahu Akbar" three times. He sat up, rested his hands on his thighs, uttered more praises, then stood and repeated the process. By the time namaz was done, Johar was shivering with cold. He burrowed under the pile of blankets near Bija.

She was still awake. "Look at the stars, Jor!" she said.

"They are beautiful," he said. He pointed to a glowing cluster. "Those stars form a goat. See the horns and beard?"

Bija said, "These others make a camel shape."

"And over there a house," Johar murmured.

"The stars build things," said Bija dreamily.

"Yes, they do! We will build a house when war is over and we return to Baghlan."

Soon Bija's breaths were steady.

Johar raised his face to the constellation. "I will build a school. I will speak up. I am not a coward." Johar repeated these words in Dari, like a prayer.

class

Suryast, Pakistan,
late October 2001

With canvas scraps from wheat bags and threads from unraveled blankets Johar fashioned a tent on the plain near
the clinic. It was comfortable, and its mosaic of colors
cheered him. The day after it was done, Johar worked with
Dr. Garland until the sun was a pinwheel of gold on the
western horizon. Then he hurried to Anqa's to pick up Bija.
When they returned home Johar dropped onto his pattu for
namaz. Afterward he and Bija ate a dinner of rice with
squash.

As the moon emerged in a sapphire dusk and lizards
slunk under rocks, he sat with Bija in front of their tent and
recited Firdausi's fantastic dragon poem:

When out from Kashaf's stream the dragon came
Lashing, it made the whole world like to foam;

Its length seemed stretched from town to town,
Its bulk from hill to hill.

He added lines about Afghanistan from the poet Durrani:

If I must choose between the world and you,
I shall not hesitate to claim your barren deserts as my own.

The last lines made him swell with homesickness. Johar longed for his talks with Aunt Maryam and for nights near Daq as they listened to the tinny strains of the oud and rubab on the old transistor radio. Finally he understood Durrani's painful yearning for home.

As Johar spoke on these evenings, children began to gather: a starry-eyed boy named Paj, a feather of a girl Bija's age who wore a poppy-red gown and a beaded ankle bracelet. Her brother, Hoqin, who could easily become an artisan with training, came too. Hoqin's drawings of peacocks and camel caravans scratched in the sand to illustrate Johar's tales could, if rendered in paint, adorn the grandest trucks in Peshawar.

And Zabit—Zabit had found them despite Romel's threats.

"Your brother comes of his own accord," Johar explained to Romel when Romel found Zabit and dragged him off. "No one holds him here."

"No one but a spineless mouse!" Romel shot back. Still, Zabit returned with black-and-blue marks. Romel, casting scornful leers in Johar's direction whenever he passed, let his brother stay.

Zabit sat especially close during Johar's knitting demonstrations. Johar had carved a new pair of wooden needles from a broken crutch to replace the stolen ones, and worked with a handful of amber and brown threads rescued from the saddle before their donkey was sold. What treasures one could cull from so little.

"What are you making?" Zabit asked.

"A hat to replace the one I traded your brother," Johar replied.

"Can I try?"

"Of course, young man. Pretty soon you'll be selling your hats at the Peshawar bazaar and earning enough riches to buy whole satchels of walnuts."

"I hope so!" Zabit smacked his gums in anticipation.

"Jor is an artist," Bija announced proudly, "and Jor is a teacher."

Hope dappled through Johar. He would never forget how he had run barefoot with Daq to Maryam's house after their sheep were safe in the paddock and her girl students had gone for the day. As the sunset spread melon-hued shafts across the dirt floor they would sit and listen to Maryam's words—words as big as worlds—describing ancient cities and the migrations of Asian tribes. He and Daq would pronounce the Dari alphabet as she wrote it on the blackboard, and copy the letters in their notebooks. And he would always remember Maryam's stories of Rabi'a, who had wandered as an orphan child from Basra to Mecca—it was rumored that she wrote so many poems she never slept! He would always compare Aunt Maryam to Rabi'a, the way she inspired people with words.

Johar gazed into the circle of young faces as he imagined Maryam had. He could fill his students with dreams for the future even if their tiny bellies were empty. "Loop around the left needle, then pull the left loop through the right," he instructed as his wooden needles clacked like a pair of hens. The children's faces glowed as they leaned forward to watch the sunburst hat emerge.

•   •   •

There were errands to do that morning in Peshawar. The doctor had sent Johar to buy clean dressings and alcohol from a medical supply store. Peshawar was crowded, and he was away until afternoon. Johar worked feverishly at the clinic to make up the time lost. Finally, at day's end, he closed the clinic door. This time was both awkward and peaceful for him—awkward to be alone with Dr. Garland, peaceful in moments when all was quiet.

Dr. Garland rubbed her eyes wearily. Her glasses dangled from a chain as she leaned her sturdy elbows on the desk. "I received a brief e-mail from my daughter, but I haven't been able to reach her on the telephone," she said. "It worries me."

Johar was cleaning the last of the instruments with alcohol. Hearing mention of Dawn, his heart quickened. He knew she was in New York. But he'd promised Dawn he wouldn't talk.

"You said that you've spoken with her," Dr. Garland ventured. "And she asked about you. Did she tell you where she goes in the afternoon?"

"No. I spoke only for minute." Johar felt a smoldering guilt at concealing so much. "She say only hello. Tell you no worry."

"Well, it's very odd. First I thought it was the time difference, but I've gotten up at all hours to call. She's never there. And my husband—" Dr. Garland's cheeks turned pink. She started searching for something in her impeccably neat desk drawer.

Johar was shocked that a man would let his wife travel

175

so far away without him. And Dawn was in yet another town. Western ways were hard to discern. Johar's family had fractured too, but not of their own choosing. Did they prefer to be apart? He would ask Dawn more about her mother.

"I shouldn't have left her like I did," Dr. Garland said suddenly. Her gaze met his as if pleading for him to speak. "I'm beginning to think my priorities are all wrong."

"Priorities?"

"The order of things, starting with what's most important," Louise explained.

"Ah." Johar thought of how he'd failed to help Daq and Aunt Maryam. "We try our best," he answered.

"Sometimes our best isn't very good." Dr. Garland sighed as she turned off the oil lanterns and fished in her pocket for the door key.

What could Johar say? Westerners were so informal that sometimes it embarrassed him, but she seemed desperate. He should offer solace. "You will find a way."

"Yes." Her hard features melted for an instant into an almost girlish smile. "I hope so, Johar." They bid each other good night, and he watched her trudge toward her tent with her shoulders hunched. Johar felt sorry for Dawn and Dr. Garland, treading their splintered paths. If that was what Western life was like, then he was glad for what little he had.

The sky was inky black. Johar had worked too late for lessons, and his heart sank at the thought of the children who must have waited for him. He hurried to collect Bija. By the time he arrived she was asleep and Anqa was readying her own children for bed. He apologized, lifted Bija up, and walked over the pitted soil to their patchwork tent.

A paper fluttered on the tent flap. Johar pulled it from the string that held it and read by moonlight: *Someone was here to see you in morning but you were not at clinic. He return in two days. Vikhrim.*

Who could it be? Johar's mind raced down the list of possibilities. Daq! No, he didn't dare hope. Was it a Talib soldier here to interrogate him, or even Uncle Tilo? But, maybe, just maybe, Daq was alive!

susie's
New York,
mid-October 2001

"Yes, of course, come over," said Susie when Dawn called. "It'll be great to have someone to feed my cats. My neighbor usually does it, but he's impossibly busy."

"Thank you so much!" Dawn said, and hurried over. She entered the walk-up and Susie welcomed her, showing Dawn to her tiny office, where a futon was set up.

"I haven't used my office in weeks," said Susie. "A features reporter is always on the road with her laptop. Your timing is uncanny, because I'm flying to England tonight on assignment for Reuters."

"What are you writing about?" asked Dawn, following her to the kitchen, where Susie offered her a chair and then scuttled around making tea.

"A report on London mosques." The kettle whistled.

Susie served green tea with muffins, and took a seat. "I can't believe I'm flying off again." She sighed. "I just got back from Los Angeles."

"How can you get up the nerve to fly after what happened?" asked Dawn.

"I must've been a bird in my former life." Susie gave a wry chuckle and ran her fingers through her brown pixie cut. "The honest answer is that the rent must be paid!"

"My foster mother is stationed overseas in Peshawar. She's an ICRC doctor."

"Really?" Susie put her teacup down and leaned forward. "That takes courage."

"Yes, she is brave," echoed Dawn.

"How I would love to interview all the people at the camp." Susie cupped the tea in her hands and inhaled its fragrant mist. "Does your mother ever take you with her?"

"Nope." Hadn't Victor said that Louise had considered taking Dawn on a mission? Why hadn't she? "Louise is too busy." She changed the subject. "How do you know Sander?"

"I was an early fan" was Susie's only comment. Was that fan as in girlfriend? It didn't matter. Dawn liked Susie, and it was cozy in her kitchen with the orange cat, Chester, and the gray one, Mara, licking their paws as they lounged under the windowsill geraniums. Sitting here in Susie's wicker chairs, by the blue gingham curtains, Dawn imagined herself in a country kitchen and forgot about everything that had happened in the city around them. The two women talked about journalism, music, and guys. As the sun shifted on the sills, Dawn realized that she was more relaxed with Susie than with Jude. *Maybe I'm learning how to relate,* she thought gratefully. Mercifully, Susie didn't quiz

Dawn in depth about her family situation. She only said, "You must be lonely in such a big old town."

"Mm-hmm." Dawn nodded, realizing that it was true. Dawn had an idea. She was almost too timid to ask, but her need gave her courage. "Um, do you think it'd be okay if I used your computer for e-mail?" She felt herself blush, but access to Johar and even to Louise was an opportunity too huge to overlook. The cybercafé had been expensive and smoky. "I mean, it's fine if you don't want—"

Susie bounced from her chair. "Of course! You must have loads of worried people to contact." She cut herself short, noticing Dawn's melancholy expression.

"I'll pay you," Dawn offered.

"Not to worry." Susie flashed her elfin smile. "I've got high-speed access and it's unlimited. That's one thing that wasn't destroyed when the towers came down." In the middle of Susie showing Dawn her computer a horn honked below, and she peeked out the window. "My car service is here." Susie stuffed a mess of folders in her laptop case, spritzed on some perfume, and grabbed a backpack. "Thanks again for taking care of my kitties. You should've heard my neighbor cheer when I said he was off cat duty." Her grin showed off dimpled cheeks. Then she was gone.

Dawn went into Susie's office and sat for a while staring at the geometric pattern morphing on the screen saver. Then she shook off her shoes, closed the window against the fall chill, and unpacked her award for musicianship. Dawn placed it on the side table, then set up the satellite phone and dialed. She felt almost ready. It was time.

"Louise?"

"Oh, Dawn, hello!" It was oddly reassuring to hear Louise's voice.

"How are you?" Dawn asked. "Did you get the message that I called?"

"Yes. I sent back an e-mail. You know, every time I call the house, Victor says you're out. How is it that you're always out? You're not cutting school?"

Victor hadn't told Louise a thing! Dawn was relieved, but it proved how uncaring he really was. When Dawn had called to string him along, Victor had shouted his typical refrain: "You'd better get back before I call social services." She hadn't believed a word. He was thrilled to be rid of her. "Cutting school? Don't be silly, Louise. I'm in rehearsals and spending time with Jude, that's all."

"Well, dear, I miss you."

Dawn almost believed it. If Louise would only lose the mannered voice and shout it! But Dawn never shouted either. *We're both so polite,* Dawn thought. *There's something messed up about that.*

"It's hard to get news over here, although we heard about the World Trade Center," Louise said. "What an unbelievable tragedy! I almost cut my trip short, but these Afghan refugees are in a terrible predicament—sick and starving. I haven't seen so many cases of malnutrition since the days of Biafra."

"Sounds awful," said Dawn.

"It really is. And think of all those poor families in Manhattan! Thank God the Red Cross there is so dedicated. They're putting in twenty-four-hour days. What do people in San Francisco think?" asked Louise.

"They're freaked! They fear the Bay Bridge might be next," Dawn guessed.

"How are *you* feeling about the attack?" asked Louise finally.

"I feel awful for the families." Dawn cared about them so much. And it wasn't in a voyeuristic way, like Jude said. She was helping out for once. It made her feel clean, good, happy. She almost exploded with the urge to tell Louise about her flute playing, about her conversations with victims' families. But Louise couldn't know. Not yet. "What about you, Louise? Are you safe? Is it scary there? Johar said that Al Qaeda has training camps in Afghanistan. And what about the Taliban? Has anyone threatened you?" Dawn was a little surprised by how worried she really felt.

"No, no, I'm fine," Louise replied. "The Taliban supports Al Qaeda mainly because Al Qaeda funds them. Even though the Qaeda group is made up of mostly Arab foreigners, both groups feel that anyone not adhering to their version of Islam should be eliminated. The Afghan people are caught in their crossfire, so to speak."

"That country seems like it's been through hell."

"Yes, and since the Taliban ordered all aid workers to leave Afghanistan, there are precious few doctors. But they have less control over us across the border in Pakistan. God, the suffering here . . ."

"What about Johar?" Dawn asked. "Does he get enough to eat? Where does he stay?"

"He was in a tent with another family, but then he made his own tent. He's lucky. Some families live out in the open. The place is overcrowded and filthy. It's a breeding ground for disease."

"That's scary. Do many people die?"

"A lot do, even though we do our best to treat them. Most times it's too little, too late. We just don't have nearly enough of the right supplies."

Dawn thought of all the people she saw down at the site when she played. Huge crowds would form to listen to her music. Some of them were there every day. "How do you handle all the sadness?" she asked.

"It's difficult, Dawn. It's really, really hard." Louise sighed deeply, and Dawn sensed how exhausted she must be. "But I'm a doctor," Louise went on. "It's my job to stay focused and detached."

"Yeah, but how can you stay detached? I mean, what about making a connection? Isn't that part of the job too?" Dawn felt a swell of irritation. When she played for victims' families it worked best when she threw her emotions into it. She didn't always know what to say, but the people seemed to gain huge relief from the feelings she poured into her music. "It's ironic," she blurted. "Johar gave me the opposite advice—not to run from things that frighten me, not to detach. What about Johar? Are you detached from him too? No wonder they can't stand Americans over there. People can't tell if you actually care or are just doing a job."

"Dawn, that's unnecessary! Of course I care about the people here. I need to keep a professional distance, though. And Johar is my assistant."

"But what do you think of him, really?" Dawn persisted.

"Well . . ." Louise paused. "His comprehension of English is quite something. He claims his aunt, who was a schoolteacher, taught him. The aunt's brother smuggled in English textbooks. Johar suspects that his uncle might even be living in the States."

"I know," Dawn put in. "His aunt's been captured. Did he tell you that?"

"No, he didn't." Louise's tone cooled. "How often have you spoken with him?"

"A few times," Dawn admitted. Why did Louise have to sound so clinical? "Sorry, but I need to go."

"But I wanted to—"

"I'll e-mail you. Promise." *Click.*

Everything seemed like a duty to Louise. Nothing seemed to matter personally. Dawn felt the opposite. Everything mattered but she could hardly ever express it. Dawn suddenly remembered that Louise had mentioned sending an e-mail, and she logged on.

Dear Dawn:

I am relieved to hear that you are fine, especially with all the dreadful things going on in the world. You asked about my assistant, Johar. He and his cousin came from Baghlan, where the Taliban were harassing the civilian population. His English is quite good, so when my regular assistant, Nils, had to travel, I hired this boy. He is a diligent worker. And yes, Johar did give me the message that you called.

I miss you very much and I am looking forward to seeing you again.

Mother

Louise did miss her. Dawn felt sick inside. Louise had been trying to relate, she really had. *Maybe it's me,* thought Dawn.

conversations

New York and Suryast, Pakistan,
late October 2001

Dear Johar—
Hi. Louise (Dr. Garland) must be mad at me. We
had an argument. Did she tell you about it? I
got so angry! But she's so formal and phony
sometimes—like a stranger with me. When she
gets that way, she doesn't seem to care about
people, only about her weird sense of duty.
After we hung up I opened the e-mail she had
sent me earlier, and felt guilty and sad,
because she was really trying to connect in the
e-mail. Before I came to New York, I couldn't
get my feelings out. Now sometimes I overreact.
How do you get feelings out without getting
burned or burning yourself in the process? I'm

still playing flute for victims' families at the Trade Center site. I'm starting to talk to them more too. It's hard, but not as tough as I thought. You've inspired me with all your poetry and encouragement. Up until now, I haven't done much for other people. Maybe nothing ever. Well, that's not true, but you know what I mean. Do you know lots of poems by heart? Rumi was an ancient Sufi master, wasn't he? We studied one of his poems in school. Are you OK over there? Are you getting food? I'm so worried about you and Louise and your cousin. XOX (that means with affection or something) Dawn

Dawn—
Good to hear from you. What abot you argu with mother? Doctor Garland work hard. She say she did wrong thing by you to come here. Say her best not good enof. Powerful emotions are difficult. Men can cry here but must be always strong. Sometimes I just want to say I give up. But that is cowards way so I say "no way," as you Americans say. But Bija and I OK. We are lucky. I feel guilty too, becase we are so lucky. So many here have no luck at all. One good thing—I start class! I teech childrin poetry and teech how to make hats—also teech English. You inspire me to leeve tent of hellish bully—now brother of bully is my student. Very funny. I laugh when clever little Zabit stand up to his mean brother and attend

class. May I ask a qestun? Why is Dr. Garland
here with no husband? Why she here without you?
Why Americans scatter like crows?
Regards, Johar

Dear Johar—
There's just so much to talk about, and I'd
like to actually hear your voice. Can I call
you at 6:30 a.m. your time? Is that early
enough for you to be alone?

Dawn—
Yes. I wait for your call.
Johar

• • •

"Dawn?"

"Johar, it's you!" His voice was warm. He was there for
her. It made Dawn happy. "E-mail sucks when you need a
real conversation," she said.

"Sucks?"

"If something sucks, that means it's bad." Dawn
guessed it was up to her to start. "In your e-mail you had
some question about us Americans, right?"

"Ah. Yes. Do not take this wrongly. Afghanis try to stay
close no matter what, yet your family is so scattered. Do
Americans prefer it that way?"

"I wouldn't say prefer, but it's something you get
used to."

"Why would they want to get used to this? You mother
seems so sad, so alone."

"You really think so? I never saw her that way." *She isn't*

187

my mother, Dawn almost remarked. "No one wants to be tied down in the States. Life is fast. Everyone is busy. Work takes people many places. We have lots of planes and highways." Dawn laughed bitterly. "I think of our highways as desperado trails."

"Desperado trails? What are?"

"It's an old cowboy term for the path an outlaw took—a bad guy from the West who kept moving so he wouldn't be caught."

Johar's rich tenor rippled into laughter. "Then you are all outlaws!"

"You could say that." Dawn laughed too. "But what is so great about staying close? From what I've read in the papers about your country, it seems that everything is clan-based, like you're all hiding inside your compounds with your own clan, not branching out into the real world, mixing with other people."

"People mix—at the bazaar, in school, in our jobs. But clan is good. We have strong families," Johar insisted. "We have cousins and uncles and aunts, spreading like vines through the villages. Maybe you hear about families hiding from the Taliban, or women hiding because not allowed out."

"Yes. I've read about that in the newspaper. But wasn't it always men versus women in Afghanistan? I've heard women aren't allowed to do anything."

"No, no, no. That is separation between public and home, not between men and women. Before Taliban, women worked—as teachers, as doctors. But like with you, it was a while before I feel comfortable. Maybe I still feel is risky to speak with you. Also, some men feel that if women doesn't cover up that is not moral, distracting—"

"Just because I am a woman doesn't mean I'm going to

bite you or put a curse on you or some crazy thing," Dawn blurted. "And if men are distracted by women, then it's their own problem. Why do they see women just as sex objects? That's so superficial. In America we have friendships between women and men. There are other things in life besides knocking boots."

"Knocking boots?"

"Sex."

"Do you think I am superficial, then?" asked Johar.

"Of course not. I'm sorry. You're smart and deep. The subject gets me mad, that's all. I mean, do you think that I shouldn't be allowed to go to college or work in the music industry when I'm older because I'm a girl? Do you think Dr. Garland shouldn't practice medicine?"

"No, restrictions on women sucks, as you say. My aunt said always that women can do whatever men can."

"Then who makes up all these stupid rules?"

Johar sighed. "I guess religion, tradition."

"Tradition sucks, then. And religion is so stuck in the past it needs a major overhaul. Spirituality should be all-inclusive, not all these religious factions fighting and killing one another. Religion shouldn't do people's thinking for them. Why can't we have a world where everyone thinks for themselves?"

"I agree," Johar cut in. "Let's go for it, as you Americans say. But give Afghanistan time. Our country may change slowly, in unique ways." He paused. "After all, Afghans are not little children playing follow-the-caliph."

●　　　●　　　●

Dear Johar—
I've thought a lot about what we discussed.
It's strange how our cultures are so different.

I never thought of family that way. Mine has always been scattered. I grew up in a foster home. It was like an orphanage. You must have them in Afghanistan. Then I went to two homes after that. Neither one worked out. So I was returned to the foster home. Louise (Dr. Garland) is my third foster parent—like a fake parent. She keeps her distance from me and I from her. She's not my real mother, and I guess that's why we don't feel close. Do I prefer it this way? No, but how can I change it? I hope you're not mad about what I said. Since you love poetry, I wanted to send you one of my favorites. It's about hobos traveling. Hobos were poor people with no home, kind of like refugees. They traveled by hopping on trains without paying. Here are a couple lines:

Down the track came a hobo hiking and he said boys I'm not turning.
So come with me, we'll go and see the big Rock Candy Mountains.

People sang it a lot during the Depression, a time when the whole country was poor and a lot of people were jobless and hungry.

It's great about you teaching!! The children must love you. You seem so patient and kind. What's your favorite poem?
xox Dawn

Dawn—
Things you tell me make me sure that change is a great thing. Those candy mountains remind me

of Afghan mountains. Too many poems are my
favrite. Here is one abot music, also by Rumi:
  Don't woory abot saving these songs
  And if one of our instruments breeks
  It dosent matter.
  We have fallen into the place
  Where evrything is music
  The strumming and the floot notes
  Rise into the atmosfere,
  And even if the whole worlds harp
  shoud burn up, there will still be
  hidden instruments playing.
I want to ask you, where are your real mother
and father?
Regards, Johar

Dear Johar—
I love the Rumi poem on music. I guess that's
why I play down at the site so much—it's like
I want to bring something beautiful there. As
far as my real parents, my dad was never part
of the equation. And I don't remember my mother
except for what she looked like. Do you know
how hard that is? It haunts me. If I remember
how she looked, why can't I remember what she
said? I was about five when I went to the group
home. Maybe my mother was too young or too
poor to keep a child. If I knew, it might be
easier. But, like you said, clan—blood
relations—probably does have some mystical
connection. I've looked for her through the
Internet and in phone books. Maybe she's

looking for me. Can anyone take the place of
your real mother?
XOX Dawn

Dawn—
I surprised that Dr. Garland is not your real
mother. She speek as if she is. My mother is
gone too. I miss her still. She die frum
stepping on hidden mine frum war with Soviets.
I get so mad. I have lost father and so many
family. And now my brother and aunt are
missing. I tell myself I will see them, but
sometimes I fear that is just a wishful dream.
I am fifteen, and in Afghanistan that is a man,
but I do not know what I am doing from day to
day. Bija gets sick and cries. I just want it
all to stop like end of hellish nightmare. Why
would you run away by choice? I wish I did not
have to run. Louise can be like mother, yes?
She care. She feed you and keep you in her
house. My aunt was like my mother. And people
in books are like mothers. Rabi'a, the poetess,
is my muse. Muse can be like a mother, yes? But
war keeps family apart. Always war. Now even
war in your country. To remember your mother.
It may help. I do not remember things my mother
say to me, yet I remember all of her songs.
Memories of her songs do help me. Pray on your
memory. Meditate on it. Wen your ready it will
come out.
XOX Johar

groove

New York,
early November 2001

Days grooved into patterns. Dawn would wake up, feed Mara and Chester, water Susie's geraniums, then set up shop on Fifth Avenue to earn money. This spot was close enough to walk to, as Dawn tried to avoid the subway and its post–9/11 litany of police investigations into this or that possible terrorist activity—a potentially anthrax-laden bag on the platform or a noxious odor on the number 6 local. Even on the street there were things to watch out for: trash cans with overflowing liquids, loonies with bulging packs, blaring sirens, or low-flying planes with odd flight patterns. The lines between paranoia and caution were blurred.

She played tunes that grabbed attention and held it. Her repertoire included jazz, rock, and classical licks with showy technique, like the Bach. Heads would turn and nod appreciatively and hands would toss dollars into her case. On a good morning Dawn could pocket thirty, even fifty dollars; on a bad morning, ten.

Sometimes she'd grab a slice of pizza and a soda, then walk up to the sheet music stores around Times Square. Dawn would search the rows with an eye to an international array—Swedish, Spanish, and French. She was frugal over final purchases—she needed to save for food and just in case she had to flee Manhattan.

She and Johar e-mailed constantly. Dawn would hurry back to the apartment in the late afternoon and log onto Susie's Mac. They e-mailed each other about poetry and music. Dawn wrote that her favorite rock bands were the Beatles and Radiohead. Johar e-mailed back, *Americans have strange names for music groups. Garden insekts and a radio on someone's head! How about naming a band Khonok? That means cool.*

She laughed as she sent off her response. *What about naming an Afghan band KabuliCool or Yakboots?* They wrote about school and friends and of the future. *I dream to start a school,* he confided in the next e-mail, *and call it Maryam School in homage to my aunt for all she has taught me.* Dawn replied, *I want to play in a concert hall, get over my stage fright.* She felt as if they could sense each other's moods. *Were you sad these last few days?* she asked in one e-mail. *How did you know?* he replied in the next. *What do you look like?* she typed in one day. *I am tall,* he responded, *but not as tall as my brother. I have black hair in curls and Daq says I shuffle like a Sufi in a trance. And you?* She typed back when she received his message, *I have blond hair and brown eyes. People say I'm pretty, but I don't think so. Louise says I have knobby flutist fingers.* She boosted Johar's spirits, and he did the same for her. *War will end and you'll return to your village,* she insisted. And Johar replied, *Your music helps many to heal.* Dawn taught Johar about the abbreviation LOL so they could laugh together online. One time she actually played him a flute rondo over the phone. Dawn felt closer to Johar than she did even to Jude.

Dawn called Victor again, just to let him know she was OK. If he knew that, Dawn reasoned, it might keep him from calling Louise. She said she was safe but didn't reveal her whereabouts.

Victor said he was relieved, but it didn't take long for the hateful stuff to leak out. He said that she was just trying to grab attention, and he wouldn't fall for it. "Because of you, I was late in turning in my research project," he ranted. "Because of you I've had to lie to Louise."

"You've lied all along," Dawn blurted. "I know how you really feel about me."

"Know what?"

"You tried to convince Louise not to foster me."

"Baloney," Victor muttered. "You can whine about this later. Get back here or I'll have no choice but to call her."

"Tell the truth!" Dawn shouted. "You never wanted me. And if you tell Louise I took off, I'll tell her you knew all along I was gone."

"Look, Dawn," he sighed, "I thought it might work out with you. And yes, I did it for Louise. I had no idea you could cause so much trouble."

"Trouble? What trouble? I'm sorry that I wasn't all sweet when it was so obvious you didn't want me there."

"Yes, trouble. Like the time you slept out on the beach all night without calling, or the times you cut school. Sending you back to Epiphany might teach you a lesson.

Heaven knows, nothing else has. But I've washed my hands of this!" Victor yelled, then slammed the phone down. It absolutely unraveled her, but if Dawn kept forcing herself to call him, Victor might keep quiet.

Today she'd tried him three times—times when he had always been home before—but it just kept ringing and ringing. Had Victor finally decided to tell Louise? What then? Louise might have started to care, but Dawn's running away would undo it all. Louise would send Dawn back for sure. Dawn was beyond upset when she decided to call Johar.

"May I help you?"

"Johar! I don't know what to do. I feel so crazed."

"What happened, Dawn?"

"My foster father finally admitted he never wanted me. I'm not surprised, but he said if I go back, he'll send me back to the group home where I was before."

"In Afghanistan orphanages are sad and shabby. There is no money for them. Why would Dr. Garland want to send you there?"

"She doesn't know. Besides, she might not want to face him. Victor is her husband. I'm not even adopted, just a foster child."

"You must talk to her. How can you help this if you don't talk?"

"I don't know. She's so distant. My real mother might understand me."

"Why more than Dr. Garland?"

"We share the same genes."

"Genes?"

"Blood. Clan."

"Maybe you share something else with Dr. Garland."

"Maybe, yeah." *Prickly personalities,* thought Dawn. "But you said how important blood relations are. You said—"

"I said also that the people who surround you can be your family."

"Okay, okay," Dawn admitted. "I guess, Louise and I share this doctor thing. We both want to help people to feel better."

"Anything else?"

"She has no other children. She chose me for some reason. She feeds me and shelters me, like you said. But it's just not all there between us." Dawn sighed. "Don't you have fights, trouble with your family?"

"Yes," he said. "I fight with my brother. We had terrible fights over which cause was right—the Taliban or Massoud's Alliance or for no war at all. And I had never cared for a child before now. Responsibility, it scare me. What does a little girl need? How can I care for Bija as Maryam did? I am so lonely with family gone that I feel I might break."

"Bija is in expert hands, Johar. Just give her love, and maybe a treat or two."

"I made her a doll."

"See? How could she not adore you?"

"Thanks." Johar paused. "Do not give up on Dr. Garland."

"It's too hard, Johar. I can't force us to be close."

"But you need—" He paused. "Do you remember things of your birth mother?"

"No. I've logged on to search lists on the Internet and checked for women with the last name Sweet. Ever since you told me to think about her, I've been sort of meditating on it. I keep trying to picture us doing something together. Nothing—well maybe one thing came up. I had a memory of riding in a car with her. It's a car ride at night, and there's snow, and I can't remember any other details, but for some reason, it gives me the creeps. It scares me, Johar. I don't know if I should even keep trying to remember."

"You seem stuck in that time. When you're ready it will come out."

Dawn felt as if she were almost there. She had come so far, but she needed just one more push for everything to become clear. She was like Winnie the Pooh in that old children's book, when he gets caught halfway out of the hole. It felt good to hear someone else say it. "Johar, you will be the coolest teacher."

•　　•　　•

Despite the nasty exchange with Victor, her loneliness, and anxiety over Louise, Dawn's life in Manhattan improved. After her concert for the Chinese family she made a sign that read Songs for Families of Victims—Free and propped it on the insurance company stairs. She had many takers. Among them was a firefighter's wife who wanted Scottish music, then a young stockbroker who'd lost his fiancée and requested their favorite song, "Here Comes the Sun." After Dawn played it, she sat next to the man as grief shook through him. Without thinking, her hand reached out to touch his arm. Dawn listened as he spoke of his fiancée—her mathematician's mind and her kayaking.

Another day, a commanding woman with graying dreadlocks requested a spiritual for her husband, a worker at Windows on the World restaurant. Dawn played "Swing Low, Sweet Chariot." The woman swayed and wept. Then she enveloped Dawn in her strong arms, saying, "My Ronald hears you in heaven, I bet he does."

There were rivers of conversations with people, and Dawn felt herself expanding like a paper flower in water. People thanked her for comforting them. They hugged her and came back to hear more. She had always thought connecting with people took some magical skill. But it was more like exercise. You could start out small and work up to the harder stuff later, when your muscles were stronger. The distance between Dawn and other people was getting shorter. It felt awesome to cross that last length she had never before been able to negotiate. After each conversation, the muscled place between Dawn's ribs loosened, and when someone said, "Play me a song," the corners of her mouth curved easily into a smile.

But the following week when a Pakistani woman asked for a song from her nation, Dawn came up empty-handed. The same thing happened the next day with a Lebanese man. The sheet music stores had songs from many countries, so why hadn't she seen music from the Middle East or Asia? People from all continents had perished in those towers, not just Americans. Dawn left frustrated.

Back at the apartment, she checked the Internet for music from the Middle East and Central Asia. There were pages and pages! She jotted down names, and that night she ventured into the world music section in the megastore on Union Square. Sure enough, there were rows of CDs from all around the globe. Dawn crammed her arms with Algerian rai, Hindi hip-hop, Turkish rock, North African raconteurs, and Egyptian ballads. She shelled out her last silvery mountain of quarters, then hurried back to Susie's.

Stretching on the futon and wiggling her toes to the music pulsing from Susie's stereo, Dawn imagined Afghanistan's ruby-colored peaks, crowded bazaars, and arbors like the one that grew the Charikar grapes Johar had described. During the tumultuous rubab run, she remembered Johar's story of winding through mountain passes as he shielded Bija from snow. With the Indian bhangra, she pictured peacocks and smoky music clubs pulsing with Hindi trance and kids dancing. She picked up her flute and tooled along to the music. Often scales were in minor keys, weighted with grief like the days following the tragedy. Beats syncopated in odd ways; scales jumped in thirds, fourths. Many instruments were new to her: the Indian harmonium, the Afghan santur, the Middle Eastern oud. And the voices! Singers' voices coiled and quavered. She'd never heard such range. Dawn imitated and experimented until the sky grew light and she had written three new songs.

The next day at the site, a woman from Bangalore asked for a song. The only thing she had left from her brother was his tie clip. The woman opened her palm to reveal it, then pressed it closed. Dawn was all set to play the Indian bhangra, but the woman asked for American jazz. "Raj liked Charlie Mingus. Do you know any?"

"Sure." Dawn played her version of "Love Chant" and Mingus' dreamy "Strollin'." Later that afternoon, her composing efforts were rewarded when the Lebanese guy returned. Dawn belted out a Middle Eastern cha-cha-raga-rai. He closed his eyes and swung his head. When it was over, he asked to hear it four more times.

After that a woman appeared whose daughter had been a financial trader—and a flute player. "You remind me so much of her," the woman said. Requesting song after song, she mopped her eyes with a sodden lump of Kleenex and exclaimed, "Giselle and I had a tiff on September tenth. We hadn't resolved it before . . . God, I feel so empty. If only we had been able to talk one more time. What a nightmare."

Dawn's response was in her music—the moody Grieg. As she sailed into its spectral waves her recent argument with Louise flooded in—how they too hadn't resolved things. If Louise died before they spoke again, Dawn would feel empty too.

When the song was over, the woman continued, "Giselle's boss was pressuring her to move for her job. I didn't want to hear it. We were so close, you see. I think I sounded angry, but I just wanted her to stay." The woman's shoulders shook in another wave of sobs. Her blond hair was perfectly coiffed. She was model thin and wore an impeccable suit with matching pumps. Such perfect visual order clashed against the vigor of her grief.

Dawn leaned in toward her. "Come back if it helps." The woman nodded, stood unsteadily, and straightened her skirt. As she walked away a scent of roses drifted up, and Dawn wondered why that and the *click-clack* of the woman's heels rattled her.

A reedy girl in a denim jacket was lingering by the stairs. She must have heard the last strains of Grieg, thought Dawn. The girl lifted her sunglasses, then quickly slipped them back when their eyes met. "This may sound silly," said the girl, stepping forward.

"Try me," said Dawn.

"So you play for victims' families?" The girl pointed to Dawn's sign.

"That's right. Something to acknowledge the life of the person they lost. Anything they want." Dawn tried to see through the girl's dark glasses to her eyes, but the green plastic was too opaque. She looked about nineteen. "Was there something specific?"

Denim girl giggled nervously. "Can you play the theme from *Dawson's Creek*?"

"Dawson's Creek?" Dawn never watched TV unless she was stuck in bed with the flu. "I'm not sure I know it."

"Oh." The girl started to tramp away. "It doesn't matter."

"Wait!" Dawn called, "Hum a few bars."

Walking back abruptly, the girl began to hum. Dawn picked up her flute and copied, missing a few notes. The girl hummed it again. This time when Dawn played it, Denim girl nodded eagerly. "That's it," she exclaimed.

"Who's it for?" Dawn invited the girl to sit with her on the stairs. "It helps me get into the song."

"It's for my stepsister. I didn't know her well." The young woman crossed her arms over her jacket and curled her body over as if to protect it.

Dawn played the song three times. *It's pretty for a TV song,* she thought as she turned toward the site, where drizzle tamped down smoke drifting up from the rubble.

"That was nice." The girl pulled on a lock of hair. "My dad said my stepsister loved her new job in the World Trade Center. She got the bank job right out of college. Dad said she was watching *Dawson's Creek* when they called to say she was hired, and that's why she liked the song. You know, I didn't like her, but I didn't want her to die." The girl began to tremble.

Dawn reached out, clasped the girl's hands in hers, and felt the warmth of her own hands firm around the girl's chapped ones.

"I thought she was mean," the girl went on. "Like when

202

my dad first took me to his new house and she was staring at me like 'This is my house and you're not part of it.' " Tears slid down her face. "Me and my stepsister, we never talked," mumbled the girl. "But one time on my birthday she gave me a shirt that she sewed herself. It wasn't my style, but it surprised me." The girl's breathing came in jerks. "I wasn't very nice to her, but I didn't want her crushed down there!" The breaths became sobs. Dawn wrapped her arms around the girl's puny shoulders and felt the girl lean into the hug, felt her muscles unfold.

Dawn thought of Louise, and not just about the flights away or about all the times Louise had shut herself in her office. "There is someone in my family like your stepsister," Dawn began, "someone I hated. She gave me things too." Dawn recalled the wooden flute Louise had carried back from Louisiana and the star mobile from Texas. "Even though she doesn't give me what I need, I think she tries."

"Really?" The girl removed her glasses and looked at Dawn with reddened eyes.

Dawn took her hands again and thought of all the times Louise talked of work. "She's a rescue doctor and loves her job too," Dawn mused. "One time she told me about a boy who'd been caught in a riptide. She said that everyone assumed he had drowned and that it seemed to take forever to resuscitate him, but she did. He opened his eyes in her arms, and she called him a little fighter. There's one about an earthquake too. She told me that she found an injured girl's teddy bear among the fallen beams, just before she set the girl's ribs in the brace. She said she was glad to be able to give the kid something to hug during the procedure."

"She sounds like a good rescue person," the girl said. "And you hated her?"

"I hated her," Dawn whispered, and swore she felt the pumping of blood inside. She felt it pump to her toes, all the way to her fingers, and out into the world as her hands warmed the girl's chilly hands. Dawn had another odd sensation, that she—Dawn Sweet—*was* Louise, that they shared some uncanny bond. That she *herself* was the doctor, the healer, and the formerly hated.

The girl sat up, stretched, and said simply, "Thanks. You've helped."

•   •   •

That night Dawn made a call. "Hi, Louise. Um, I wanted to call and say hi."

"Good to hear from you, Dawn."

"Hey, I'm sorry we got into it the other day."

"Me too. It's unfortunate."

A rush of feelings—missing San Francisco, the ocean, and even missing Louise—washed over Dawn. "I didn't mean to put down your doctoring," she said. "It's different from how I would think of it. But I haven't been doing it for years like you, and everyone's entitled to their own approach."

"Well, I understand your point too," said Louise. "At certain times, connecting emotionally with patients is the right thing for a doctor to do."

"I think so. But you *are* a talented doctor," Dawn insisted. "I never forgot how you bandaged that man in Oakland, you know, after the car accident. And maybe sometimes it's good to distance yourself, as long as you can connect at other times."

"That makes sense," said Louise. "Finding out just how horrible some patients' lives are can be unsettling. I try just to focus on treating the patient. I imagine myself fixing them and push the rest out of my mind. But I suppose that's unrealistic, dumb. . . ."

"It's not dumb," answered Dawn. "You're doing your job, that's all. What do you treat most patients for?" she asked with real interest.

"Malnutrition, which is complex because it contributes to a host of other diseases, including pneumonia and malaria."

"Why?"

"When people, especially kids, are weakened by malnutrition, they pick up whatever is going around. In Suryast, unfortunately, there's a lot going around."

Dawn thought about all the people in New York who weren't physically sick but were so devastated. "What about psychological problems?" she asked. "In New York since the attack there's a lot of depression and post-traumatic stress disorder."

"Oh? Has there been a lot of news coverage of New York?"

"Yeah, I guess so." Dawn paused. "Did you know that Johar saw his dad being shot, and that a land mine blew up his mother? I mean, God, how can a little kid handle that?"

Louise seemed surprised. "He hasn't talked to me about that."

"He's a tough guy. We haven't been talking for that long, but the stuff he tells me . . . He doesn't even feel sorry for himself." It felt good to Dawn that Louise was listening, maybe caring about the same things Dawn cared about. She went on. "Johar says he's lost without his family, but that taking care of Bija is freaking him out."

Louise went silent. Dawn wondered if she'd lost interest

or was angry about something. "It's hard," Louise said finally. "I didn't know both his parents were dead."

Dawn asked, "Do you ever get over losing your parents?"

"Truthfully? No," said Louise. "I lost my mother five years ago to kidney failure. And two years later my father died of cancer. I'm still trying to make my peace with it."

"I didn't know." Louise had dealt with huge loss right before Dawn's arrival. Was that why she wanted a daughter?

"Do you speak with Johar often?" asked Louise.

"Yeah," Dawn admitted. "Do you? I mean, more than just about doctor stuff?"

"Sometimes. Maybe it's good that you talk with him, Dawn."

"Yes. It is."

•　　　•　　　•

Dawn opened the door to the blare of rock and a shrill whistle.

"Hey, hi," Susie called. "Could you turn off that silly teakettle for me?"

"Welcome back," said Dawn. She switched off the burner, poured water into a waiting cup, came into Susie's room, and placed it on her bedside table.

"Thanks." Susie swished the tea bag in the hot water. "Dawn, you've got to see these guys." She pointed to the TV.

Dawn leaned against the door frame. An MTV VJ was interviewing young men in loose shirts and pants. "They're handsome," Dawn remarked. "Where are they from?"

"Afghanistan. They're interviewing kids in Kabul about music, about their lives."

The skin along Dawn's back prickled. A glimpse into Johar's world!

The guy who was being interviewed had expressive hands, which he waved around as he spoke. "I like rock music and adventure films, but now, no Western films. Too bad for that. Still, we sneak in Hindi films," he said. The VJ asked him if he prayed five times a day and if it was hard to get up so early. "Yes, I pray five times in day. Not hard to rise in morning. I *like* to rising before sunup."

His English is almost as good as Johar's, marveled Dawn. Suddenly she wondered what Johar really looked like, what it would feel like to see him and sit together rather than just talking on the phone. She imagined how cool it would be to sit close and read poetry together.

Susie plumped a pillow. "Come. Get comfy." Dawn plopped down, and Susie handed her a bowl of charred popcorn. The VJ was interviewing a cluster of young Afghan girls now. "Such grace," Susie said. "Those flowered scarves. Too cool."

"They *are* beautiful."

The next TV clip was a close-up of a woman. "Look at that awful burqa," Susie remarked. "But the way she drapes it, and her proud voice. Such dignity."

"From the news reports," Dawn said, "it's only a matter of time before the Taliban is crushed. The allied forces are almost to Kabul. But it's coming at such a huge price. We're clueless in the States to their level of pain." Dawn couldn't believe how much she sounded like Louise. "My foster mother's translator tells me such awful stories."

"Yeah, the stories those people would tell," Susie exclaimed. "I'd love to interview them." Her pixie grin spread as she turned to Dawn. "And I've got to admit, I'd love to get my hands on a few bolts of that floral fabric."

"Wouldn't it be fantastic if we could go over there?" Dawn blurted out.

"Yes!" Susie exclaimed. "You know, ever since you told me your foster mom was stationed over there, I've been trying to work an angle on a news feature. Maybe I could interview the ICRC doctors and their patients."

"Yeah, probably."

Susie took a bite of popcorn, made a face, then spat some burned kernels into her palm. "What a rotten cook I am. What do you say I treat you to dinner? You've done such a smash-up job of watching Mara and Chester."

"You're not a rotten cook," Dawn said as she eyed the burned popcorn. "On second thought–you are." They laughed. "I'll take you up on that offer," she added.

Susie jumped up. "Let's go," she said and dumped the popcorn into the trash. "You've got to tell me every detail of what's been happening."

daq

November winds snapped at the folds of Johar's pattu beneath him. He turned his head left, then right while reciting praise of Allah's mercy. With that, the early morning namaz was done, and Johar rose restlessly, recalling the note on his tent. If it was Daq who had arrived, what a miracle it would be!

"The man said he was family," Vikhrim said when Johar hurried into the office. "But he wore the black turban of a Taliban. You are a Tajik from the north. What was I to think?"

The turban ruled out Tilo. He would have worn a Western suit. "My brother, Daq, may be fighting with the Taliban. What did the man's face look like?" Johar asked impatiently. "And why didn't you tell me this earlier?"

"I did not want for you getting eager, for who knows if this man is who he saying he is?" Vikhrim examined Johar's face. "He was square-jawed like you, but taller."

It must be Daq! They would have much to talk about. Yet despite his anticipation Johar was unsettled. Vikhrim said that the man had appeared ill. War could make a man sick, even insane. And what if Daq's arrival *was* a Taliban ruse—a trick to take Johar by force now that the snakes had begun to lose their stranglehold on Afghanistan? Still, every muscle in Johar's body longed to grasp his brother in a long embrace.

Johar inhaled the acrid smoke of fires, which with the onset of cold weather had replaced the reek of open sewers. Finally the Alliance, with help from the Americans, had liberated the northern strongholds of Mazar-i-Sharif and nearby Taloqan. Maybe soon Kabul! The news had spread from tent to tent, and most had been overjoyed. Only the southernmost farmers, whose Pashtun families formed the Taliban's loyalist ranks, were upset by the news, for if the Alliance marched on Kabul, the balance of power would surely shift away from the Taliban. The Americans, Vikhrim said, were pleading with the Alliance to hold off from taking Kabul until a coalition government could be formed. It made sense that each tribe should be represented in any new government. Otherwise, quarrels would never cease.

"Bija, let's hurry. I'm late for the clinic." Johar helped tie the sash on her gown.

"I'm hungry," Bija whimpered.

"You had a bite before dawn. And you wanted to be like the grown-ups and fast. During Ramadan we grown-ups wait until sundown to eat again. Besides, Anqa will feed you later." Lately Bija's demands rankled his raw nerves.

"But my belly hurts."

"Enough!" he snapped. Children weren't required to fast. Johar crouched down and dipped his hand into the rice bowl. He gave her a mound, which she popped in her mouth.

"Jor, tell me about Ramadan," she said, happily chewing.

Johar sighed. He began to comb out her tangles with his fingers. "Prayer and fasting purify one's body so that Allah shines through. Ramadan is about charity to others, and about family." He remembered when his family would pass out coins to the beggars near the bazaar. He envisioned the candles at night and his father's soothing voice reading the Quran.

"Then where is Uncle Daq?" asked Bija.

"We don't know if it was Uncle Daq who wrote the note. Have patience." Johar had made a stupid blunder in telling Bija. If it wasn't Daq, they would both be crushed.

"What about sweets?" asked Bija. "You said children get sweets on the last day."

"Yes, on Eid al-Fitr, the festival at the end of Ramadan, which breaks the fast. I have no sweets, my pearl, but how about a ride on a swing? Maybe I can fashion one." Johar finished braiding her hair and covered it with her print scarf.

"A ride on a swing! Promise?" Bija ran outside with her dolly. A moment later she screeched, "Look! It's Uncle Daq!"

Johar tripped over the edge of the tent flap in his haste. It was Daq, loping towards them in a black turban and dirty shalwar kameez! Johar ran to Daq and hugged him. Bija was already hugging his legs.

Daq laughed. "No need to fall over yourselves to greet me." His ribs stuck out like old camel bones and his flesh was cold yet damp. Stepping back, Johar stared into his brother's eyes. They were yellowish, sunken, and bloodshot. "Well, what do you see?" asked Daq. Johar recalled that look in the eyes of men who had crouched like apparitions along Baghlan's most crime-filled street. No, it couldn't be—the yellowed whites of a drug addict? "I saw the note you sent, brother. Wedged in her door."

"Was Maryam there?" Johar's heart leaped to his throat. "Did you see her?"

Daq shook his head, and Johar's heart sank.

"It's a relief to see you," Johar said. "But are you ailing, brother?"

Daq's face creased with irritation. "I'm fine." Bija climbed silently into his shrunken arms, arms whose muscles had once rippled like the flanks of stallions. "The Taliban took care of me. See, new boots, as Naji promised." Daq held up his foot with a boot once shiny, now clotted with dirt, its seam parting at the toe.

"Handsome boots." Johar attempted a smile. "You're here! I can hardly believe it. Where are you staying?"

"I'm staying behind the old bazaar stalls south of the Khyber Pass." Daq lurched forward, then backward. "I'm here to bring you back with me."

Even in his dilapidated state, Daq was still imposing. It would be good to have him along when they trekked back to Baghlan through the mountains, with its wild bands of luti hidden behind every curve. Johar said, "Thank Allah you're done with the war."

"The war? The war is just beginning. I'm taking you back with me. Little brother, it's about time you learned to fight as a soldier."

"But the Taliban are almost done for," said Johar. "Thank the heavens you're still alive for soon their forces will be driven from every village."

Daq laughed. "They are only taking a break and will return to finish the job."

"What about me?" Bija asked. "Where will I go?" She wiggled from Daq's grip, scurried to Johar, and hid in the folds of his garments.

"We'll take you with us, to Ramila's," Daq said.

"But I want Mama," Bija demanded, and began to cry. Daq was silent.

"No one's heard word from Aunt Maryam?" Johar asked. "Are you sure?"

"No." Daq muttered, gazing unsteadily at the ground. "I told her to stop her teaching, but she wouldn't listen. I told her—"

Johar's skin prickled along his arms in a dark sense of foreboding. He stroked Bija's head to soothe her. Dawn's words echoed in his mind: *protect life in your own unique way.*

"Let's go, brother. Pack your bags. Time to move on," Daq demanded.

Bija peeked from the folds in her cousin's robe. "Johar needs to work at Dr. Garland's today," she explained in a grown-up voice.

Johar smiled almost apologetically. Maybe this would stall things—give them time to change Daq's mind. "I have a job at the Red Cross clinic. Come along, I'll introduce you."

"Red Cross clinic? An American organization?" Daq uttered with suspicion.

"It's international, actually," Johar replied. As they walked on, Johar tried to overlook how gaunt Daq had become, how he stumbled, his rattling cough. He pictured them walking to Maryam's together before the war had begun.

Johar let Bija come along instead of taking her to Anqa's. As he watched her skip up ahead, he worried what Daq would think of Dr. Garland.

Daq eyed the bedraggled patients lined up by the Red Cross compound. "Before the Americans came here, people were happy in their villages. Now look at our people. They are injured, hungry, lost."

"It's not just the fault of Americans. Some Americans are trying to help–" Johar began, then stopped himself.

"Trying to help?"

"Forget it." It plagued Johar that Daq and he had ended up on such opposing sides. Couldn't Daq see how the Taliban warped the laws of sharia for their own brutal purposes? Couldn't he see the inhumanity in their public assassinations, in the mothers begging and the torching of entire wheat fields? Dawn and her people had suffered too–from Al Qaeda's fiendish destruction of the American towers. But Johar kept his mouth shut. He refused to start arguing. Nothing would get in the way of being with his brother again . . . nothing except being coerced into joining the Taliban ranks.

They stepped past the crowd into the ICRC's whitewashed building. Daq gawked at the shelves of medical supplies and the colorful satellite poster of the world.

"Why, hello," said Dr. Garland. "And who might this be?"

"My uncle," squealed Bija, grabbing Daq's arm in excitement.

"My brother, Daq," added Johar.

A gray strand escaped Dr. Garland's scarf as she leaned

forward. "Salaam alaikum, Daq." She held out her hand, but Daq refused to shake it.

He's repulsed by the way she offered her hand and the hair peeking from her scarf, thought Johar. This is the same brother who could curse in English, the same brother Johar had worshiped. Well, Daq embarrassed him now. He watched the doctor's smile fade. "Dr. Garland," Johar said, struggling for courage, "I haven't seen Daq for so long and, well . . . I wonder whether I could have the day off. If you please."

She busied herself opening shutters and then shuffling charts. Johar sensed Daq's rage at the audacity of this working American female. Johar imagined his brother thinking that she took an impudently long time in answering. When Dr. Garland finally turned to them, Daq's gaze fell to the floor. "I suppose, Johar. But first could you let a patient in and interview him?"

"Of course, Dr. Garland." Johar turned to Daq. "It will take only a minute. Please, sit." Johar pointed to a chair.

"I'll stand," Daq said firmly. Bija scurried into the corner with her doll.

Johar led in the first patient—a new arrival with an ugly shoulder wound. As he questioned the patient and took notes, Daq tapped his boot on the floor impatiently.

When Johar was done asking his questions, Dr. Garland bound up the patient's wound. "One more thing," she requested. "Could you please talk to the truck messenger behind the building? He needs the supply list—"

Daq cut her off in midsentence. "Are you coming?" he demanded, facing Johar. Johar looked from Louise to Daq and back to Louise, who was silent, waiting. "Coming?" Daq repeated. "As for me, I'm leaving." Daq's eyes held

rage. "I'll not stay another second with this American infi-
del, this ill-mannered female who dares order my brother
around like a street sweeper!"

"No one accuses this woman of being ill-mannered,"
Johar retorted. "This woman gave me a job. She saved our
lives!" Bija whimpered and clutched her doll.

"So be it, brother." Daq stalked out.

Johar dashed after him and grabbed Daq by the arm.
"Don't act crazy! Think about what you're saying." Daq
thrust off Johar's hand and swerved away. "I will come to
where you stay," yelled Johar. "We'll talk later, after you
calm down."

"You have chosen the wrong side," Daq called over his
shoulder. With that he was gone.

Johar waited until Dr. Garland went out to give the
trucker an additional list, then dialed Dawn's number. He'd
always waited until she called him, but Daq had unnerved
him. "Dawn, where are you?" he mumbled to himself as
the phone rang and rang. "The war has ruined my brother.
He's a specter of his old self. His skin is all yellowed.
Kherab!"

confessions

New York,
late November 2001

Dawn twisted the flute pieces together and flipped through the sheet music. The blond woman had come back–the one with the rose-scented perfume and the model's graceful poise. She was already softly crying when she asked for the Bach–her daughter's recital piece. Playing for families was always such a meaningful occasion, but something about this lady burrowed under Dawn's skin.

"Please, play another," insisted the woman after Dawn's last notes. "Just one more," she begged when that was done.

Dawn felt so bad for her, barely sopping her tears with the wad of Kleenex before another flood came. Although Dawn sensed there were people on the edge of the crowd who would have liked a turn, she could hardly refuse this woman. But when she requested a third song, Dawn finally asked, "Don't you need to get back to work?"

"I make my own hours. Can *you* take a break?" Dawn's eyes locked into the woman's blue ones, onto her powdered forehead and perfect chin. She couldn't look away—that face seemed so familiar. Spurs of baffled recollection shot up through Dawn. There could be no way, but this lady was a spot-on match for her ruby-lipped, blond birth mother, or at least for Dawn's memory of her. But this woman was too old, probably pushing sixty. She had deep crow's feet, and her hair was dyed platinum over strands of white. Still, the resemblance was spooky.

"I'll take you for a coffee or something." The lady clamped onto her hand with spidery fingers. "You look as if you've seen a ghoul."

Against her will, Dawn let her sneakers shuffle along the pavement next to the lady's clacking heels. The woman led her around the crush of bodies on the sidewalk and guided her into a dark restaurant. Dawn took a croaking breath, inhaling the rich aroma of burgers and coffee. They sat in a booth, and she looked across at the lady. She felt ridiculous asking, but couldn't help herself. "Did you ever have any other kids? Did you have one who went to an orphanage or a group home?"

The woman looked startled. "No other children, just Giselle. Why?"

Dawn felt herself sink. "It's just . . . it's just that you look like someone I used to know." There was no way. This woman was too old.

"I hope that's good. By the way, my name is Vera." The woman fished in her purse and pulled out a photo. She held it out to Dawn.

"Mine's Dawn," Dawn said, then looked at the pretty girl in the photo who was dressed up for a school dance or a holiday. "Your daughter was beautiful. She was . . ." Dawn struggled to find the right words. "Asian!"

"Yes. She was from Korea. She'd been in an orphanage. That's why your question surprised me." Vera held out a menu, and Dawn took it. "Hungry?"

"Not very. Well, actually, yes." Vera was offering to feed her. She was paying attention. It made Dawn feel sad and happy at the same time. "So, your daughter's adopted?"

A tentative smile revealed perfect caps. "That's right."

"And you felt like she was really yours?"

"She *was* mine! You mean because I didn't give birth to her?" Dawn nodded. "I didn't think about that, only when someone looked at us cross-eyed. Then I had to feel sorry for them." Vera smiled again, a patient smile.

"But wouldn't you have a truer bond if you were re-lated?" The question was crude, but Dawn had to ask. She'd heard all the standard lines about adopted kids being no less loved than biological kids. Those were just so many words, though. She'd never heard it from a real parent of an adopted kid.

"Clones are a bore," Vera said with a tiny smile, flicking her veined hand forward in a dismissive motion. "Besides, genes are no guarantee of similarities or bonds. The kids of some of the people I know—well, you wonder how they could ever be related. Giselle and I, we connected over music even when she was small. Well, you know what I'm talk-ing about. I'm sure you and your mother have things in common."

"An interest in doctoring." Dawn said.

Vera nodded. "How nice."

The waitress came over. Vera ordered fruit salad and tea. Dawn ordered soup. "Don't you go to school?" Vera pressed a lemon wedge against her spoon.

She seemed nice enough, but Dawn figured that the less she said the better. "Sure. I'm in an Internet school. You know, classes online." She tried to steer the conversation Vera's way. "Tell me more about Giselle."

"She was talented on the flute, like you. I bet your mother's proud of your playing."

Dawn scrunched up her napkin and lowered her head. Her real mother had never heard Dawn play. *She wasn't there.* Dawn tried to picture her, but an unexpected memory of Louise floated in, of her beaming awkwardly in the front row of the auditorium as Dawn played. Was it Louise that Dawn missed, or just anyone being there for her? How could you know what to miss if you'd never had it . . . or if you'd never let someone try to be there? Louise *had* tried. Was it a sense of duty that led Louise to Epiphany House, or emptiness or desire? Maybe none of it mattered except what came after.

Lunch came, and they were mostly silent while they ate, both hungry, both thoughtful. When she finished, Dawn glanced at the wall clock. One o'clock; almost too late to play before lunch hour was over. "Thanks for everything. I have to get going."

"You're very welcome." Vera straightened out her skirt, and the rose scent wafted up.

Dawn waved as she walked away. She was sure of it now: that rose scent was what her mother had worn.

•   •   •

At midnight Dawn dialed the number. Thoughts whizzed like darts as she listened to its ring. *What if Vera had been my mother? She's so different from Louise.*

"Hello, ICRC Peshawar. How can I help you?"

"Hi, Johar."

"Dawn! I tried to call you."

"Really? What's up? I've been out a lot lately." It must be very early there.

"My brother Daq is alive!"

"Seriously? That's awesome, Johar. Is he there with you? Have you guys talked or had time to plan? I mean, this is huge!"

"Yes, he is alive. But he is very sick."

"What do you mean?" Dawn had called for Louise, but that must wait.

"He is acting strange, not himself. He is like skeleton and eyes are yellow. He want to take me to army. Americans drive the Taliban back. Kabul is finally free! Soon even Kandahar. But Daq want to stay fighting."

The capital city was free—Dawn had heard it on the news. It meant Louise might return sooner rather than later. But Johar couldn't go back and fight now. "Join the army? I thought you didn't want that! What about your poetry, the school?"

"No want army. Is everything I hate—killing; death."

"So don't go with him."

"I try not." Johar's voice was high-pitched, faint.

Dawn heard a woman in the background ask who was on the phone. Hastily she added, "Johar, you're strong and you're no coward. Remember that."

"I try."

"E-mail me with every detail, and be careful. Promise?"

"Promise."

"Was that Louise? Can I speak with her?"

"Yes, one moment." The phone clacked as Johar put it down and then Louise's voice.

"Dawn. How are you?" Dawn had thought so much about Louise lately that it was weird to hear her voice. Maybe Louise wasn't feeling the same at all.

"I'm fine. I miss seeing you. How's the clinic?" Dawn felt suddenly unsure of herself.

"The clinic is quite challenging. It doesn't get any easier." Louise paused. "I miss seeing you as well."

Dawn had only asked her next question once and hadn't gotten a straight answer. "Did you ever learn why I was at Epiphany? Do you know anything about my birth mother?"

"They told me next to nothing," said Louise quietly. "Why are you thinking about that now?"

"I guess it's just that this whole Trade Center attack made me think about family, about losing people. I mean, things are starting to bubble up. I've been remembering things."

"Some family history is better left unexamined." Louise's voice was hesitant. "But not always. What did you remember?"

"It was pretty vague. I was in the car with her, and I was scared and I smelled her perfume, rose talc. It made me feel sick, like I wanted to cry. I thought I would faint."

"The past is the past, and they didn't tell me much," said Louise. "It's hard for me to think about what happened to you before you came to live with us."

"But I need to talk about it. It's like I'm stuck and I need to move on, get it out. If you want to be close to me, you would try to understand—"

"I'll try," said Louise. "When I get back, I promise." She sighed. "Trust me when I say that I don't know many facts. But if you think it's preventing us from having a better relationship . . . if it'll help to get the feelings out . . ."

"Thanks." Dawn felt almost like a traitor, but that was silly. Talking honestly with Louise felt good. "Is Johar right there?"

"Not here in my office. Why?"

"I want to ask you something without him overhearing. What did you think of Johar's brother, Daq? Did he threaten you?"

"Johar mentioned that to you?" When Dawn didn't reply, Louise went on. "Daq didn't dare threaten me. I'm pretty tough, you know." She laughed wryly. "He was furious at me for ordering Johar to do chores. He was furious about the war casualties. He was an angry guy in general. Truthfully, he seemed to be on drugs."

"Daq wants Johar to come north to join the army. Don't let him do that, OK?"

"The war is almost over," Louise said sensibly. "Coalition forces took Kabul. Now they're headed to Kandahar. It's only a matter of days until the Taliban surrender. Then it'll be months of skirmishes here and there, but the major fighting is over."

"Well, his brother doesn't think so."

"He's deluded," Louise insisted.

"Either way, I'm scared for Johar. What if you take him back to the States? He needs a family. All his relatives are gone. He said it was hard to care for Bija on his own. And now, with his brother so agitated—"

"But his brother is his family too," Louise pointed out, "and it would be very difficult to get an Afghani through U.S. immigration since the attack." She paused. "It's a nice idea to bring Johar back. Maybe it *would* be good for him and his cousin to have a break from the suffering. We don't understand the scope of it in the States. We've been protected, cut off . . ."

Except at ground zero, Dawn wanted to say. She felt an irresistible urge to confess, to share her trials and her new insights. She wanted to tell Louise about the trip east, about the excitement of her first night in New York. She wanted to describe the terrible September day, her terror, and the heavy aura of pain that had enveloped the city. But most of all, Dawn wanted Louise to understand how those days of playing flute music for victims' families had transformed her into a person who was finally connecting with the world—like a blind girl learning Braille. It was impossible to hold it in anymore. The rush of feelings began to breach her self-restraint. "Louise?"

"Yes, dear?"

Should she tell? Louise seemed more open. It was time she knew who Dawn had become. "I have to make a confession. I'm in New York. I'm doing something deep and wonderful. I'm playing flute for victims' families. I'm learning so much!" There—she'd said it, but Louise's silence was palpable.

Even before words came, the phone crackled with tension. "*What?* Are you all right? How long have you been there? Do you know how dangerous it is in New York right now?"

"I promise you, I'm fine." Dawn's confidence faltered. "What about you? It's way more dangerous over there. Don't you think I've worried about you?"

"Yes," Louise said wearily. "But . . . but it's different, Dawn. I know what I'm doing. This is crazy. What possessed you to run away, and where is Victor in all this? Why didn't he tell me? I haven't been able to get through to him for days."

"He knows I left," Dawn replied, and heard Louise's

sharp intake of breath. "Truthfully? He doesn't care. I have no clue where he is. And he doesn't know where I am either. He hasn't answered my calls for a while now." A breathy silence weighted the space between them.

"So he's been lying to me."

Dawn's tone softened. "I don't know what he's told you, but yeah. I'm sorry, Louise."

Louise's voice regained its urgency. "What part of the city are you staying in? You're not staying anywhere near ground zero, are you?"

"No, I'm in a safe place. A friend of a friend's."

"Good. But you're going down there to play your flute for people?" asked Louise.

"Yes. It's weird, but I've never been so happy. I've just never felt like I've done something this important."

"What's your friend's address, dear?" Louise's voice grew shrill.

"I can't tell you yet." Dawn said, "but I'll stay in touch." She hesitated for a moment, and then the words came flooding out. "If it weren't for you going away all the time, I wouldn't have come here. I was mad at first, but it's not about that now. I'm using my talent for something good– helping people. I'm growing up. I know you care about me, but please don't stop this."

"I'm not trying to stop you from growing up." Louise was yelling now. "But I'll have to curtail my work here to find you in Manhattan. I can't have you running around on your own. It will make things easier if you tell me. Now!"

Dawn was too spent to fight. She imagined a protective layer surrounding her, like snow, to drown out the shouts. "Louise, I'll be in touch. Promise." She hung up and sat on the bed, shivering. *So maybe she does care. Maybe she believes in what I'm doing,* thought Dawn. *But she doesn't want me here alone. She doesn't trust that I'm safe. She got too mad. I couldn't explain. And Johar might leave.* She hadn't convinced Louise to help him before she hung up.

Dawn fell back on Susie's bed. She decided to try meditating, as Johar had suggested in his e-mail. As she slowed her breathing, her muscles loosened and she began to feel sleepy and calm, yet her mind was aware. For a moment she imagined Johar reciting poetry, but she couldn't hear the words. His soft voice gave her courage. Dawn let her head sink deeper into the pillow. She thought, *I'm almost unstuck,* and took a long breath in. As she breathed out, ever so slowly, a thought formed, delicate yet as pointed as snowflake tips: *I may not want to meet my birth mother. Ever.*

warrior

New York,
late November 2001

Dawn's emotions bubbled near the surface. Tears pricked her eyes at the sight of homeless people, and she went all jelly-legged when she bumped into Sander on St. Marks. She told him about playing for victims' families. "You're brave," he said, and offered to come down and play with her. He encouraged her to try jamming with his band again. Instead of panicking, she chatted eagerly and even said a proper goodbye.

She had contacted Jude and asked him to check the house on Santa Marisa. He'd rung the bell at all hours, but no Victor. Finally he'd let himself in with Dawn's hidden key and tripped over a pile of mail. In the bedroom, Jude had discovered Victor's note.

Louise
   I tried to search for Dawn. I tried to talk

sense into her when she called. I had to take a
break from this.
Victor

He's gone, Dawn thought. Inside her, it opened up huge
spaces.

These wobbly new feelings were good, but when they
got intense she sometimes pined for her old reflexes—ones
that could shut her emotions down as automatically as her
knee jumped when the doctor tapped it with his little
hammer.

Meanwhile, she e-mailed back and forth with Louise.

Dawn—
I am coming to get you. Please tell me where
you are.

Louise—
Please, please give me another week or so. I'm
staying with a woman friend. She's older. She
keeps me safe. I'll give you her address soon.
Trust me on this.
Dawn

Temperatures had been dropping steadily, but Dawn
still went to the site almost every day. One overcast morning she wore a new red sweater and hat she'd gotten
on sale.

"You look so lovely in that red sweater. Like such a
proper little lady," Vera said as she approached the concrete stairs. "Do you know any Telemann? My daughter
used to play that so nicely." Vera held the clump of

Kleenex, already dabbing at her mascara, and she reeked of the rose talc.

Telemann was brilliant—ordered yet fierce. Dawn began to play, stewing with precarious emotions—fear, doubt and sudden bursts of elation. Images flashed in and out like strobes: Louise in her office, an image of her birth mother staring into the distance. Without warning, Dawn's impressions swelled and sharpened. For the first time ever, the still portrait of her birth mother shifted. They were in a car. Her mother's chilly stare led Dawn to lower her eyes to the hands with their red nails clutching the steering wheel.

"When you're ready," whispered Johar in her mind.

Vera gazed toward her and said, "Such a proper little lady."

Memories sizzled, loosened. She drew out a high G on her flute.

Mama's got things to take care of, said the voice.

I'll listen to you, just to end this thing, thought Dawn. The shutters of her chest broke apart, and two voices emerged—Dawn's, so young, and her lost mother's.

"We're going to a place where you'll stay for a while," Mama *says.*

"Why, Mama, aren't you coming?" I ask, alarmed.

"No, Mama's got things to take care of." Mama always has things to take care of.

"Can't you take me with you? I'll be good. I won't fuss." Mama hates it when I fuss. The punishment is Mama not speaking for long times after fussing.

"No, Dawn, I can't take you." Her jaw is hard and tight. She won't look at me, but stares straight ahead at the road.

I grab on to her coat. It smells like roses. "Mama, why?" Is punishment time starting? I cry in chokes, tugging at her scratchy coat.

She pries my hands open and smoothes down her coat. The only sound after that is of my crying and the click-clack *of the wipers pushing snow off the windshield.*

The notes of Dawn's flute soared.

We drive to a house with two porch lights and a sign in between the lights. Mama jerks the car to a halt. She opens my door and yanks me out so hard, my hands have red marks. My legs sink in tall drifts and the cold flakes burn my eyes like pepper.

As I rub them, my coat falls open, showing the new red dress Mama bought me for this trip. "Something to help you look like a proper young lady," she'd said. I was so proud of my dress that every day before this trip I had opened my closet door to make sure it was still there. Now that I'm a big girl, almost five years old, I thought Mama would be taking me somewhere very special—maybe to the movies or to the ballet, but this is scary.

"I don't want to stay here, Mama," I cry, refusing to take steps.

She doesn't answer, but drags me toward the house. My boots scratch trails in the snow. "Sometimes we must do things we don't want to do." She presses the bell.

"I'll be a good girl. Promise. I know I've been a bad girl," I shout.

"Stop it right this instant," she scolds.

The door swings open. A lady with gray hair in a bun leans her big body forward, and waves for us to enter. It smells like pine soap and there is old furniture. A clock ticks.

"My name is Mrs. Donovan. Take your coats off and let's get started." The lady points to a coat rack. I'm afraid to look at her. I run to Mama's coat and bury my face in its rose smell. She pries my fingers off again, as if they have mud on them.

Vera's voice rippled up. "Go ahead and cry." Her hands enveloped Dawn's, but not spidery like before, just holding. The flute waited patiently on the concrete while

Dawn's tears mixed with Vera's—spilling and sloppy and such a relief. "It must be difficult to come here, day after day. Cry now," Vera crooned, and held Dawn, shivering in her red sweater.

Dawn didn't care that people stared. Raindrops began to patter. She pictured the snow, the ice daggers under the curve of Epiphany's eaves. Sun glinted through them, increasing their beauty—an icy beauty like her mother's. Dawn realized her face had frozen too. She had become an ice queen. It had been all she had left of her mother. It had protected her.

"Child, are you all right?" Vera asked, worry in her porcelain-blue eyes.

"Bad and good."

"Kleenex?" Vera asked, holding out a dry bunch.

"Thanks." Dawn took them and blew her nose. She opened her mouth, loosened the muscles in her jaw, then picked up her flute and stroked the raindrops off.

family

Suryast, Pakistan,
December 2001

"You've got mail!" piped the computer voice. Johar sat at
Nils's desk and fumed over what he'd heard Dr. Garland say
to Dawn on the phone the other day. And later in the clinic,
the way Dr. Garland had seemed to hint that he should go
to America. He knew they meant well, but how dare they
make plans for him without asking? He and his cousin
weren't stick dolls to be tossed around—they didn't need res-
cuing. Even an exciting trip could be terribly wrong if the
timing was bad. Maybe he wouldn't read Dawn's message.
He had to think about things. In his desperation for a friend
maybe he'd opened up too fast. Curiosity overcame him,
though. Johar clicked on the e-mail.

Dear Johar—
I remembered! All this awful stuff came back

to me about my real mother while I was
playing at the site, and I remembered what
you said—"When you're ready it will come out."
And it did—it poured out of me. There's no
reason to candy-coat it. My real mother was
cold. Or maybe she just hated kids. Anyway,
it's a relief to remember the facts. She was
haunting my imagination, but I think she's
gone now. When I finally decided to stop
searching for her was when it all came out.
Isn't that weird? I guess fantasies fall on
their face for good reasons, and what you
thought was flawed is really pretty solid.
Life is truly like riding one of those freight
cars in "Rock Candy Mountain"—careening like
hellfire into dark caves, then swerving out
and around into breathless vistas. I told
Louise I'm in New York.
Dawn

Johar was shaken. Dawn seemed different—more confident. Some of his irritation seeped away. He called her, but she wasn't there. He logged on and clicked Write Mail.

Dawn—
I am glad to hear that you finaly remembered.
Dr. Garland did tell me you were in New York.
This quite upset her. I have a matter to
discus. Can you call me at your time midnight?
Johar

"Hi, Johar?"
"Yes. Hello, Dawn. How are you? I read your e-mail."

233

"You did? I'm sorry to lay all that on you. I'm still shaken. But everything's much clearer."

"Did you have more bad memories?"

"No. Maybe I will later. But the search for her is over. That much is clear. I just want to put it behind me."

"Yes. Maybe you can do that now."

"Yeah. So, what did you want to ask me? Are you still worried about Daq? Did he come back?"

"No. It's not Daq." Her voice made Johar both glad and angry. "It's about your last phone conversation with Dr. Garland."

"She told you about it?"

"Did you tell Dr. Garland that she should bring me back to the States?"

"I did! I know it would be a huge change, but isn't it a great idea?" Johar was silent. "Was there something wrong with that?"

"Yes, something is wrong! I thought you understood me."

"I think I do."

"Not if you think I want to flee from my country! What have I fought against all this time? What is it I've been dreaming of?"

"You've been dreaming of a family reunion. And now Daq is at the camp, and Bija, and you could go see your aunt first–"

"It's true, most of my family is here. But tell me, what else I have spoken of all these weeks?"

"I don't know. You tell me." She sounded defiant.

"I thought you were not like any others. I thought you understood."

"That's not fair," she said.

Johar sighed. "I want to go back to Baghlan and start a

234

school. I want to be with my aunt if she's still there. Not run away to America like all the million refugees who flee their homes."

"But I thought you and Bija . . ." Dawn started to mumble. "I thought you would like to be part of our family, at least until Afghanistan is stabilized."

"People like me will stabilize Afghanistan!" he shouted. "If all people run, there will be none to rebuild." His anger shifted to weary frustration. "They say America bursts with refugees from wars. They say these refugees stay, make money, and make new life. Maybe some should go back to rebuild their countries, not hide out in lands that already have plenty."

"That's a really negative way of putting it," said Dawn. "I wouldn't say anyone is escaping here. Your uncle Tilo is teaching abroad, right? I'm sure he does a lot of good as a teacher—opening people up to other cultures. And immigrants work very hard in America. I think it would be so tough to start out here brand-new." Dawn's voice lowered. "I hear what you're saying, though. You are a stubborn dreamer like me."

"Yes. But I used to think I was different from my people." Johar paused. "I am no different. Thinking of myself as separate, misunderstood—that was my fear speaking."

"Fear? You are the least fearful person I know. I couldn't do what you're doing." Dawn chuckled. "Maybe someday you will visit—not to live here, just to visit."

"Yes, someday when my country is not hurting."

"Can I come to help you, then?" Dawn asked. "Or would an American be unwelcome at your school?"

"All students and all teachers will be welcome at my school."

gig

New York,
December 2001

Dawn scurried through the East Village. She was thinking about how things peeled off in layers like onion skins. Just when you thought you had peeled off the last dried-up piece, another layer of unfinished business revealed itself from underneath. Sander was unfinished business—all the times she had shied away from his offers to play in the band after that first awful time. She passed a row of Indian restaurants, a health food store, and a hardware store, all the while murmuring to herself, "Yes, I *want* to play my flute with the guys, even though I'll have to deal with Pax's superior attitude. It's not going to freaking *kill* me! And yeah, it's scary how when I think of jamming with Sander, my insides hum. But hey, terror never felt so good, because it's a *feeling,* dammit! Pulse the feeling through me like Pax's mad bass and Sander's percussion."

Dawn buzzed his doorbell. Footsteps pounded down, and Sander opened the door. "Perfect timing," he huffed. "The band's rehearsing. Want to come in and listen?"

"This time I'm here to play."

"You brought the flute? Excellent!" They clomped upstairs to the apartment.

Dawn called over to Pax, "Is it okay with you that I play?"

"Whatever." He shrugged and waved her in with his bony hand.

Sander's coffee table was littered with chip bags and empty soda bottles. There was hardly a spot to open her case. Dawn twisted the flute together and wove her way around the chaos of pillows, bongos, and guitar picks poking their plastic nubs through the shag. She eased into a spot between Pax and Sander, plugged in the flute, and began.

As Sander hammered the snare for the song's climax he called to her; "Sounds great! You're soaring!" Then he turned to Pax. "Lighten up on the bass, guy. You're drowning out the flute."

This time Pax is the one being bawled out, Dawn realized. They practiced Sander's tune and a cool Incubus song. She taught them her compositions: the bhangra and a Middle Eastern rock song she had titled "Arabesque."

Sander had to run through Dawn's songs a dozen times, adjusting to their novel beat. "These tunes rock!" he remarked. "How did you come up with this stuff?"

Dawn shrugged. "I wrote it for ground zero. I needed all kinds of music."

"It's fresh," Pax said. "We need something fresh." He started jiggling his head like one of those bobble-headed car accessories. "We could do a September eleventh benefit gig with some of that material." Pax was coming around in full colors. Who would've thought?

They played "Arabesque" over and over as the shadows crept over the sills, and hypnotized themselves with its orbital mantra. Streetlights hissed on, neon storefronts flashed, and Dawn realized abruptly how late it was. She suddenly remembered that she needed to call Louise and Johar. Dawn lay the flute on Sander's amp and unearthed the sat phone from her pack. "Got to make a call. Can I have some privacy?"

"Sure." Sander pointed to his room.

Dawn walked in and sat on his bed, the scent of sandalwood wafting up. She had tried to call earlier, but no one had answered. They must have been celebrating the Taliban's release of Kandahar, their last southern stronghold. She dialed, thinking about how her feelings had been shifting toward Louise in increments so tiny she had hardly noticed at first. Shifts toward Louise. Louise was sort of like a tree. Her bark was tough, but she had been there, in plain sight. You could lean on a tree or climb its leafy branches and feel the sun warm on your shoulders. Still, it was high time Louise understood how crummy it was to have a parent always flying away. Dawn would work to find the words to tell her how that felt. *Decent words for a change,* she thought.

The phone rang and rang. Where was everyone? Worry began to drain away the pleasure of band practice, the sandalwood, and any world beyond Peshawar. Was it the celebration at the end of Ramadan? No, that had gone by. Maybe they were out to get supplies. Why hadn't they told her where they were going? She dialed again. On the fifth ring, someone picked up.

"Salaam." It was a strange man's voice.

"Is Dr. Garland there?" asked Dawn. There was an uncomfortable silence. "Who is this? May I speak to Johar?"

Finally the man responded. "I'm Nils. I work here for the ICRC. Neither Johar nor Dr. Garland is here." He had an accent, unlike Johar's. "May I ask, who are you?"

"I'm Dr. Garland's daughter. Where are they? They're usually here at this time."

"Yes, but the clinic is shut."

"Why?" Had the army seized the clinic?

"The clinic was sacked, I'm afraid."

"What? What do you mean?" Hysteria rose in Dawn like a stormy tide. "Was anyone hurt?"

"No. Apparently it happened late last night after the clinic was closed. They stole the computers, the supplies, and most of the satellite phones and did quite a bit of damage to the walls. I managed to salvage this phone. Thankfully, it was tucked away behind a desk. This place will stay closed until repairs can be made."

"Can you get Louise or Johar? I'll hold the line."

Nils sighed. "I have yet to speak with them myself. Your mother was not here when I returned from my trip, and neither was Johar. But stay calm. They'll return soon."

"Stay calm! Shouldn't you figure out where they are?" Dawn was shouting now. "How do you know they weren't hurt? I need to know where they are!"

"I understand your worry. Give me your number and I will keep you posted. I'll call as soon as I have information."

Sander peered in, then came to sit by her on the bed. Dawn gave her number to Nils, clicked off, and threw the phone on the bed. "What's wrong?" Sander asked.

As he held her, Dawn began to weep, her tears dampening his shirt. Dark images filled Dawn—of Louise's body in a ditch, of Johar lined up and shot. Why hadn't she realized how much danger they were in every day? Everything had seemed sort of stable—she could call and they would be there. But the situation was precarious. Johar had been a stranger just a few months ago. And Louise—Dawn hadn't known her either. She had willed herself into total denial. But now—now these two were more important to Dawn than anyone else in the world.

• • •

She hadn't returned since those early September nights. Dawn entered St. Peter's, tiptoed along the marble floor to the altar, and knelt before the candles. Stuffing a wad of bills into the donation box, she whispered, "What can I do?"

She switched on the first candle. "For Louise. Please, bring her back to me." She switched on the second. "Keep Johar safe." And another. "For Bija." Dawn switched on all the rest. They flickered in a fierce rectangle like the candle flag had at Union Square's memorial. The glow cast ruby light on the statues of the saints. "For Johar's aunt Maryam and his brother, Daq; for Sander and Jude. For all the people I hated and all the ones I loved but never told, for America and the world and our messed-up lives." With closed eyes she felt the breadth of her own emptiness.

escape

Johar left Bija with Anqa, then hurried along the path, eager to work. When Dr. Garland had let him off early he'd felt uncomfortable every time he pictured her alone with the patients. That was two days ago. After Daq had stormed off, Johar had sat on the ridge to mourn the rift between him and his brother. He recalled rosy images of Baghlan—of them as boys playing mansur in the dirt, of steadying the sheep for Daq so shearing could be done. He made silent apologies for Daq's behavior; he'd had a difficult time as the eldest, and Daq missed Father the most. The day before had been just as bad. Johar's anger toward Dawn had frightened him. She had only been trying to help.

Before he knew it, Johar was at the clinic, circling around the gathering crowd of patients. He swung open the door only to find the place was in a shambles! Papers were scattered on the floor, and the laptop and phone were missing from the desk. The supply shelves were bare, and it looked as if a stick had been taken to the flimsy chipboard walls.

"Dr. Garland?" called Johar. "Dr. Garland?" He knew she wasn't there, for he'd spoken to her this morning at Anqa's. The doctor was on her way to visit a family who had moved outside the camp, and had asked if he would mind holding down the fort, as she put it, for a few hours. She mentioned that Nils was returning but that Johar was such a help he would remain on. Johar surveyed the damage to Nils's office. The satellite poster was ripped from its wall clasp and trampled, as well as most of the files. And Nils's computer was gone. No more e-mails. The thought depressed him.

As Johar returned to the main room something crunched underfoot. He picked it up. It was Dr. Garland's photo. The frame was broken, but Dawn's face gazed out soberly, challenging the viewer. Daq must have done this! Johar's mixed feelings for his brother flared into pure rage.

No more excuses for Daq. A deadly resolve settled in Johar as he marched through Suryast's warrens of tents, along its ditches, and through the grasses to the road north. Johar felt for his gun and was repelled by it. He hadn't thought about it for a while, though he always carried it. He couldn't imagine using a gun against Daq, but he might need it for protection. To calm himself, he chanted a poem Dawn had e-mailed him: *Escape is not a safe place; escape is not a safe place; escape* . . . Musicians called Pearl Jam had written those lines. *I can't escape fear,* he thought. *I can't escape my disgust. I can't escape my duty.* Daq had put him in his place long enough. Today Johar would not escape the pain of setting his brother straight.

The sun baked through his shalwar kameez as Johar flew past trees spurred with devotional nails. Fields of camel thorn scraped his feet.

How far was the pass? Daq hadn't said exactly. It could be five or ten kilometers. Daq had said his hut lay behind a stall with a red sign south of the Khyber Pass. On his trek south Johar had traveled not through the pass but through gaps in the border patrol to the west of it. These stalls would be new to him, so he must keep a keen eye out.

Johar was weakened from last month's fast, and he had managed just a bowl of rice earlier. He trudged along the trail for what seemed like hours, his side aching. He passed a rusty stall, but behind it lay only sand. He passed a no-mad further on, who requested a charm to guard from injury. *The man must think I'm a dervish of some sort,* Johar thought, shaking his head. The nomad raised his cane in anger, yet moved on.

After a few hours, a structure bearing a dusty red sign loomed ahead. Johar hurried toward it. Fifty paces beyond the stall, a guard leaned against the door of a mud hut, Kalashnikov by his side. He was young, maybe Johar's age. Johar hid behind the stall. Again, the thought of handling the gun made his stomach lurch. There must be another way to defend himself. He tried to devise an approach. The cramp in his side sickened to waves of nausea. Johar stepped to the side of the stall. He could see the boy in his black turban, his body taut like a lynx's.

Talk to him honestly, thought Johar, *say I'm here to visit my brother.* He took another step and his stomach heaved. The rice he'd eaten earlier gushed onto the sand.

"Who goes there?" The guard raised his gun, searching the perimeter.

Johar wiped his mouth on his sleeve and stepped from the shadows. He walked forward, hands outstretched, each step a death sentence. "Asalaamu alaikum. I come as an ally."

"What is your business?"

Johar stared down the metal barrel: "My brother rests inside. I must speak to him of family matters."

"And who is your brother?" The boy had the dark skin and long nose of a Pashtun farmer, yet his stance was that of a soldier.

Johar felt another surge of nausea. He breathed cautiously, with his mouth open. "My brother's name is Daq. Daq from Baghlan, sahib."

"Daq from Baghlan. Ha!" The boy laughed, his angular cheeks rounding a bit. The smile faded, as he looked Johar up and down. "You mean Daq from the *Taliban*."

Johar took another queasy breath. "I suppose. My brother told me he was here."

"Wait." When the boy returned, Daq walked by his side, lurching back and forth as if he were drugged.

"Brother, how are you?" Johar asked, forgetting how ill he felt.

Daq broke into a woozy smirk. "I expected you'd come here, pleading."

"Should I send him away?" asked the guard, raising his Kalashnikov.

"No," cut in Johar, "this is a private matter. In fact, my brother does not need your services at the moment. Take a break. Catch up on some sleep, sahib." Johar's voice was firm. He felt fury and fear and pity all at once.

Daq's lids fluttered open. He stared at Johar with surprise, as if viewing him for the first time. Then he turned to the guard. "Yes, take a break. I will handle this matter." The guard glared back with suspicion as he strode toward the road.

"So, what do you want?" demanded Daq.

"I came for our stolen supplies."

"Your tainted American merchandise!" Daq snarled.

"Let me by." Johar started for the door. Daq stumbled after him. He seized Johar's shalwar, but Johar pushed him off and barreled inside. A rat's nest of syringes, spent ammunition, and candle wax littered the dirt floor.

Daq lunged at him a second time. Johar caught his brother and pushed him backwards, knocking him to the floor and scattering debris.

Johar was surprised at his own strength and Daq's flimsiness. He swung open the interior door. There it lay in a pile—the computer, the phones, medical supplies. "Have you no respect?" Johar shouted.

A surge of Daq's old strength seemed to return as he hurtled toward Johar for a third time and slapped him against the mud wall. "It is you, brother, who have no respect," shouted Daq. "You spend your time with infidels who order us to perform like slaves, who bomb us, and then retreat like cowards."

Johar's resolve faltered. Americans *had* raided the country. It was true their bombing raids did not always hit the right targets. He'd seen the wounds that proved it. And there would be chaos if they left before order was restored. But that didn't change what Daq had done—to Dr. Garland, to the patients who waited for her help.

Johar stood facing his brother, whose hands still

gripped Johar's garment. "Would you rather Aunt Maryam starve in her house because the Taliban decree she cannot teach?" Daq's eyelids lifted, then slid closed. His grip on Johar loosened. Johar jerked away. "You're sick, brother. Let's talk. Let me help you."

Daq wavered like a drunk. "I don't need your help. You'll not talk me into your weakling ways." He reached into his vest, pulled out a knife, and held it to Johar's neck.

Johar froze. His breath caught in his throat. Talk was all Johar had. He refused to be poisoned by the gun in his pack. Even though Daq held a knife, he was still Johar's brother. "Remember Mother?" asked Johar, "her songs pure as a flute? Remember Father? The way he held us in his strong arms? You remind me of him, Daq. You could be strong too, if you stopped this insanity. Warlords who ruined the lives of their own people killed Father. It's crazy, Daq—killing your own. How are you different? And the Taliban?" Daq's blade scraped the soft flesh of Johar's throat. Terror and adrenaline surged through him. Slowing his breath so the knife wouldn't pierce him, Johar experienced a moment of strange calm, as if he were floating above his own fear. He said, "Brother, fight your hate. Fight your anger. It's killing you as surely as this gun has tried to poison me."

"What gun?" Daq eased up on the blade and regarded it with glazed eyes.

Johar inched his hand toward the pistol in his pack. He remembered Dawn's words: *if you have a weapon, a criminal can use it against you.* The gun's weight disgusted him. "Daq," he exclaimed, "I'll never escape the fact that I like poems and weavings and flowers." Johar rested the gun just inside the opening of the pack.

"Little weakling, what does that have to do with it?" Daq's eyes shot open again as if a spark had taken hold. He wavered forward on his heels, the knife swinging wildly.

"Brother, you are lost," exclaimed Johar. "We all know your strength, your bravery, your ferocity, but it's not your rage that makes you alive. It's your love, your joy like Father's. Like when you shear the sheep or dance to your music. Why do you hide that away? Do you want to be just a hard, bitter shell?"

"You lie." Daq began to whimper. He spotted the gun in Johar's hand, and his yellowed eyes glittered with terror. "You're going to shoot me!"

"No, never. This gun is poison!" Johar thrust it onto the dirt floor by Daq's feet. "Take it. Kill me if you want. But you need to know one thing. I am no coward, and I have *never* been a coward!" Johar watched as his brother gaped at the gun. "I won't fight back with vengeance," Johar continued. "For me that is the weakling's way."

"Brother?" Daq muttered, as if emerging from a dream. He stared at the knife in his fist, then looked up at Johar. Tears swam in Daq's eyes, and he was trembling.

"Why are you crying?" Johar asked.

Daq lurched forward. He hurled the blade onto the floor. It clattered against Johar's gun. "Nothing. It's nothing," he muttered, roughly brushing away his tears.

Johar touched Daq's shoulder. "Tell me. Are you sick from drugs?" Daq spun away. His shoulders shook. "I have no doubt you were a great soldier," whispered Johar. "I only mean that one can find other ways to fight; not from hatred, not for vengeance."

"Aunt Maryam is dead," Daq cried. "She was killed by American bombs that fell on the Taliban jail."

Johar felt the life drain from his body. "Is it true, brother?"

"It is true." Daq crumpled to the ground, sobbing. "The Taliban, they should not have put her in jail. They should never have stopped her teaching."

Johar fell on top of Daq among the needles and the trash. He strained to listen for Maryam's voice whispering poetry in a deep, soft corner of his mind. But there was only silence. Johar began to weep.

fly

New York City and in flight toward Asia,
late December 2001

Dawn lunged onto Susie's futon for the satellite phone. "Hello?"

"Dawn!" Louise cried out.

"Louise, you're all right!" Dawn yelled.

"I'm fine. It's just that the clinic . . ." She sounded exhausted. "Nils said you called."

"He told me you were gone," Dawn said. "Where were you? I've been calling the whole day. I was scared you were hurt, or . . . I didn't know."

"I went to visit some families outside the camp in the morning, then to get supplies. I didn't find out what happened until this evening. It's so depressing."

"Yes, but at least you're okay. What about Johar? Is he . . ." Dawn could hardly speak the words.

"Johar is unhurt."

"Thank God you're both all right. Who robbed the place?"

"Johar's brother," replied Louise. "He came to Suryast a couple of days ago. He was furious at Johar for working with an American. I guess he decided to get his revenge by robbing the clinic." She paused. "Heroin has almost destroyed him."

"It's lucky you weren't there. Was Johar there when it happened?"

"No. Johar discovered the robbery the next day. He went to where Daq was staying and confronted him. It must have taken every shred of nerve. Daq was so deranged he was violent."

Dawn swept away all other emotions. "Is Johar in shock?"

"No, but he's grieving. His aunt was killed."

Dawn inhaled sharply. "How?"

"In a prison near Baghlan. An American bombing of a Taliban compound. Daq gave him the dreadful news."

"God, that's really awful. Tell him I'm sorry. Tell him to call me when he can." Dawn's heart was aching and racing all at once. "Louise, I want you to know that I feel terrible for the stuff I've put you through."

There was a pause, then Dawn heard sniffling. "That's good to know."

"I'm sorry for being mean, for running away."

Louise's sniffles turned to sobs. "You had me so upset! Especially with all that's going on in New York."

Dawn's tears slid down too, warm on her cheeks. "At first it was terrifying. Who knew if a bridge would get blown up, or some nut would spray anthrax in the subway." She paused, then continued warily. "But I'm not sorry I came. I've learned so much. And I feel like–I feel like I've done so much too."

"I can't imagine what you might have learned that was worth all that."

Dawn gazed at her garnet ring. She vowed that this conversation would stay kind. "Remember that memory I started to have about a car trip? I finally remembered it all."

"What do you mean?"

"It was my birth mother. She was taking me to Epiphany. I remembered her yanking me from the car so hard that my hands had red marks, and refusing to talk to me. I remembered her pushing my hands off her coat and leaving without looking back."

"Nobody should have to go through that."

"True," Dawn sighed. "But I'm so relieved to get it out. Get it behind me."

"But that's so hard."

Dawn said, "I never would have left a kid with strangers. I would have loved my child, no matter what. Maybe my mother was sick; maybe she needed a shrink. Maybe I'll forgive her someday. But Louise?"

"Yes, dear?"

"I had already made up my mind, I mean before that."

"What do you mean?"

"She wasn't the one who fed me. She wasn't the one who was there. . . ." Dawn felt shy, and shifted her train of thought. "At the site, when I played, I started to feel other people's pain. I wasn't the only one hurting anymore. Helping them made me strong. Maybe I had to get away to quit blaming you."

"I'm proud of you," Louise said softly. They were quiet for a time.

"It's not to say that you haven't hurt me," said Dawn.

"I'm sorry that I hurt you," said Louise. "I'm learning things about myself too."

Dawn recalled the note Jude had found. "Have you heard from Victor?"

"He left," said Louise. "He got in touch with me about a week ago and tried to explain. But there's no excuse for him not calling the police when he knew you were gone. And no excuse for not telling me! You should know that I plan to file for divorce."

"What did you see in him?" Dawn's anger swelled.

"That's a hard one," Louise admitted. "I married late, so maybe I didn't take the time to know what I was getting into. I was desperate for a child, and then we couldn't have one. Victor definitely had his moments, but he wasn't cut out for children. Truth is, I should never have married him."

Dawn was suddenly alarmed. "If you get a divorce, does that mean you can't keep me? You won't get rid of me? You won't send me back to Epiphany House?"

"Never!" Louise's words came in jerks. "I couldn't imagine giving you up."

There was more silence. Dawn's emotions played havoc, veering from fear to panic to fury. "It will be hard enough to convince social services that you can handle me without another parent. But they'll never let me stay if you keep traveling all the time." Heat flared through her. "I hate it when you leave!"

"Dawn, I'm so sorry about that. After those towers fell I imagined that happening in San Francisco. . . ." She paused, and Dawn heard more sniffling. "Being so far away, I've missed you—*truly* missed you, and missed all I want for us. I've made a decision to only take local assignments in the future. I've been distant and, well, just plain avoiding you." She sighed. "Getting close to people is damn scary!"

Dawn realized that fear hid behind Louise's harsh shell,

behind her sense of duty, even behind her pity. Dawn would never have guessed that when she first saw her standing like a dour general in Epiphany's halls. "But what's so scary for you, Louise? I mean, I know relationships can be scary, but I just figured I was messed up from moving all the time, from not having parents."

"You're not messed up, dear. Or maybe we both are." Louise was silent for a moment, then said, "My parents were missionaries who were constantly traveling, teaching languages, building medical centers, showing tribes the ins and outs of irrigation and things like that. I got used to them being far away even when we traveled together." She sighed. "They taught me how to be the classic type who can save the world but can't deal with her own family."

"Why did you want a kid, then?" asked Dawn.

"Maybe it's selfish, but I wanted someone to connect to. Then I didn't know how."

Dawn chuckled ruefully. "I was good at disconnecting too. I was so out of it."

"In what way?"

"All this time when I was searching for my mother—or wishing I was with her—I imagined there was some mystical blood bond, that we'd have some instant understanding. I even fantasized that she might be a musician." Dawn laughed. "Sometimes connections form when your head is turned a hundred and eighty degrees the other way. You and I, it's surreal how alike we are."

"You're right," said Louise.

"We're both trying to help people. We're both runners." They laughed together. Then Dawn said, "One more thing."

"Yes?"

"I want to keep doing what I've been doing with flute playing—maybe join a band and play music for sick people, maybe in hospitals, cheer them up, connect with them. I've sort of figured out a way to help people. I'm actually good at it! I know it's idealistic, but . . ."

"Hey, you're talking to the queen of idealism here. And who could complain about another healer in the family? But when I come for you in New York and we go home to California, you'll need to make up all the school that you missed. You'll also be grounded for a couple of months. Running away is no small thing."

"Ground me?" Dawn couldn't remember Louise ever punishing her.

"Dawn, I've been thinking about your idea to bring Johar to the States."

Dawn felt a wave of apprehension, recalling Johar's anger, but she was nervous about spoiling the mood. "Yeah?"

"What if we bring Johar and his cousin to San Francisco to live with us, to be a family? I want us to be a real family; I've been thinking a lot about that." Louise paused. "I asked Johar about it and he didn't say much, but you two seem to have formed quite a bond. We have the room, and at least Johar knows enough English to go to school."

How could Dawn tell her how wrong this was without hurting her feelings? How could she say it in nice words? "It's an awesome idea, Louise, but—" She broke off.

"I thought you'd be thrilled."

"Well, actually I suggested it to him myself, but that's not what he wants. He wants to return to Baghlan and start a school."

"But he's only fifteen. Didn't he say that caring for Bija was too difficult?"

"He gets overwhelmed sometimes, but he sees Bija as his responsibility. With his parents and Maryam gone, and Daq off as a soldier, Johar is the head of the family. He told me that in Afghanistan at fifteen, even at fourteen, a boy is considered a man," Dawn explained. "Johar wants to stay and take care of things. He thinks that running off to another country would be like running away from his problems."

"Well, what about a visit to the States, at least until Afghanistan is stabilized?"

"He doesn't want to leave at all, even for a visit," Dawn replied. "To Johar that would be cowardly."

"He told you all this?"

"Yes. I guess he was afraid to tell you. He doesn't want to seem ungrateful." Dawn paused, then said, "I've got a great idea."

"What is it?" asked Louise.

"Do you promise to keep an open mind about it—to really, really consider it?"

"Maybe." She paused. "What is it?"

Dawn took a deep breath and began. "My roommate, Susie is a reporter. She writes features on cultural and political issues. She recently interviewed Muslims who worship at this controversial London mosque. And she's been angling for an unusual assignment on how Muslims interact with westerners. She's come up with a story idea."

"What's that?"

"Interviewing the ICRC doctors and their patients in Peshawar!" Before Louise could react, Dawn plowed forward. "If she interviewed you guys, I could fly over with her. She travels with translators and security people and the whole nine yards, so it would be relatively safe. She'd do her interviews, and when she was done, we would all travel

255

north to Baghlan to help Johar clear his compound and start his school. And the best thing, Louise, is that you and I and Johar and Bija could all work together. It'd be like a family—this weird, crazy family. We'd have such a *blast*!"

There was an uncomfortable silence. Then Louise shouted "You are incorrigible!" She began to howl with laughter. It kind of shocked Dawn. She'd never heard Louise laugh like that. Ever!

•　　•　　•

Dear Johar—
It's really happening! As soon as I get my passport in a couple weeks, we're coming to Peshawar! Then we'll travel to Baghlan with you. My heart is so full it feels like it might pop. I'm sorry that I'll never meet your aunt. She sounded like a beautiful person. But I can't wait to meet Bija! I have a special dolly for her. My friend Susie made the doll's clothes. Bija will get a taste of American fashion. By the way, you must get used to Susie slowly. She's kind of over the top, but she's a sweetheart. How to explain "over the top"? Um, she's bubbly and perky and talks really fast. Speaking of fast talking, boy, did I ever have to do some fast talking to persuade Louise. Actually, Susie helped. She's hiring guards and translators and photographers. We'll be in a veritable caravan. I told Louise that she is my mentor as a risk-taking field doctor (all true). I never appreciated how organized Louise was until she and Susie arranged everything

down to the airplane meal. She is starting to *love* the plan and has even arranged to get chalk and a blackboard up there for you. Johar, it will be an honor to help set up Maryam School.
XOX Dawn
P.S.—How is Daq?

Dawn—
I cannot beleev you come here! It best dream I have had! I sure I will like over the top Susie. I admit, have never talked to a girl like you so neer. But nothing in Quran says a guy cannot have a female frend. Anyway, the world is changes. I impatient for your arrivel each day. Maryam School will be way cool as you Americans say. And blackboard extra, extra cool! I will arm student warriors with books, not guns. Also armed with cleen socks. LOL!!! Thanks for kind words on Maryam. I miss her. And sorry I was so angry during last talk. Daq is OK. He recovers in my tent and Nils convinced him to see addiction Dr. in Kabul. Daq is considering this and actully speak to me today abot coming with us north for this.
XOX Johar

•   •   •

Sander borrowed a car and drove Susie and Dawn to the airport. He helped them haul bags and escorted them to security. He pecked Dawn on the cheek, and kissed Susie too. Sander had probably kissed every girl in Manhattan on the cheek. That's how it felt to Dawn, at least. But hey,

Sander had taught her how to stand up and jam. More than anything, he was the guy to call when it came time for landing professional gigs. They sat and gulped caffeine and talked about the madness of the last few months. Then, while Susie and Sander scurried off for newspapers, Dawn wrote Jude a postcard.

Dear Jude,
Truth is surely stranger than fiction. My life is living proof. I will be returning home with Louise after a little side trip to Afghanistan. Hee hee! Details to follow. Manhattan says hi. Can't wait to see you in the Haight.
Love and spacey jigs, Dawn

Dawn gazed at the people streaming by. Probably many were New Yorkers braving flights for the first time since 9/11. So much had changed in Manhattan. Ground zero's fire was finally extinguished. The mountains of metal debris had finally been cleared, transported on barges to other resting places. An observation deck had been built so that people could pay their respects. Weeks of anthrax scares seemed to have passed but some rescue workers had fallen ill with lung ailments from working in the toxic air.

Many downtown businesses had gone bankrupt, and landlords were still spending a fortune to repair damaged buildings, yet most people had settled into holiday shopping. Plans for a memorial were batted about. Tourists ventured warily back.

Dawn's thoughts were pleasantly interrupted when Sander and Susie returned with armfuls of snacks, magazines, and newspapers.

It was hard to leave Sander as she and Susie rode down the escalator. He'd taught her so much and protected her. Dawn looked back once, and he was waving, blond mane encircling his face.

•   •   •

They were over the Atlantic, almost to England. It was night, and the sky outside the plane was black and impenetrable. Most of the passengers were out cold, their snores rumbling down the aisles. Only a few business types on laptops and a guy playing a video game were still awake with Dawn and Susie. Susie elbowed Dawn. She pulled out two gorgeous blue scarves from her oversized shoulder bag. "Pashmina wool," she explained. "Normally they cost a fortune, but I got them as a present from someone in London. It's to show our respect in a Muslim country. Try one on."

"Thanks, Susie!" Dawn tried to arrange hers like a veil. It wasn't quite working.

"Wind it like this." Susie demonstrated. "This journalist for the London *Times* who's been to India and Iran and everyplace showed me how. So, what does he look like?" she added slyly.

"Who?" Dawn asked.

"Who? Who do you think?"

"I don't have a photo of Johar," Dawn replied, shifting for the umpteenth time in her cramped seat. They had been on this plane for an eternity, and her nerves jangled every time she pictured facing Johar and Louise in the flesh.

"I can't believe you have no idea what he looks like," Susie said. "What does he sound like? You can tell a lot from the voice." Susie had already asked versions of this question a million times. Still, it was an endless source of entertainment for both of them.

"Well," Dawn mused, "it's soft, but not in a feminine way. It's a rich tenor, if you think of it in terms of where he'd be placed in a choir." Dawn felt herself blush.

"Ah, the sensitive type. He sounds adorable," Susie gushed.

"Susie! You're embarrassing me." Dawn covered her head with the skimpy fleece blanket the flight attendant had handed out.

Susie jiggled Dawn's arm. "So, what did you guys talk about most?" she asked, also for the umpteenth time.

"Johar recites poetry," Dawn remarked, peeking out from under the blanket. "He's turned me on to some incredible poems." Dawn's cheeks were still hot.

"You've got it bad," Susie said.

"He's a friend," Dawn protested.

"You've got it really bad," Susie repeated, shaking her head.

The flight attendant began to roll down the aisle with the food cart, and when Susie ducked out for a pit stop, Dawn's gaze fell on a father, a mother and their two sons, two rows up. She'd studied them whenever she could. She watched how the little boy clasped his mother's neck with his chubby arms. She saw him lean his mop of curls on his mother's shoulder. Dawn noticed the older boy gazing up at his father as his father explained a book they pored over together. The family leaned toward one another, as if gaining sustenance from the huddle. Dawn wanted that. She wanted that a lot.

Susie hurried back just as the flight attendant came by with the food tray. He served rice and lamb kebabs. Dawn savored the spicy concoction. Johar had said this was what people ate in Afghanistan! Her back prickled with excitement. She could taste how close they were.

home

Johar

Johar bristled with anticipation as he stood by the arrival gate in Peshawar's airport. He hardly felt the jostling crowd or heard their loud chatter. Dr. Garland stood by his side; they both waited for the same girl. Johar wondered if this was against the laws of sharia. The sharia allowed human communication, spiritual love beyond desire. He'd gone over this problem of logic hundreds of times, each time piecing together a different justification. But he refused to feel shame. *It's just dawn music.* Under his breath, he composed poetry: "I am building a novel world in which to walk. This is no fantasy, but fact. My universe has many voices born from one cradle, one altar, and buried in one grave. The voices sing the music of all tribes. I welcome you to join me."

A steady stream of passengers flowed toward the gate.

"People are coming out!" Bija squealed in Dari, jumping up and down.

"This must be Dawn's flight!" Louise exclaimed.

Johar's heart beat wildly. He searched the multinational crowd for a woman with hair the color of desert sand, pale skin, and pink cheeks.

"I'm so nervous," he heard Dr. Garland say, as if from across the room. "I wonder if she looks the same."

"Look! A tall white lady," Bija remarked in Dari, pulling on Johar's arm. "Is that her?" The woman was tall, but the hair poking out of her scarf was brown.

"It's not Dawn," answered Johar. This woman did not match the photo.

But wait, right behind that woman strode Dawn. Johar was sure of it! She was even more radiant in person— boyish, yet delicate. Strands of blond escaped her blue scarf, and she had the same brown-eyed gaze that had jumped from the photo, though in person it was livelier. Dawn wore the cowboy jeans and sneakers he'd seen in newspaper photos of westerners. The passengers advanced like a formation of boisterous revelers. She looked at him. He saw her blush.

"Dawn, over here!" called Dr. Garland.

Bija took one of Johar's hands and one of Louise's. She jumped up and down between them. Inside, Johar did the same. "Dawn! Dawn!" squealed Bija.

"She's almost here," Louise said to Bija. Bija nodded eagerly as the crowd fanned out, connected with friends, hugged lovers, hurried to the escalators, and departed in great clumps. Dawn was fifty paces away and getting closer.

Johar rehearsed words in his mind. *I am pleased to meet you. I have looked forward to this occasion. How was your flight?* It sounded so stiff. He'd known this girl's essence—how could he stumble back to formalities after that? *I have just a few seconds to compose myself,* he thought. *She will greet Dr. Garland first.*

Dawn

Was that Louise past the door of the waiting area? Dawn hurried along the narrow hallway with Susie leading the way. "Oh, my God, there she is!" she exclaimed.

"The one with the wire-rimmed glasses?" asked Susie. Dawn nodded. Susie took her friend's hand and squeezed it. "Don't worry. It's going to be great."

There was something so different about Louise. Was it that she had lost lots of weight, or that her gray head scarf accentuated her pallid face? She did look run-down, but there was something else. She looked exuberant, and her military stance had yielded to a softer, less certain one. For the first time ever Dawn wanted to hug her. Louise's mouth opened slightly, while her brows creased, as if she were trying to puzzle something out. Dawn recalled seeing that look the first day on Santa Marisa, when they had been washing dishes in the kitchen. They'd both tried so hard that day.

Now, as Louise drew closer, that memory faded and Dawn's old apprehension clenched her throat. "Susie, I'm panicking. Hold my hand?"

"Sure, honey." Susie took it and kept it gently in hers.

The guy next to Louise wore loose pants, a cobalt shirt, and a black vest, which accentuated his raven hair. A tiny girl in a long yellow dress peeked out from behind him. It must be Johar and his little cousin! To utter the first hello would be indescribably sweet. And Dawn had Bija's doll tucked in her pocket. But she needed Louise first.

At twenty steps away Dawn sensed Louise's slight hesitation. At ten steps Dawn witnessed the whites of her owlish eyes. *She's terrified too,* Dawn realized. At four steps away, Dawn ran into the crush of her arms. "I'm so glad to see you!" Louise's plain cotton dress smelled of campfires and sweat.

"Me too." Louise's voice was muffled and teary.

Holding and being held, pressing their hearts close, felt to Dawn like drinking pure, cool water. And she had been so thirsty.

"My girl," Louise whispered. "My Dawn." They swayed as they hugged.

"You look different." Louise held Dawn at arm's length. "Grown-up."

Dawn laughed and smoothed down her head scarf. "I took an intensive course in that this fall." She introduced Susie. "Here's the woman who's been helping you with all the arrangements. She's my best friend in New York." Susie flashed her elfin smile.

Louise eyed Susie's new paisley pants suit and pashmina head scarf. "Pleased to meet you, Susie. You're right in fashion."

"Thanks. I try." Susie's manicured hand shook Louise's square one. "Your daughter's an awesome flutist and a very cool lady," Susie said. "And thanks for letting her come on this assignment. I can't wait to interview you and your staff."

"Well, we're delighted," Louise began, and glanced hesitantly at Dawn with that quizzical look again, almost asking permission. Dawn realized that she had liked that gaze that first night in the kitchen but had been too wary to understand it. She'd convinced herself it was disdain. She saw now that all of Louise's awkwardness, her fumbling talk, and confusing expressions were signs not of a cold heart but of a warm one.

Susie broke the silence. "Excuse me, Dr. Garland." She leaned toward Dawn and whispered, "Go. I'll keep your mother company."

Dawn murmured, "Thanks." She saw that Johar had stepped back to make way for her reunion. Bija, a tadpole of a girl, clung to Johar's hand. He was mysterious in his shalwar kameez, like some Afghan rock star—unclassifiable and so handsome. Johar seemed radically different from other guys she knew. He was practically a stranger, yet she felt closer to him than anyone else. Johar was her poet. He would soon walk with her. They would talk. He would show her around Afghanistan. It mattered hugely how he saw her, and yet it didn't matter at all, because they already had something real. *A connection.* Johar's gaze darted from Dawn's shoes to Louise's to Bija's. Dawn realized, *He's nervous too.*

Johar

Dawn was coming his way. He lowered his gaze to the carpet and watched her sneakers move toward him. Bija, as if sensing Johar's alarm, scurried behind him and hid herself in the folds of his tunic. Words left him as Dawn drew close. His face grew hot. *I must relax,* he advised himself. He peeked and realized that this was most decidedly not dawnmusic@usa.com. This was the woman Dawn. His friend; his musician. Her smile dazzled him, and there was a moment before he found words. "Hello," he said finally. "I am Johar."

Dawn

Dawn looked up, then down. Johar's was a sinewy, lofty strength, giving him an aristocratic demeanor. Over his black curls he wore a skullcap decorated with sunbeams. He wore a woolen vest over his garments, and sandals on his feet.

"Hi. I brought you some presents." She held out the brimming satchel.

"For me?" asked Johar.

"Music for your new school. It's the first music book I played from at ground zero." She regarded his steady hands with their crescent nails, the way his cheekbones sloped out under his almond-shaped eyes as he flipped through the books.

"Music, Jor!" Bija rolled the English word on her tongue as she stood on her toes to get a look.

"What honor." Johar seemed confused as he examined the musical notes.

"It's American notation. Maybe I can transpose it."

"Transpose? Ah, like to translate, but music. Of course." Johar reached into a sheepskin pack. "I have present for you also." He held out a woolen cap.

"Thanks." Dawn stretched it out. "The moonbeams are fantastic."

He smiled back shyly.

"And who do we have here?" asked Dawn. "Is this the awesome Bija?"

"I, Bija!" she chirped. Her wide face dimpled, and one dark ringlet fell from her scarf. She hopped over to Dawn like a rabbit.

"I'm happy to meet you." Dawn drew out the English words. "If you want to, you can call me Aunt Dawn. Would you like a gift too?"

"Gift," Johar repeated in Dari. Bija nodded. She took two more bunny hops and leaned in eagerly. Dawn reached in her pocket and pulled out the dolly.

"Jor, gift! Aunt Dawn!" Bija said in halting English. She took it and lifted the doll's coat to examine its skirt, then removed the plastic shoes and put them back on, prattling in Dari all the while.

"She likes it," explained Johar. "She says, 'Funny shoes.'" They both laughed.

"Oh, I almost forgot." Dawn pulled out a thick paperback. "I'm not much with poems, except for songs, but I remembered one poetry book from lit class that blew me away." She handed the book to Johar. On the cover, an old man with a white beard and brimmed hat leaned on his cane. "Hope you don't mind that I marked my favorite passages."

Johar read, "Walt Whitman, *Leaves of Grass*." He flipped open to the place Dawn had marked with pencil, and read slowly:

I celebrate myself,
And what I assume you shall assume,
For every atom that belongs to me as good belongs to you.
You shall no longer take things second or third hand,

You shall listen to all sides and filter them from yourself.
It is not the violins and the cornets,
Not the men's chorus nor those of the women's chorus,
It is nearer and farther than they.
The old forever new things . . .
The closest and simplest things—this moment with you.

Johar's hand came away from the book, gesturing with his upturned palm. "Remember when you invited me to be part of your family?"

"I remember."

"I would like that. And you are part of mine. In spirit, yes?"

"Yes." She smiled. There was something clean and warm in the way he said things. There was no guessing.

"Coming?" called Louise.

Johar, Bija, Dawn, Louise, and Susie zigzagged through the airport lobby and out its wide exit door. "We've got the coolest extended family in Peshawar," said Dawn.

"In Afghanistan," said Johar.

"In Asia," said Louise.

"In the East," said Susie, "and all the merrier when the crew arrives in a couple hours."

"We play!" squeaked Bija.

Dawn slipped her hand into the crook of Louise's arm. "Want to go for some chai, Mom?"

"Yes, love." Louise pressed Dawn's arm with her own, and her gray scarf rustled lightly as she nodded.

They stepped into the Peshawar streets—streets of mosques and beggars, of spice bazaars and a concerto of conversation.

GLOSSARY
of Afghan-Persian Words and Phrases

AAB, *water*

ALLAHU AKBAR, *Allah is the greatest*

AFGHANIS, *Afghan money*

ALLIANCE, *United National and Islamic Front for the Salvation of Afghanistan, or UNIFSA, an anti-Taliban resistance movement formerly headed by Ahmad Shah Massoud, comprised mostly of Tajiks, but also Uzbeks and others; Americans mistakenly refer to this group as the Northern Alliance*

AMNIYAT NIST, *it's not safe*

ASALAAM ALAIKUM, *peace on you*

ALAIKUM ASALAAM, *and on you, peace*

CALIPH, *a spiritual leader*

CHAIKHANA, *teahouse*

CHAI, *tea*

DAQIQI OF BALKH, *well-known poet of the tenth century*

DARI, *Afghan dialect of Persian, one of the two main languages of Afghanistan*

(AHMAD SHAH) DURRANI, *Afghan poet, 1747–1773, founder of the Afghan empire*

FIRDAUSI, *one of the writers of the epic poem* Shah-namah, *A.D. 974*

FARRUKHI, *poet and lute player in the court of Mahmud of Ghazni, A.D. 1000*

GABLI PILAU, *meat in rice mounds, often cooked with raisins, almonds, pistachios, and carrots*

GHADIS, *a horse-drawn cart*

HAZARA, *the third largest ethnic group, mostly in the central area of Bamian, persecuted for their Shiite way of worship, may be related to the Mongols*

HIJAB, *a woman's head covering*

HIZBI ISLAMI AND JAMIATI ISLAMI, *multiclan local political factions particularly active after the Soviet withdrawal*

IMAM, *religious leader*

INGLEESI, *English*

INSHALLAH, *God willing*

JAZAKULLAH, *may Allah reward you, thank you*

JIHAD, *Holy war; literally means "struggle"*

KAFIR, *unbeliever*

KAMEEZ, *loose-fitting overshirt*

KESHMESH, *mixture of nuts and raisins*

KHERAB, *ruined*

KHUB AST, *literally means "it's fine," but said cynically when things are going badly*

(KHAN KHATTACK) KHUSHAL, *great seventeenth-century Pashtun poet*

LUTI, *a bandit, thief*

MADRASAH, *a religious school*

(AHMAD SHAH) MASSOUD, *the beloved United Alliance leader who fought the Taliban; critically wounded on September 9, 2001, by an Al Qaeda operative with an incendiary device hidden in a television camera, and died on September 14*

MULLAH, *village holy man*

MUEZZIN, *equivalent to a minister, one who calls people to prayer*

NAAN, *bread*

NAMAZ, *Afghan prayers*

NURISTANI, *a small, separatist ethnic group residing in the mountains of Nuristan, the last of the tribes to convert to Islam*

PASHTO, *one of the two main languages of Afghanistan*

PASHTUN, *the largest of the ethnic groups, mostly in the south and southeast of Afghanistan*

PATTU, *prayer rug, cloak, blanket (used as all of these)*

PIR, *religious leader*

RABI'A BALKHI, *a beloved woman poet, lived around A.D. 900*

RAMADAN, *sacred holiday beginning in November—fasting during daylight hours*

RUBAB, *Afghan violin*

(JALALUDDHIN BALKHI) RUMI, *a Sufi poet, born A.D. 1207*

ROUSSI, *Russian*

SAFAR-E KHOSH, *happy travels*

SAHIB, *mister, sir*

SALAAM, *peace, hello*

SAMOSAS, *fried pastry crescents, with leek and spices and served with yogurt-mint sauce*

SANTUR, *a musical instrument similar to the hammered dulcimer*

SHALWAR, *loose-fitting pants*

SHARIA(T), *Islamic religious laws*

SHIITE, SHI'A, *a branch of Islam that believes that imams must be conferred by heredity, practiced in Afghanistan by the minority Hazara group*

SUNNI, *a branch of Islam that believes spiritual leaders can be elected; the majority of Muslims in Afghanistan are Sunni Muslims*

TALIBAN, *a mostly rural group of Pashtuns who rose to power in 1996 and imposed a strict Islamic regime*

TAJIK, *second largest ethnic group (25 percent), of ancient Persian origin, who represent many of the educated in Kabul and who also cultivate the lush areas of the northeast*

TANBUR, *Afghan flute*

AFGHANISTAN UPDATE

Afghanistan is now a country with more freedoms but many continuing struggles. These struggles are compounded by the fact that Afghanistan was, even at the onset of the American war to oust the Taliban in autumn of 2001, a country that had already been fighting—civil war and a war against the Soviets—for approximately twenty years.

Post-Taliban reconstruction is well under way. Hundreds of new schools are being built, and girls have flocked back to class. The University of Kabul has had an unprecedented number of women applicants with heavy enrollment in its new computer curriculum, and women continue to gain a voice in media, journalism, academia and medicine. The main highway between Kabul and Kandahar is being rebuilt, a new currency was introduced in 2002, and a national census is under way. Afghanistan's reconstruction has been and continues to be a truly global endeavor, with nations from around the world donating millions for reconstruction. Many countries have stepped in to create job programs, train a national army and police force, develop agricultural alternatives to poppy cultivation, and train lawyers and judges in a push for law reform. The North Atlantic Treaty Organization (NATO) took over the peacekeeping force in the summer of 2003, and the United Nations continues to provide an enormous array of services, including inoculations across the country.

On the political front, the Bonn agreement, a road map for the future, was created in Bonn, Germany, by members of a new provisional government. A new constitution was completed and adopted in January 2004 and national elections were held in June 2004.

Security issues remain a serious hindrance to peace and reconstruction. Pro-Taliban Pashtun and extremist Arab factions undermine the peace process by sporadic acts of violence, particularly in southeast Afghanistan and along the Pakistani border. In Kabul, unsuccessful assassination attempts were made on President Hamid Karzai, and his vice president was fatally shot. Afghan civilians demonstrated in Kabul against what was declared as "Pakistan's continued undermining of the new government." Many in Pakistan continue to support the Taliban and other radical Islamic elements. Local warlords still engage in illegal taxation and forced recruitment and it will take many years to clear buried land mines leftover from decades of conflict.

During the American-led war to oust the Taliban over 3,000 Afghans were killed by U.S. bombs. Almost 2 million refugees have returned to their homes, although there are still about 480,000 displaced persons inside Afghanistan, most of them in the south. Most Pakistani camps have closed, although refugees still remain in both Pakistan and Iran.

For the peace process and the instigation of a new constitution to be successful, there will need to be more relief in the daily struggle of the average citizen. Areas outside of Kabul must receive protection from a national police force.

Afghanistan will continue to require both financial and practical help for a number of years to come. It is essential that poppy cultivation and drug trafficking be replaced with lucrative agricultural alternatives. In 2003, Afghanistan was the largest opium producer in the world. The Pashtun majority must have their concerns met, for part of what fuels pro-Taliban uprisings is a feeling among Pashtuns that they are politically underrepresented, treated with prejudice in the north, and not receiving their fair share of benefits under the new government.

Many troops are still stationed in Afghanistan.

MANHATTAN UPDATE

At any one time up to 50,000 people in 430 businesses from 26 countries worked at the Trade Center complex until September 11, 2001. In addition to One and Two World Trade Center, the twin towers, seven other buildings were destroyed: Four World Trade Center, the southeast plaza building; Five World Trade Center, the northeast plaza building; Six World Trade Center, the U.S. Custom House; and Seven World Trade Center. The Deutsche Bank Building sustained major damage and will be torn down. In Washington, the Pentagon also sustained major damage, but has since been repaired. The exact number remains elusive, but approximately 2,800 people lost their lives in the attacks that day.

The Federal Emergency Management Agency (FEMA), the Red Cross, the National Guard, and many volunteer services devoted months of invaluable aid after the disaster. Thousands of civilians gave blood and contributed food and bedding to makeshift shelters. Construction workers and retired firefighters volunteered to help clean the site. The fire at ground zero was finally extinguished on December 19, 2001. It took another few months to clear the site. Schools offered to host closed high schools in the affected area. For example, Brooklyn Technical High School hosted students from Stuyvesant High.

In response to the disaster, the Department of Homeland Security was created and the Federal Bureau of Investigation (FBI) was remodeled. Major grants were awarded to study health effects, ranging from air filter samples to pregnancy outcomes of exposed women (Columbia University noted a significant increase of smaller babies). Most of the damaged subway tunnels have been repaired. The South Ferry and Rector Street subway stops were reopened in September 2002. Metropolitan Transportation Authority (MTA) engineers used the original 1915 blueprints as the basis for the tunnel's structural design. The Cortlandt Street station, directly under the site of the towers, will not open until the area is redeveloped. On November 23, 2003, the World Trade Center Port Authority Trans-Hudson (PATH) stationed reopened.

The September 2002 anniversary of the attacks was commemorated with concerts and speeches throughout the five boroughs, including a bagpipers' march into Manhattan at dawn. New York City commemorated the second anniversary in 2003 with a private ceremony at the site for the families of the victims, where children related to the victims read the list of deceased. There was a citywide tolling of bells to mark the end, and a temporary display of the Towers of Light, two beams of light directed upward to represent the towers and the victims. Families of the victims were consulted at every step of the program's design.

In the years following the tragedy, some New Yorkers chose to relocate. There were lawsuits over the amounts of victim compensation, controversy over air quality safety, insurance frauds and accusations over misappropriation of emergency funds. The area around ground zero has become a huge tourist draw. Its atmosphere offends many New Yorkers, where vendors sell everything from 9/11 T-shirts to refrigerator magnets. The transcripts of the 9/11 tapes were finally made public in August of 2003, after the *New York Times* sued for their release.

Architects Daniel Libeskind and David M. Childs form the design team for the Freedom Tower in the new World Trade Center complex. It includes angular, light-filled towers and a 1,776-foot-high memorial spire, housing airborne gardens. Libeskind took his inspiration partially from the mathematician and architect Christopher Wren, who was given the opportunity to redesign London in 1666 after a great fire ravaged the city. Some details of the design are still in flux. An advisory council, which includes family members of the victims, oversees the redevelopment plans.

Santiago Calatrava, the "world's greatest living poet of transportation architecture," was chosen to redesign the PATH station complex. Calatrava, best known as a designer of bridges, airports, and train stations, is a native of Spain. There was a global invitation to design a memorial at ground zero. Michael Arad, a young architect for the New York City Housing Authority, was the winner with his design "Reflecting Absence," which features two huge reflecting pools on the towers' footprints. Peter Walker of Berkeley, California, an experienced landscape architect, was chosen to "green" the surrounding plaza. The two men share the design credit. Davis Brody Bond, LLP, the firm that designed Lincoln Center, will work with the design team. Plans also call for office space, a cultural center at the northeast corner of the site, and a memorial center.

About the Author

Catherine Stine grew up in Philadelphia. She received her BFA from the Boston Museum School/Tufts University and earned her MFA in creative writing, with a double focus in writing for children and fiction, from the New School in Manhattan. She is a painter and illustrator as well as a writer. She often thinks of crafting scenes as painting with words. Catherine Stine lives in New York City with her husband and their two sons. This is her first novel.